IMMORTAL WROUGHT

Judgement of the Uneven Throne

By Jarrod Garceau

IMMORTAL WROUGHT
JUDGEMENT OF THE UNEVEN THRONE

Jarrod.Garceau@gmail.com
Instagram: Immortal_Wrought
Facebook: Immortal Wrought

Cover design Art Grafunkel
Instagram: artgrafunkel
artgrafunkel@gmail.com

ISBN 979-8-9885874-0-8 Hardcover
ISBN 979-8-9885874-1-5 Paperback

Dedicated to my wife Cigdem.
A special thanks to my Dad and Wes for the editing

Darkness kneels before the light. Full moonlight encircles the show of the evening. Hidden in the hay were two sets of brown eyes in a loft above, awaiting tonight's performance. One pair of sapphire blue eyes has a front-row seat to the concert for the first time. She has waited to be a part of tonight's show. A broad figure, a veteran of the stage, prepares his instruments for the night's chorus. Alchemical steel of all types creates a blend of tones. A forbidden flame comes to life and color.

The forest around him goes silent and still as he begins. He raises his hand to bring forth life in the forge; flames light up the night sky, and patterns fall upon the mountains. The steel rings out, calling on the elements of the flames—the soul of the wielder. The steel changes tone with every color of the flame when struck. The master's blend calls forth another flame from the rock face in the forge, and a roar from the mountain adds a beast flame to the mix. The blaze is pounded into the flesh of the steel. The flames are now encased in the steel as it takes shape.

The eyes in the loft squinted from the brightness in the room but kept watching in awe. As the closing act begins, the flames enshrine the blade and it tries to escape. It's time for the master to tame the blade. He pulls the flames back in with his bare hand and seals them with runes in his other hand. Subdued, the fire returns to the steel. The blade went silent, and the forge grew dark. A new set of golden eyes appears in the loft behind the two.

"Time for bed, you two." "We have an early morning."

Chapter 1

Olcay laid in his bed, staring at the ceiling. His brother was snoring in the cot next to him. He could hear his sister and father coming in the front door. Mom was complaining they were bringing too much soot into the house. Olcay's mind began to wander as he started thinking of what he wanted to do for his apprenticeship in the coming year. He wished he had inherited either of his parents' skills, then his decision would have been easier. He turns over and tries to sleep. He can see the light from the fireplace flicker through cracks in the floorboards. His eyes begin to close as he forces himself to sleep.

Their house sat on a cliff behind the Golen Mountain, overlooking a small plateau before the valley. The family used the plateau for their livestock and a small crop field. The path around the mountain was wide enough for a cart with two oxen, which led through the forest to the main village. A few barriers along the path kept the home safe from raiders.

Olcay arose early before sunrise to get his chores done. He tried to occupy his time rather than give in to his thoughts on his present issues. He checked on the animals in the morning, tending to a modest flock of sheep and chickens. The area on the cliffs they lived on was quite small, and the animals needed to be rotated regularly. He could see a few neighbors below them in the valley. As close as they were, they were still too far around the mountain to ever visit his village. One of the farmers in the valley had a home below theirs. Sometimes Olcay's family could send a bucket down on a rope to do some trading if they needed something and did not want to head to town. Olcay's thoughts betrayed him as the sunrise brought together two things that reminded him of what he could never achieve: gold and heat. He sat on the edge of the cliff as the morning shadow passed over them.

"Are you still sulking, Olcay? Father would be infuriated if he saw you like this." Orion's voice was still rough with the fresh mountain air. He was adapted to the city air near the water.

"No, just trying to put things together." Olcay pouted. He crossed his arms and looked deeper down the cliffside.

"You mean sulking then; you know how the family feels about this." Orion lifted Olcay and turned him around. "I just wish life was clearer. Even with my path laid out before me, I am still trying to figure things out." Orion slapped his brother's shoulder in encouragement.

"Look, you know how I feel. Your penmanship is good, you could do well as a scribe. I know you are smart; you can be one of those scholars, or you can work with one of the book merchants at the guild. Mom and dad know people. You have till next month before dad figures it out for you." Orion then started to guide Olcay back towards the path home.

"I wish I could get into something fun and exciting like you or Oriel."

"Well, mom never looked into your future, so you could decide it on your own. Plus, the guild takes time to move up; my eyes are more for show than anything." He gave Olcay a hard stare and smiled. You could see rings of gold around the irises of his eyes shine and almost move.

"I just feel left out sometimes." Olcay kicked a few sticks out of the way.

"Left out? You are all we can talk about. You will need to apprentice somewhere soon or end up with something chosen for you. "At the very least, YOU will have a choice."

Olcay knew his family meant well, but his mind began to wonder again. He could hear his mother finishing the packing in the house, and he knew they needed to get ready.

The mother, Fenya, looked out the window and could see Olcay and Orion preparing the cart, stacking their father's work, and wrapping them so they would not make noise on the trip to town. Fenya's eyes glowed, and then she covered them with her hand. "It will be a normal day, no need to muddy it up." She then looked back to Olcay, the youngest in the family; he has some height and is stocky from working the fields. He inherited brown hair and brown eyes. "I can only hope for the best from here with him," she said to herself. Orion is the middle child with thicker, darker hair and brown eyes as well, with gold rings around the iris from his mother's side. The ring itself never really bestows power. In some circles, it is a sign of luck and fortune. He is skinnier than his brother, and his beard has started to grow in. He took up an apprenticeship as a trader the previous year and came back for a short stay until the summer. "I wonder when he will talk to us about the girl he meets later this year, I may need to get a new dress for the occasion." Fenya rattled on with her thoughts. "Oriel, you need to get down to the cart before we leave. I see a big day ahead."

Oriel could be heard rolling out of bed. The late night in the forge takes a toll on the body. Oriel ran past her mom and grabbed some bread and cheese from the table. "Sorry mom, I was up late again and couldn't sleep." Her hair was red, and her freckles were quite pronounced. Her body was muscular from working the forge but kept its feminine shape.

Fenya's eyes flickered for a moment, and she covered them. "Best get with your bothers and load up the cart. It will be a busy day in town."

The cart was loaded, and the family settled Demir, the father, stepped into his forge for a moment. Unsheathing a small blade from his belt, he makes a small cut to the back of his hand. The blood trickles down as he mumbles an incantation before it falls into the burning embers of the forge. The blood sizzles on the embers. He then wrapped his hands with a bit of cloth and left the forge to join his family at the cart. His stature was massive and filled the doorway. He had a beard that was so red, it looked like he was bleeding from his face.

"Did you set a barrier, Hun?" Fenya asked. "You know you don't need to build such a strong barrier out here." Most of the barriers around their land could be seen through like frosted glass. The one around their home that Demir made was clear until you touched it. Father climbed into the back seat to take a nap, while Orion took the reins and began the ride into town. The ride going around the mountain path and through the woods is short for the family.

The path was smoothed down after years of the family traveling to and from town. They had no problems driving at night because the cliffside path always had a shoulder. Only the occasional flooding along the roads ever kept them from getting to town. An old guard station lay at the end of the path into the forest. The roads converged there for the town's backside entrance. Not many took this path unless they were coming the long way around the valley or they were guests of the family. The guard station was never really manned since no one other than the family used the road. Today, as they passed, a single guard was asleep at his post. The rustle of the cart going by startled him back to attention, and the family laughed at the sight. He waved good morning to them and went out back to make himself breakfast before his shift change.

The forest before the town is always quiet, as very few creatures could live in the cursed environment. The family passed a clearing in the middle of the woods, the site of the last great war before the empire united. The imprisonment of Immortal King Ebedi by the Heartless Council ignited the great war as a power struggle ensued to replace him. The ground was cursed and dangerous to walk on. Magic items, armor, and weapons littered the field. There's a fortune to be made if you could get to it and be able to hold it long enough to sell it. The fool's treasure was either infused with magic to increase the power of the wielder or cursed to prevent it from being taken on the battlefield. The spoiled ground could take decades to recover.

Regardless, the few pieces near the edge have already been hoarded, and the coveted pieces lie farther away than a rope can be thrown to get to them. Just grazing one of these items could set off an explosion that would kill a small platoon. The ground was cratered and scorched by many explosions. The trees in the area were fallen and splintered, as if mangled by a natural disaster. It was thought to clear the forest of the troublesome items, but it only led to items being stolen before disposal for black-market sales. The town itself leaves the cursed forest alone, creating a makeshift wall around them for protection. Further in, smaller fey have taken up residence, making small towns in the trees and allowing the cursed ground to protect them from those who would do them harm.

Freshly decaying bodies of fools littered the ground, and fallen leaves piled on those already dead from the changing seasons. Still, many have tried; the family notices a few foreigners in the area near the edge of the field. Tossing lines with hooks, shooting arrows, and using light wind magic to get ever closer to the valuable pieces, the family could hear some curses discharged in the distance as they left the woods heading into town.

The family's main shop is near the center of the town of Golen. The main forge had to remain isolated outside of town in case of a magical discharge from the volatile magical steel and to protect the family's forging secrets. Demir, who was once the King's grandmaster blacksmith, has since retired to this town to raise a family. Demir mastered all manner of steel forging, from the elegant art of the dwarves and elves to the beast-made steel of phoenixes and dragons. His large build is a remnant of his craft. Demir's red beard and hair concealed most of the scars on his face from the beast's forging. Tattoos encompass Demir's body as a sign of his guild, status, and craft. "Hun, I am going to run a few errands around town, do you need anything?"

Demir turns to her "Fenya, my love, any way you can grab meat and ale for tonight."

He looks into her eyes. Pools of pure gold shined brightly amidst her dark hair. A former oracle and adviser to the king, she fell in love with Demir while they worked together at the castle. Her homely, hand-sewn white linen dress was a far cry from the white silk robes she wore in the capital. For Demir, it did not matter what she was wearing, he only saw her.

She placed her hand on his cheek and brushed through his beard. "We will see. You need to bathe today, you have too much dust in your beard." He holds her hand to his cheek. She sees the metal scaling on the inside of his hands. The outsides of his hands were covered in glyph tattoos for his trade. Finally, she sees the fresh cut he made at the house for the barrier.

"You know that you don't need to place that barrier every time. The home is already protected well enough." She smiled while holding his hands.

Demir's home was guarded by the kingdom because he was the first complete grand master Smith ever born, having held every station in the guild. Most smiths in the world are specialists in specific types of forging. Demir could forge anything with fire and magic, from demons to dragons and phoenixes to fairies. His daughter Oriel was the only one that inherited his ability. She still needed time to build stamina like her father does to resist the flame's feedback. Olcay and Orion could only forge some creatures, but nothing that could be imbued with magic. For the kingdom, his abilities were valued and protected. Demir's ability was a blessing and a curse. A person seeking his skills were not looking to make farm equipment. They desired weapons of the most dangerous kind.

Demir placed his large hand behind her ear and felt the waves in her hair lovingly. "Looks like the weather will be good today, your hair feels soft."

"Don't get cheeky right here," she said, grabbing his hand, going in, and kissing the exposed part of his cheek. Fenya grabbed her basket for the market and waved goodbye to Demir.

The town itself had three blacksmiths besides Demir's. Being on the border meant that a lot of trade passed through the area. The other smiths in town were decent enough in their craft. Their trade was mostly the care of the tools or decorative stuff. Demir limited his work when it came to weapons or tools, allowing the other blacksmiths to obtain work easily. His stipend from the kingdom kept him from wanting. Each of the blacksmiths was famous in their own right, adding to the town's prosperity.

Fenya walked among the crowd of people in the market square in search of the evening's meal and ale for her husband. She knew there would be some celebration and wanted to make sure it went well. As she passed the stalls, the vendors would greet her with a solemn bow of respect, and she was not hassled like other customers. Along the border, trade was just as good as in the capital cities. In some cases, the prices were better on perishable items that might not make the trip to the main bazaar.

"How much for a barrel of ale?" Fenya inquired softly to Brewmeister

"Around 20, malady" He smiled and stroked the end of his beard.

"I see you giving it to me for 10" as her eyes shined in the light

The brewer gave her a chuckle heard across the market. "It never gets old; I will do it for 15 and deliver it to your place tonight after the market closes."

She smiled, nodded, and handed him the 15 silver coins for the ale already wrapped in the coin purse. Fenya turned and felt a small tug at her skirt from below, she smiled and knelt to see two small blue-eyed children, one no older than five and another no older than six years of age.

"Can you tell us about our future? Will I become a big and strong warrior?" The boy's little voice was full of happiness and glee.

6

"Will I be rich?" said the second just as excited.

Fenya smiled and turned her eyes quickly gold and back again to give them a shock.

"Well now… are sure you want to know?" "Yes, please!" They said in unison their voices rang out in the street. Her golden eyes flared open in a sparkling light. She then leaned down to meet their gaze. "I see your mother being upset about her missing pies and two very red bottoms."

Their smiles turned to dread as they ran off. A few of the villagers that overheard her smiled and laughed at the exchange.

Back at the forge Demir ritually prayed before entering. This was also used to check the stability of the forge's barriers to prevent explosions.

"Oriel! You're working with the fairies today. See if they are up." Demir yelled to her. He could hear Oriel giggle with glee inside the shop running to the back room.

Demir was in a rush and started collecting his tools haphazardly, he wanted to open shop before the market started to get busy. Olcay already put the horses up and Orion started to empty the wagon of the products for sale and patrons' custom orders. Oriel went through the shop to the forge. Above the forge was a small home. "Stix ...Hix are you up yet?" "We need to get started."

The little home's windows lit up. "We're up. Did you bring breakfast?" A high-pitched voice blurted out from the house.

Oriel placed a small pouch at their door. A tiny hand reached out and pulled it into the little home. The sounds of belching and eating filled the room. "Father has said I will be working with you today." Oriel's voice was enthusiastic. The eating stopped. Two small figures stepped out of the little house. The identical twin fire fairies, Stix and Hix, were both dressed in leather garb like blacksmiths. Their wings gave off an amber glow, and a flame appeared above their heads. In the dimly lit room, they appeared to be candles.

"Are sure you are ready?" Stix asked, voicing concern.

"I have to learn some time." She replied with assurance.

"Then we will start with just a simple dance today, nothing needing imbuing magic…" Hix started.

"She will be doing a full forging today." Demir bellowed from outside.

"Sir, she is still young for this." They protested in unison.

"She has already worked the dwarven forges and can forge with salamanders and a fire mare. "She is ready for the fairies to dance." Demir reassured them. "It is not like she is forging with a demon or a dragon." He said sarcastically.

7

"Then we will prepare the forge after breakfast. Oriel we are proud of you and look forward to our dance." The twins said in unison.

Oriel was giddy and went upstairs to change. She stripped down to her linens and put on her smithing gear. Her freckled skin was still free of scars, unlike her father's. She was tall like her mother and had a mild build that was quite feminine. She tied up her red hair and placed a leather cap over the bun. She was always excited when it came to a new forging and was looking forward to working with the twins for a while.

Forging required several things. First and foremost, the fire source had to be willing. Forcing a creature to produce fire could cause the metal to be tainted or fail at holding in the magic. Fire fairies were some of the safest beings to work with, yet one of the hardest, since their fire magic required a dance.

Demir yelled out the window. "Olcay, Orion… prepare the shop for opening and prep the tools. You will both be assisting today!"

"Really?!" you could hear them both say in excitement from outside. They both grabbed their leather garbs hanging on the wall. They may not have inherited his ability, but Demir never left them out of being part of his work.

The sun was starting to rise above the tree line between the mountains and the town. Golen sat on the outermost part of the kingdom, about a full day's ride from the main capital of Telson. The impassable mountain range protected them from invasions and raids. The main road pass was the only way through the mountains to the other kingdoms of the west. The prosperous town traded in mining from the mountains, artisan crafts, and an array of fine smithing. The main pass to the west made Golen the first or last stop before going to the capital. Demir's work was also a main attraction for the town, as many would love to possess anything from the kingdom's master blacksmith. Demir kept nothing of value at the shop to prevent thieves from nicking anything. Besides, imbued or not, forged steel would be dangerous in the wrong hands.

Oriel came down from upstairs and saw her brothers in their positions. Her father was dealing with customers outside the window. He was keeping an eye on her and keeping his distance.

"Stix and Hix I am ready… Orion and Olcay let's begin"

Olcay grabbed a pouch with the alchemist steel and handed it to his sister. She grabbed her hammer and struck the lifeless steel. The sound rang out in the forge.

Hix and Stix disrobed, and their leather garb fell to the ground. Their forms were thin and muscular, and their wings sprouted up as clear as glass. Their wings ignited and started to burn brightly. Oriel started to pound the cold steel rhythmically. The twins embraced and plunged into the heart of the cold forge. The room instantly heated up as the heart of the forge came to life. Inside the fire, two forms danced. It was reminiscent of an Elvin ballet. Oriel took the cold steel into her hands and placed it in the forge without hesitation. Her arm lit up with runes up to her shoulder. The heat even activated the ones in her neck and chest. She knew it was going to be different.

Demir watched in awe from the window, ignoring his customers. Gradually, the other windows began to fill with the faces of the townsfolk. Oriel began to sing in tune with the twins' movements.

A thousand-year the fire forge will rage
Bringing life and death to all that age
Stealing time and rewriting their page
All written and danced on a smith's stage
Giving the farmer rule over his field
Arming the oppressed swords and shield
All with the power I wield
Turning the world with what I yield

The twins danced on top of the steel, making markings in rhythm to the beat. Oriel pulled the heated steel with her bare hands from the forge. The runes begin to spin around her arm and create circles. They started to sound and resonate with the twins' movement. Olcay hands Oriel the hammer she needs while Orion holds the steel to the anvil with a pair of tongs.

There are several ways to imbue steel with magic. Steel can have the magic put into it ahead of time as an ingot. However, magic can be lost when the steel is heated and not treated correctly. This is the preferred method as it is low-risk and does not require a magic caster to be present nor a special creature to move the flame. The fire can give off natural magic that can harness a wielder's will. Powerful creatures like demons and dragons produce magic this way and are highly sought after. The risk is great, as not many dragons are willing to work with a smith; even then, not many can survive the process. Demons require contracts or blood to forge and cannot be trusted. Magic can be imbued directly from the source. In the case of the twins, they dance the spell right into the blade. In all cases, the blacksmith must decide how the metal is used, the magic required, and the seal on the metal. The seal acts as a framework in the metal to keep it attached.

Oriel continues in rhythm as the blade takes shape into a small dagger. The metal begins to sing in the chorus. The runes begin to move down the blade from her arm.

9

The blade took on a white glow. The final words are danced onto the blade as Oriel takes a final dip into water.

Demir shakes himself from his awe and walks into the forge, grabbing the cooling blade with his bare hands to inspect it. Demir saw the imperfections and the misspellings by the twins, as they may have been drinking the night before. However, the seal was holding, and the framework was solid. Demir smirked at the now exhausted, sweating, and hungry trio.

"Excellent work, I might be able to butter my bread with this tonight" He laughed. They knew he was kidding, but it was still embarrassing as the township joined in on the joke. Demir hands the blade to Oriel. "Fine first attempt, remember next time the source has to be willing and sober." Demir glared into the fiery blaze, looking at the now uncomfortable twins.

"Sorry sir, we found a couple of dwarves, and things got out of hand," Hix said reluctantly. Demir wanted to scold them, but he dismissed them to sober up and turned to his daughter.

Oriel looked at her first fairy blade with amazement. The patterns gave off hues of color. "So, what do you want to do with it?" Demir asked Oriel.

"I want to work it again with Fico at home," she said, shouting in excitement.

"Sorry, Oriel, you are not yet ready for Fico. He is still resurrecting, and you have not built up the resistance nor stamina for the task." Demir raised her chin with his right hand. "Give it some time."

"Father…" Oriel's voice cracked.

"We will not discuss Fico!" Demir's fatherly face turned to concern. "You still have a few years before you are ready for high tiers of magical forging." He placed his hand over her shoulders. "A phoenix is just too much right now for you."

"But you let me play with Fico all the time and I have never been hurt once." Oriel rebutted

"Oriel, look at my hands, the insides are completely torn apart still from my first time." He held his palms out to her. His hands were caked in calluses. His glyphs showed through, and the metal in his hands sparkled. "Once we get you doing steel with a few more beasts, we will see. I would hate for you to have hands like mine too soon."

She saw his wounds and scaring as beautiful and the embodiment of their craft. He continues to mentor her "Your scars will come in time." Demir rested his hands on her shoulders. Oriel sulked in disappointment yet understood her father's wishes.

"Olcay and Orion go take care of the customers and we will clean up in here before your mother gets back with lunch." Demir's voice bellowed out across the shop.

The market square had just come to life with townsfolk, traders, merchants, and travelers. All manner of races also came to this open town. Vendors were shouting to attract customers, announcing fresh produce, potions, and baked goods. Olcay knew that he did not need to shout as customers from all over the world came down the market street for one reason only. They came for a House of Demir weapon, or at least to see one. Foreigners also came to see his sister and ask if she had been given indoctrination as a Master Smith yet. An early work of hers would be quite valuable to noble collectors. Oriel worked tirelessly in the forge on the pre-commissioned requests from customers.

Olcay negotiated prices at the shop front with customers needing orders and repairs. A few traders from the western pass needed some tools, a dwarf from the mines demanded a hammer be repaired, and a Lycian needed a purification blade for his rituals.

Next in line was one of the foreigners he saw on the way to town. A tall, lanky man with a limp, dressed in the ritual robe of a western god, Olcay thought to himself, 'They probably got the limp from the explosion they heard.'

"Olcay, son of Demir. How can I help you, sir? Catch anything?" Olcay wanted to have a bit of fun but could see the man's face was lacking a sense of humor.

"Holens, son of Burtran. I need something purified, and I am in a little bit of a rush." The man replied flinging his sack onto the counter.

"Well, let's have a look." Olcay reached under the counter to grab his gloves. Nothing that came out of that field was safe to touch. Opening the sack, he saw a blade. "From the looks of it, we have a cursed demon steel blade. Great condition from being in the field. Olcay could see from the inscriptions that it was made for a berserker, and handling it would not end well. The raw power alone would kill the wielder after a single use.

"So how much to purify the blade?" The man's voice was snarky and condescending.

"Purification like this would need dragon fire, but I don't have that in the back. Or a phoenix and ours is dormant right now…" Olcay was explaining and then interrupted.

"What are saying?! The great shop of Demir cannot handle a simple purification?" Holens said mockingly.

"Can I help you, friend?" Demir bellowed from the window. "Olcay, I will handle this." Demir's large frame overshadowed the skinny man. He grabbed the cursed sword barehanded, and the sword's guard began glowing with life. The skinny man jumped back in fear, screaming, "Are you mad?!"

Olcay was in the corner of the counter, trying to hold in a laugh. Demir's arm runes activated, and the guard returned to normal and became lifeless. "Let me educate you on cursed swords. Doesn't do a smith much good if the blasted thing is going to activate when working with it." Demir wraps it back in the sack "Next, as my son was explaining, I can purify the blade after our phoenix egg hatches on the next crescent moon. Payment is due upfront."

Holens, now humbled by the scare, brushes himself off. "How much then to also inscribe a power boosted incantation?"

"20 silver for both." Demir's voice was firm

"That is absurd! I will pay you 15." Holens looked like he was about to have a tantrum.

"Look you pulled it out of the field, and you can't handle it, so you want to sell it. You need it cleansed since the curse is only good for the black market. The nearest blacksmith that may be willing to handle this is a week away."

"Fine! I have business in the Kingdom anyways and will be back after the crescent moon"

The angry customer paid his 20 pieces of silver and shook hands for the deal. The man leaves, with Olcay barely able to contain his laughter. Demir managed a chuckle as well. He always tries to discourage people from grabbing items from the battleground by overcharging. Purifying them could bring big business. However, stealing from the dead brings one's honor into question. "Olcay, keep it in the bag. Place it in the cart with a tag so we don't misplace it." Olcay put his glove back on and took the blade to the back. Olcay always worked in the shop as safely as possible. Even with the forge's safety measures in place, many of the items could prove deadly.

The day was ending, and the family started to close the shop. Oriel managed repairs with the twins on farm equipment and some elven armor. Fenya returned from her errands in town. She had the meat and mead delivered earlier that day. She managed to bring a container of honey for the twins and an old cow being led by a rope. Her children were excited to explain the day's events to their mother as they loaded up the cart for home and tied the cow to the back. The road wound its way through the forest before turning around. They could see a few more bodies being claimed by the forest and paid no attention to them. The sun was setting as they saw the silhouette of their home come into focus. "Olcay hitched the cow to the post near the cliff for tonight. Orion clean up the cart, I have work again tonight before dinner, and Oriel you will need to assist me," Demir instructed his brood.

The forge at home always burned brightly. The room was spacious to allow ample workspace for complicated projects or beasts to move around. Tiyron, a large, blazing salamander, slept in the corner of the room. In the back was a large door to a stone stable. A fire-mare peered out to see what they were up to. Oriel went over and pulled fresh meat from the pouch she brought in. "Here you go, Phyo good boy." The fire-mare took the meat from her hands and went to the outside corral.

In the middle was the forge and within it was Fico's egg on a fiery altar. The egg gave off a permanent blaze and allowed the forge to always be heated without the need for fuel. The fire had no magical properties; it was still useful for regular work. Underneath the inner forge was a hole that ventilated the forge naturally from the caves within the mountain. "Oriel... Fico will hatch tonight if you want to watch" He turned and put his hand on her shoulder.

"Really father?" Oriel said excitedly. The last time she missed it was because she slept in.

"Yes, the color of the fire is right tonight." He guided her down and pointed into the forge. Pointing out the hues bouncing off the forge walls

"Does this mean I will be able to work with Fico tonight?" The big child's eyes came out to pull at his heartstrings.

"No, we already discussed this. You can watch the hatching only." Demir scolded. "Maybe when you can chant in tune for once."

"Understood." Oriel pouted.

Demir had Oriel stand back and reach into the forge to grab the egg. As he held it, the runes on his arm resonated. The heat was intense and woke up Tiyron in the corner. The flames of the egg went from red to blue. The glyphs on Oriel's arms activated just from the heat alone. A painful screech came from the egg as it began to crack, and a bright, searing light enveloped the room. A little beaked face emerged from the egg. The heat subsided, and a tiny feathered figure stood in Demir's hand. "Welcome back, my old friend," Demir said with a smile.

Fico's small frame was no bigger than a fairy or imp. His feathers shined like tinted glass and sparked tiny blue flames.

"Father, he is blue this time, what happened?" Oriel was captivated.

"A phoenix rebirth is exactly that, a rebirth. He can come back each time different." Demir started to pet Fico "This time is special."

"I thought his rebirth was not for a few days."

13

"Technically, it would have been, but today was different. We have a star alignment tonight that favors for the rebirth" Fico started to become drowsy. Demir placed him back into the forge and opened the vent to the cavern. Fico started to spark as he slept in the inferno.

"He will fully grow in a few days, and we can get the bigger projects done." Demir gave her a nudge out the forge door. "You will get your chance."

They went in and retired for the evening after supper. Oriel was restless as she could only imagine the forge and working with Fico.

Chapter 2

The next morning. "I do not feel well today," Oriel said to the family at breakfast. Her face was mildly pale, and her voice was groggy.

"It's normal after your first time with fairies. Take the day off." Her father stated.

"They probably gave you their hangover during the connection." Demir let out a chuckle.

"But I wanted to try to work with the twins again." Oriel was able to stand but felt weak and light-headed.

"You heard your father; Gods above know he went through it before with fairies." her mom stated. Fenya remembered that Demir also partied with them the night before that incident. He had an additional hangover after the connection.

"Bet the twins partied last night again so no lost work," Olcay said jokingly.

The morning routine stayed the same as they all prepared the cart for their trip to town. Knowing Oriel would be home alone, Fenya did not object to the barrier being set. As Oriel waved goodbye to her family in the distance, she turned to the forge. She never noticed the back post of the house was empty.

After time passed and boredom started to set in, Oriel found herself restless. "I might as well get a few projects done," Oriel said to herself as she got up out of bed. Her weakness and headache were still there, but she could not lay down all day. Oriel disrobed and started to look over her markings. The patterns of the tattoos can just be seen under her skin, encompassing most of her body. Only a few places on her shoulders and chest were left. She took a moment to reflect on each one and the future they held for her. In a bit of fun, she activated all she had on her. The writings began to come to the surface of her skin. They moved around her body in waves of patterns. Oriel took the time to hug herself and smile. Every mark was earned, and she was proud of them.

She found her work clothes already prepared on the chair in the next room, along with some breakfast and some powdered root for her headache. "I guess mom was expecting me to get up."

The medications gave her some relief, and she was able to get dressed and head outside to the forge.

Fico was still resting in his inferno bed, and the other beasts started to stir when she entered the forge. She laid out the projects her father had picked up the day before. She saw the sack that had the cursed sword that her father needed to fix with Fico. She only overheard the conversation. She unwrapped it from the sack. The eye in the hilt fired up and tried to activate. Then Oriel's arm markings resurfaced, and the barriers in the forge activated in shimmering light, and the hilt went dark.

"Nasty little curse you have there." A little voice spoke from the forge.

Oriel turned to see the full-sized splendor of Fico. "Fully restored, I see," Oriel replied with a smile. Fico's form was impressive. He was as tall as Oriel; the plumage was mature with a full spectrum of blue hues. Small blue flames smoldered underneath. "I doubt Demir would allow you to play with such a thing," Fico said.

"I was just looking and studying," Oriel replied. She placed the sword down by Tiyron's stable.

Oriel embraced Fico. "How was your slumber?" The full-sized phoenix rested his head on her shoulder.

"It went well, it has been some time since I was blue. Does it suit me?" Fico asked as he turned around. His plumage was reflective like glass and small flames emanated from the folds in his wings.

"Of course, you look magnificent. My brothers will be in awe when they get back." She was reminiscing about the last time she saw him in golden yellow and wanted to compare the experiences.

"How is the family doing? Not much I can account for when I am cooking." Fico asked as he settled himself on a piece of stone next to the forge. He heated the stone between his claws to make a better hold.

"Mother and father are the same. Orion is back from his apprenticeship and will start working in the trade guild at the end of the year. Olcay… we are waiting for him to grow up." Oriel said with a smile. She sat next to him to get more comfortable. The radiant heat from him caused a few of her clothing runes to activate.

"Olcay owes me a few new stories still," Fico said. He started to look about the room to see the changes.

"Olcay needs to get his nose out of his books and pick an apprenticeship." Oriel retorted. She crossed her arms as if to brace for an argument.

"He never inherited the deific gifts of your parents, so you must give him some pardon. At least he still works hard." His voice was as soothing as that of an old wise man. But it was not a relief to Oriel.

"I guess, it is just frustrating to see him with his head in the clouds." She stood up and kicked a stone and her arms flared in the air in frustration.

"Well, I do rather enjoy the clouds myself." Fico laughed.

Oriel turned to the forge behind Fico and saw that the inferno was still ablaze without fuel. "Fico, is that something new with the fire?" She asked. Fico turned to look at the back window toward the post outback. "No worries, it will be fine. Just need to close the vent." Fico replied. Oriel went over to the vent lever next to Tiyron's pen. Reaching over, she accidentally knocked some tools onto the floor. The crash on the floor startled Tiyron and his tail lit ablaze and heated the cursed sword. A second eye opened in the hilt, and a seal formed on the floor.

"Get back Oriel!" Fico yelled, as he pushed her out of the way and was thrown back a bit himself by an unknown force.

As a thin-faced man appeared in the seal, Oriel ducked behind the counter. Fico took a defensive posture, igniting his feathers. The room heated up instantly. "You came to the wrong house, friend."

Oriel peered around the counter and could see the same frail framed customer from yesterday that her father argued with.

"I was hoping that I would appear here." The man chuckled as he licked the blade slicing open part of his tongue.

"What business do you have here?" Fico demanded. The flames between his feathers started to take shape and his plumage looked fuller. They started to stare each other down and circle around the bench in the middle of the room.

"I am here for the secret of the unknown flame that is in that forge." He sneered.

Fico chuckled. "Not much of a plan, how did you plan to leave with that information?"

"I was hoping that I would appear at a better time or at least in a position to take a hostage."

Holens lunged at Fico with the blade, and Fico withdrew into the air to draw his attention from Oriel. He swung wildly at Fico but was too angry to see where he was going. Holens started knocking around the ingredients on the table and they started to smoke on his clothes. Fico sensed something was wrong and posted himself over where Oriel was hiding.

"Oriel, you need to activate all of your markings right now!" Fico commanded. Oriel did as she was told and braced for an impact. Fico turned his sight toward the intruder. "You are not the first person to get this far, hence why the master of this forge always sets up something special for unwelcome guests." A magic circle encompassed the room, and the air became heated. "Don't move, I would hate to have you make a mess all over the room," Fico said maniacally. The man sensed that he was in danger and grabbed the cursed sword and tried to activate it. He held it in both hands, awaiting the explosion in power, and ... nothing. Fico laughed, "You are a moron, you should have known that would not activate here." Oriel sat in the corner of the table nearest to the forge with her protection barriers up. She knew if something were to happen, Fico would protect her; she only needed to stay out of the way.

Holens, in a fit of rage, tossed the sword at Fico. Fico smugly dodges the flying blade...

"We need to go home now!" Demir yelled to the family. "Olcay grab the king's guard at the garrison barracks. Orion unhooks the horses from the cart; we need to ride back now."

Demir could only feel his heart at this point; he only knew he had to stay calm; he had to hold his breath to regain it.

"What's happening, Hun?!" Fenya was in a panic as she had not seen Demir like this since the war. His face went hard as iron, trying not to show her his fear.

"I sensed the forge barrier had been breached and the traps activated... now nothing."

He grabs Fenya and hugs her saying, "She will be ok. My beast brethren at home will protect her." Demir had no time to fully console her; he saw Orion coming around the house on his horse with the other in tow. Demir mounted the horse and rode off without looking back. Orion wanted to ask his father what was going on, but he knew that he would not get an answer. He prepared a blade from his saddle.

On approach, they could see smoke above the tree line. They raced to the homestead and saw that Tiyron was on the ground near the forge, and Phyo was running around scared. They happened upon scorched remains close to the house. Demir turns it over to see the half-burnt remains of the rude customer, Holens, from yesterday. The cinder began to consume his flesh where he lay. Nothing could be done for him, and he would not provide it if he could.

His eyes opened wide in agonizing pain. Demir and Orion jumped back. A cursed mark ran widely over his body. "What is in the flame?" He said with his dying breath.

Demir looked to the forge "Oriel?!" His breath now was taking him as he turned.

They both ran through the broken door of the forge. The blackened room and rubble are offset by the bright plumage of Fico in the middle of the room. "Fico are you alright? Where is Oriel?!" Demir panicked. Fico turns to see them and moves his wings to reveal the tattered body of Oriel. Fico shielded her from the main blast. "Fico what happened?"

"The idiot tossed a cursed sword into the forge... it was purified and instantly released the curses without a seal. The sudden release caused it to run wild all over the forge. Somehow it overrode the forge barrier as well." Fico struggled to stand; his body was a complete mess. Fico's broken parts began to reset themselves. He was thankful he would not need to regenerate fully this time.

"Curses?" Demir was confused. Even with barrier down Oriel should have been safe with her runes and glyphs.

"The sword was a trap made to infiltrate and also remove witnesses." Fico sighed. "I don't think I have seen anything like it since the war. Only another smith from that time could have made it."

As Fico fully healed, he stood up. They could see Oriel's body was covered in curse marks like tattoos. Some started to interweave within her flesh.

"Orion go outside; secure Tiyron and Phyo," Demir demanded. Orion didn't want to argue and left to find them. He moved Oriel over to what remained of the forge's circle. He placed some hay under her head to make her feel comfortable.

"I stopped the spread and prevented the activation. This is beyond my ability to remove without killing her." Fico got up to stretch out his newly healed body. "Only the king can remove such a thing." Fico then leaned into Demir's ear. "He was looking for the secret to the flame."

Demir looked at Fico with horror, he then nodded to Fico in understanding. Demir started to feel the ground shake, horses were approaching. The king's guard; Olcay must have brought them already. "Fico, will you be alright?" Demir asked.

"Yes, a fiery bath will fully revitalize me." Fico walked back over to Oriel and moved the hair out of her face. "I am sorry young one that I could not save you." He began to cry, the tears sizzled as they hit her face. Not even they could help her.

Demir placed his hand on Fico's wing. "You kept her alive, now we will do the rest, my ancient friend."

From outside they could hear the guards surrounding the home. "Secure the house! Secure the barrier." They started to scatter everywhere, surrounding the house and forge grounds. The assailant may have met his end, but others may be around.

"Demir is the forge secure?" The captain of the guard yelled from outside.

"Yes sir, it is safe to approach!" Demir shouted. "Bring a stretcher!"

Two other smiths from the town came with the guards to help secure the forge's barriers. They may be on the cliffside, but the explosion was loud enough to have the town worried and rushing to their aid. Demir let his fellow blacksmiths get to work as he attended to his daughter.

Fenya and Olcay came barreling down the road in their cart. They borrowed horses from the neighbors in town. Fenya could see the guards surrounding her home in the distance. She could see Demir speaking with an officer near the forge. Orion saw them and intersected their path. "Orion, what happened?" Fenya asked with her lips curled, fearing the worse.

"We had an unwelcome guest. Everyone is fine for the most part." Orion could not make eye contact with her to even give that comfort.

"Where's Oriel?!" Fenya screamed. Pulling her son's shoulders to meet his eyes as they shined brightly in the light.

"She is with Fico in the forge mom." Orion's words did not bring her any more comfort. Fenya's eyes started to glow, and she rushed towards the forge. Demir stopped and held her in place.

"You can't go in yet; Fico and the smiths are restoring the barriers." He held onto her, knowing she may never forgive him. Demir could see his wife's eyes glowing in fear of an impending future. Tears ran down her face, motherly tears that shined on her face like glass.

"I am going to need you to stop trying to see the future right now. Calm yourself for Oriel's sake." Demir knew that when an oracle peered into the future, it ran the risk of writing fate. "You know there is only one person that can handle this, and we have to ride now if we are going to save her."

Fenya looked into her husband's eyes looking to see if he had gone mad. The horror of returning to his Majesty King Hakim of the Uneven Throne! They both feared the day they would need his help. Demir's mind was in turmoil on seeing the King. However, he could not hesitate at this moment for Oriel's sake. He knew that there would be consequences.

"Fico, I need you to stay here to take care of matters. Orion, you stay at the shop and deal with the customers until we return." Demir instructed. "Olcay prepare for the journey, ready the cart with Phyo we need to get to the King by the morning."

No one hesitated and got to work. The guards helped load the cart with Oriel's stretcher. Olcay grabbed what he could from the house, some lanterns, food, water skins, and blankets. Fenya made sure she was comfortable. With everyone loaded, the guards escorted them into the night with torches.

Chapter 3

The night was long, Olcay worked with his father, riding like madmen, until the sun began to rise. The great wall that surrounded the main city was in view. The guards broke off to ride ahead to the main gate to expedite their entry. Olcay could see the grand bazaar from the hillside, which was stirring as vendors started opening. He looked behind to see his mother asleep next to his sister. His father, who drove the first leg of the trip, was still wide awake. His brow was furrowed, tired, and heavy with worry.

Olcay was aware that his father and the king had fallen out but did not know the reason why. They approached the gate, and the vizier of the king was there to greet them. A short, chubby man, wearing red robes, and a square red and gold hat. "Master Demir I am Vizier Tyrak. "What brings you here before the drunkards go home?" he scoffed, arranging his robes to keep warm.

"I have an emergency and need to speak with King Hakim!" Demir bellowed. He felt he did not have time for formalities with a useless bureaucrat.

"Watch your tone. His majesty is asleep still, and I will not have him awakened for trivial matters." The vizier gave a cocky smile and went to dismiss them from the gate.

Demir's face was already pushing the emotions started to add one more as he turned red. "You..." He could only think of snapping the man in two and dealing with the consequences later.

"You know as well as I do that King Hakim never sleeps and never leaves his throne." Fenya interrupted. Her golden eyes shone through the dawn's light. "He would welcome old friends." Her voice conveyed both calm and malevolent caution.

The vizier was shocked to his core and took in a breath to gain his shaky composure. He stood back from their path and then motioned to the guards. "Let them in and lead them to the palace main gates." He did not want to start his day with a foreboding omen.

The streets were coming to life; the street carts were already starting to be moved into place, and the apprentices were already prepping before dawn. Thankfully, they came before the streets were too crowded to move. Even with the splendor of the dawn and all its color, they could barely make out the castle since it was made of only dark gray stone. You couldn't tell what was a shadow and what was a wall. Several towers are positioned at the corners of both sets of walls. The main entrance was down a stone path surrounded on both sides by walls. As they approached the end of the path, they were met by the palace guards, who were already prepared for their arrival. On the front of the castle, Olcay could see a grand metal door. Even at a distance, he could see the fine detail. It was exquisitely ornate and the size of a dragon. He noticed his father's mark on the door, as well as the marks of several other smiths. It must have taken months to collect enough metal for this door, he thought.

The guards that rode with them all night waited for them at the stairs. "Go to the inn, gentlemen. Thank you for the escort." Demir tosses them a satchel of gold coins. "The inn will be better than the barracks." The guards could not argue or fight the sleep they needed. "Olcay, help me carry your sister on the stretcher." Olcay secures the brake and runs around to help. Oriel was still unconscious; her face was red on one side from the incident.

"Olcay what do you know about the king?" Demir asked as they began to situate her.

"He is the King of Judgment. Following the defeat of the Immortal King by the Heartless Council, there was a power struggle over the kingdom. Lord Hakim ended the war with the other factions wanting power and forced a stalemate with the council. Hakim's rise to supremacy came from the power of his weapons, fashioned from you father and the oracles." Olcay responded with what he could remember.

"History books and bards do like to spin the tale. After the war, I requested an unpopular reward; my retirement with Fenya. King Hakim allowed it if I continued to work for the kingdom when called upon. He has been grumpy and spiteful since." Demir then muttered under his breath, "…also quite mad."

Demir looked Oriel over, he could see the fragments from the blast were throughout her skin. Fenya led them both up the stairs to the main door as they carried Oriel. The main door opened and inside were great halls both left and right. The halls were decorated with stone figures and statues. The main throne room's door was made from metal as well; adorned with art of the war and beasts. In full armor, the guards were as tall as the ceiling itself. "Master Demir and Lady Fenya, King Hakim is expecting you." Giants would be required to push doors this large, Olcay reasoned.

Olcay did not know what to make of the situation. He was there for his sister and yet was awestruck by everything he was seeing.

"Olcay"

"Yes, Father?"

"Don't do anything unless I say. I had no time to prepare you for this."

"Yes, Father." Olcay could see his father's cold sweat roll down his face.

The giants pushed against the mighty door; it creaked and cracked. The ground trembled. The giant to Demir's right whispered. "The gods be with you."

"Thank you, my friend, we will get through this." He gave a friendly tap to the giant's knee as that is all he could reach.

Olcay felt at that moment the massive door and the giants were just for show and whatever was in the room needed no such protection. Olcay followed in; the massive room had a temperature change that was quite cold and bitter. The room was brightly lit, but he couldn't see a light source from anywhere. The grand hall was entirely covered in polished white stone. It was like a blank canvas with specs of glint and muted color. The kingdom's crest, ornaments, and curtains; are all made from carved stone. It was as if everything was frozen in time. The room lacked carpet, furniture, and treasure of any kind. Overall, from a distance, it looked rather somberly barren. They all started the walk through the main throne room. Olcay could start to make out the massive figure sitting on a broken throne.

King Hakim was a massive, bearded man, semi-clothed in leather garments. His right hand was holding the hilt of a massive double-sided ax. His left arm looked withered, mummified, and decayed; it was resting with his palm facing upward on a small pedestal. The uneven throne he sat on was beautifully carved on his right and newly polished. The left side was cracked, destroyed, and decayed. Demir led Olcay over to a small altar on the right side of the room and placed Oriel atop it. They all went to the middle of the room and bowed down. The tension was uncomfortable, and the room was quiet. Only a few guards and serfs were in the room, and you could only hear their breathing echoing throughout the large chamber. "Old friend, what brings you before me at this early hour?" The king's voice broke through the silence, and it was terrifying. Even the familiarity of the voice was unsettling, haunting and bellowing in Demir's gut.

"Sire, my home was attacked last night, and my daughter was injured in the incident." Demir got down on his knees. "The kingdom's barriers were breached." Demir's words were straight to the point.

The king leaned in with intrigue "How?" His massive frame leaned forward but his left hand never left the column.

"Unknown; that got past mine as well," Demir replied.

King Hakim was stalled by hearing this. "I will send my people out to look over the barriers." Hakim motioned to his guard, a fully plated knight, and whispered to him then turned back to the room. "Now the matter of your daughter, what happened?"

"Her injuries were mild; however, the assailant tossed a cursed sword into my phoenix companion's fire and released a curse abruptly. She was hit with the feedback." As Demir pleaded, he saw something he had only seen once before.

23

The king stood up from his throne. The room attendants were thrown back. It has been some time since the king moved from his throne. "Well, let's have a look." The King's full height towered over Demir, and his presence cast a shadow over the room.

He walked past them and over to Oriel. Olcay looked over and saw genuine fear in his father's eyes. The king uncovered one of the bandages covering Oriel's arm. He walked slowly back to the throne and stood in front of it. He reached to the right side of the throne with his left hand and grabbed his ax. He slammed it down on the ground, cracking the stone floor. "Clear the room now! Seal the great hall!" Hakim commanded. Guards, attendees, viziers, and court members clamored for the door and sealed the room. The doors, windows, and cracks in the walls fused and became solid.

Hakim sighed "What are you doing Demir? Who else knows?" The king seemed annoyed and rather disappointed at the situation.

"No one, your majesty." Demir's eyes could not look up to see the king's gaze. The king sat back on his throne and placed his left hand back on the pedestal. With his right hand, he rubbed his forehead in disbelief.

"Even if I overlooked everything, you still violated the guilds' rules and they're a pain as it is. I almost should let things happen as they are to teach you a lesson."

"Please sire, Oriel just got caught up in the incident. It was no one's fault. She is innocent." Fenya cried out in panic.

"Fenya you are too soft and naive; this might have been avoided if you honed your abilities better. Demir I am surprised you kept such a large beast hidden so well." Hakim chuckled."

Fenya turned to Demir her eyes in tears wanting answers. "What is he saying?!" He was silent and avoided her gaze. 'Why will you not answer me?!"

From their side, they heard, "Fire used in forging or incantations have several properties. Fire from magical beings or beasts can inscribe, amplify, or nullify magic. However, high reward comes with great risk, and Fico's flame could not release the curse from a blade in that way." Olcay spoke up.

Her eyes turned to her son as he continued. "I figured it a while back, there is no way we went through so many cows with our Fire-mare, and I just confirmed it after seeing the aftermath. Father is bound by a pact that he cannot break so that is why he cannot speak on it"

Hakim's left hand squeezed down on the pedestal ever so slightly. Hakim's eyebrows lifted, "Smart boy, now Olcay son of Demir what happens next?" Fenya and Demir were now confused about why the king was addressing their son.

"Sire, you can cure my sister for a price of judgment. Or so I hear from stories told by visiting bards"

"Son, I told you..." Demir tried to speak.

"Quiet Demir!" Hakim commanded; his voice bellowed throughout the room. The king turned his attention to Olcay. "You are brave; most of my court no longer speaks in my presence. Your father wishes to offer his judgment to your sister."

Fenya's eyes were still in tears and confused from being left out of the conversation about what was going on. She did not know who she was going to lose at any moment and was too afraid to see for herself.

Olcay turns to his mother and answers her. "There is only one creature that could have caused the damage and could unfuse spells from metal at such a rapid pace." Olcay paused, not wanting to say more, but in that room, he felt he needed to speak. "Father has a dragon below our home in the cavern and has been using it to heat our forge. Dragon fire is not illegal, just dangerous and reckless."

Fenya's eyes turned to her husband in rage and tears. As the room started to rumble her anger was overshadowed and lost.

Demir fully prostrated himself before the king "I wait for your judgment." He wanted to refocus everything back on himself and leave his family out of it.

"Your judgment will be too easy, certainly your judgment would provide the catalyst to cure her. Your sins during the war alone would be enough. But your death would be bad for the kingdom. Besides, your contract with your dragon would be nullified and I cannot have that thing angered. Your wife's scorn is enough for you." Hakim moved his blade to his left hand. "Your daughter's and wife's judgment would not be enough. So, Olcay what am I to do?" The king gave a grin and Olcay could see why his father called him mad.

Fenya tried to move but could not and then she tried to say "Your Majesty! Please he has not apprenticed yet, his beard has not even come in." A mother's plea falls silent.

"SILENCE!" King Hakim stood, and the room started to phase. The feeling he emitted was nauseating to them. The glint and color in the stone of the room started to brighten and move like a school of colorful fish in a crashing wave.

Olcay was spared the feeling and stared into the king's eyes. He saw darkness, a void of souls. Demir and Fenya could not move or speak. Hakim grabbed his ax and walked back over to their daughter. His blade eclipsed Oriel's body as he passed it over her, and an aura of darkness was pulled from her body. The color returned to her face, relief for the family was short-lived as the King stood before Olcay. "She lives Olcay, now what do you have to offer me?" His body was hunched over and staggering. The death in his arm began to spread throughout his body and shift from flesh to bone.

25

"You are my King, I will not fear a man whom I should follow, and divine judgment awaits everyone in the end." Olcay kneeled before the king. "I offer my judgment or my servitude to your blade."

Olcay did not break eye contact, he did not blink as he stared into the void in the king's eyes. He found darkness, emptiness, sadness…

His parents could not scream, and they could not reach for him. They were held in place as if the air around them was solid and then darkness took them from his view.

Olcay could see the king's left arm as an aura surrounded it, a ghostly shadow of its former size and build. The ax glowed and sparked as the energy built up inside, the walls began to crack and the ground shook. Small pieces of the ceiling came down and hit the ground next to him.

The king's ax fell upon the boy, as light, pressure, and energy were released. The blade contacted Olcay and stopped against his face. He could hear a voice from the blade "Free me Olcay."

The room settled; the murderous pressure subsided. King Hakim was upon his throne as he was when they entered the room. The room was warmer than before, and the air was calm. Olcay looked to the left to see his family all kneeling before the king. The walls were restored to their polished state. The people from the court were all still there as if nothing happened.

His father and mother returned to consciousness as well and could see Oriel between them, also kneeling. Her wounds and curse were gone as if nothing had happened. They all embraced Oriel and cried in relief. Olcay realized they were all being judged and that what he was seeing was not real.

"No Olcay, it was very much real," Hakim stated.

Olcay was in shock, 'did he read my mind?'

"No Olcay, it's just the same feeling everyone has." Hakim laughed. "It's my favorite part of this… if the participants live long enough." He relinquished his ax to a leather holder next to his throne.

"Now this was interesting. Your parents offered themselves for judgments, and your sister offered her life to protect her family from her irresponsibility; all very foolish gestures that would not have saved her. "His tone was almost mocking them.

Hakim paused and looked Olcay in the eyes again. "You offered your servitude."

Fenya and Demir's happiness turned to horror. "What have you done?" Fenya asked Olcay. Demir could not say anything as this could have been a worse outcome for all of them.

"Olcay is to return home, gather his belongings, and return to my court by the next phase of the moon." Hakim declared. A scribe in the corner wrote a declaration and offered it to the king.

"Your majesty..." Fenya tried to speak and was held back by her tears.

"You stated your son needed an apprenticeship. He will be returned once his beard has grown fully. Hakim motioned to his scribe to give the scroll to another aid. It was as if he had returned to business as usual and was ignoring them.

"Demir, you are not hiding anything else below your house?" Hakim asked in a stern tone.

"No Sire." Demir could only bow his head.

"Steward Olcay, I will place you under a house banner suited for your station, please bring honor to your lord and king." Hakim lifted the ax with his right arm and provided a small gesture.

"Steward? Your majesty...?" a Vizard spoke out of turn.

Hakim's blade cracked the floor when it was replaced and the room for a moment was the hell-scape it was earlier and then gone. The man fell to his knees and was huddled with his eyes blank.

"Please retire to the west wing of the castle before you depart tomorrow." Hakim's mood had changed again as if nothing had happened. The family was escorted from the great hall, relief returned for the moment; there was much to discuss. Demir rushed them from behind pushing them quickly out the door.

The king motioned to his bodyguard. The large, armored knight was Sir Pasha. He was head of the royal guard and personal bodyguard to the King. He came to the King's right side and tilted in ever so slightly, "Yes Sire, how may serve you?"

"Pasha, I will have the young Olcay serving under your house and crest when he returns. I see much potential in him." Hakim's eyes glazed over as if he was exhausted from what happened.

"As you command my king." Pasha saluted by grabbing the hilt of his sword and then returned to his post.

Chapter 4

Fenya smacked Olcay and Oriel in the back of their heads. "What were you two thinking?!" she asked in disbelief. Then she hugged them both. "You both took risks you are too young to make. Anything could have happened to you. Oriel why did you ask for judgment? We were there for you." Her tears were streaming down her face. She felt as if she had lost them both already.

"Hakim told me you both committed so many sins during the war and your judgment would have killed you both. I asked for you to be spared as you both are needed to keep the kingdom safe." Oriel could not hold back herself as well seeing her mother in such a state; she cried in her mother's arms.

"None of what you experienced was real, the King's judgement experienced by each of us was different." Demir explained. "From the outside we all would look like we were just sitting there. The room changing, the people leaving, and even the king standing was not even real." Even though Demir was aware of the façade it did not make it less real for him.

Demir placed his hands on her shoulders. "There is no kingdom for me without you both in it, Oriel," Demir said to her. He teared up and embraced them both together. It was a heartfelt moment that was so close to being a tragedy earlier. None of them knew what had transpired and it was as if it had never happened.

"Each of us saw different things. What were your verdicts and sentences then?" Fenya asked as she distanced herself just enough to look into her daughter's eyes. Then looking her over as if she was waiting for something to happen.

"I was found to be too young to be judged and found to be innocent," Oriel answered as she took out a cloth and wiped her tears. "What happened to you both?"

"Your mother and I were found innocent of our crimes, which were in the name of the king himself." Demir crossed his arms. "Fenya it's ok. The judgment is over; you can stop looking her over."

"You don't tell me about the judgments, I watched him toy with someone for hours trying to get a verdict." Fenya retorted. She then started to look Olcay over as well.

"Then what about your judgment father? The dragon you keep is not a crime?" Oriel asked.

"Of course not! I just should have registered the information before making the pact with it. Besides, we have known each other for decades. Long before the king was in power and before the rules were set by the guilds." Demir abruptly answered. He was more upset about being caught than about anything else.

"Mom, why are you still looking me over? I am fine as you can see." Olcay asked while she continued to make sure they were real as well as safe.

"The King's judgment magic is complicated. It is indiscriminate and almost always does not end well. It also grants a wish at unspeakable costs for some." Fenya explained. "It functions similarly to your father's forging magic. The room is his forge, the ax is his hammer, the people are his materials, and the emotions provide the fire." She hugged Olcay tightly. "The result places a magical hold on those on trial."

"So, the curse is still there, just sealed," Olcay concluded as he stared down at his chest and placed his hand over his heart.

"We don't know son; this is why almost no one does this," Demir interjected. "Even criminals will take the executioner's block rather than an appeal to the king." Demir hugged Olcay tightly again as if he had already lost him.

"Why would you both do something so crazy for me and put Olcay at risk?" Oriel asked in tears.

"Olcay did not listen and spoke during the trial; thus, we could do nothing." Demir snapped. He was angry but could not bring himself to scold him. "Why did you speak son?" Demir asked holding his son's shoulder.

"I felt like I was being compelled to speak. Also, I knew you were being held back by your pact. It was the only thing I could do to help. It was like I needed to say something, and I had no choice." Olcay could not tell for himself if it was his will or another's. His mind replayed it in his head as if he would never know.

"The king would have called him in any way. He was already aware that we had brought him. "We should have looked at the results before we came." Fenya consoled. "This is why we left the court, the King's ways are almost madness, yet his power keeps the other great factions at bay." She sighed as she stepped back.

"Honey, looking ahead would have gotten us all muddied up in ifs. Olcay what was your verdict? What happened at the end?" Demir asked with concern in his eyes. He braced himself and his lower lip trembled as he could only relive what he saw in the great hall.

"I do not know, only a voice asking to be freed," Olcay said with a look of confusion.

"Not much is known of his power and hallucinations are possible," Demir replied. "It is best we get to bed. We have a long road tomorrow."

All the belongings they came with were in the room and a meal was prepared as well. None wanted to change clothes, and no one had the stomach to eat anything.

The family could only settle in for the night. The castle itself was quiet besides the occasional changing of the guards. Someone came down each hall and lit up some enchanted lanterns. Outside the hustle of the streets in the early morning the people settled down, then were replaced by the nightlife of the pubs and brothels. Olcay was laying in his bed thinking again about the throne, the king, and the voice he heard. Olcay decided to get up and walk the halls of the castle to calm himself. The halls were long, without decorations or accents. The design was functional and prevented the enemy's ability to hide. Olcay walked by several guards without hindrance and found his way to the library. Outside the entrance was a life-size figure of a man covered in segments. Each segment was impaled with a sword, a painful image in Olcay's mind. He thought to himself, 'Why would this be in a library?'

"The 'Final Betrayal', it's called." A sweet voice could be heard from behind Olcay. He turned around to see a female figure with an enchanted lantern. "Sorry to have startled you, Olcay is it?" The voice spoke as the figure came into view. Olcay could see the figure more clearly. It was one of the people in the room during his trial. Her long hair reminded him of his mother's. She was tall, slender, and her eyes were silver as the moon gave away her identity.

"Princess Lua!" Olcay began to kneel.

"For the fates' sake please don't." She scolded. "I deal enough with formality in court." She gestures for him to rise. Olcay complies with her request and is still hesitant after this morning's event. "You have nothing to worry about here. You completed your trial, unscathed and that is something to be celebrated." Olcay did not think of it that way.

"I will have to talk with him, my father sometimes gets eccentric when he gets bored." Lua laughed.

Olcay felt it was not amusing but tried not to embarrass himself and joined her laughter. She looked him in the eyes, and it brought him some comfort. He heard stories of the princess with a mighty king wrapped around her finger. She was the face of the palace as her father never traveled. She also had a grace that her father lacked in speaking with people. He looked into her eyes and saw the silver moonlight, an oracle of the past. Just like his mother's eyes golden for the future.

Oracles have lost much of their role in recent years. The future was always dangerous as it could write history before it could be changed by fate. An oracle from the past could go insane by touching the wrong thing and never return from the void into which they peered. He knew the immortal Ebedi would collect them but never knew why.

Lua saw that the conversation was starting to stall. "There are no guards, viziers, or titles right now." She grabs his hand. "You have much to learn since you will be living here with us in the capital." She gave him the cutest smile that he knew spelled trouble.

She started to pull and then run down the hall with Olcay in tow. She took him to the back of the library and pulled a lever behind the bookcase. "Shhh… you did not see anything," Lua whispered and smiled. A well-lit hallway appeared, and she took him through the innards of the castle wall.

"Where are we going?" Olcay asked. He started to keep up the pace and was no longer feeling like he was being dragged. They rounded the hallways and turned a corner where they met face to face with a gnome fixing one of the exit doors.

"Princess! Out late again I see." The gnome smirked.

"Just a stroll to the kitchen tonight and maybe a few other places." She smiled and giggled.

"Hmmm" He looks over to Olcay and back. "Scapegoat or co-conspirator?" He asked.

"It depends on how fast he can run." She started to continue to pull Olcay down the hallway. The gnome started to fade from view as he waved goodbye. Olcay started to regret this evening's stroll. They appeared to have walked almost the entire length of the castle. Olcay started to think of taking the nearest exit. "We're here," Lua whispered.

"Where is here?" Olcay asked quietly

"The kitchen. The bakers are making fairy cakes and I need to snag a few from the oven while they are hot."

Olcay looked a little puzzled and had to ask. "You are the princess, just ask for them. This is crazy." Lua placed a finger on his lips.

"Shhh. What is the fun in that?" she asked. Lua started to look through a small hole in the wall, preparing to make her move.

"How long have you been doing this?" He inquired further.

"As long as I have known about the passages in the walls." Lua started to tie off her dress so she could sprint faster.

"What if we are caught?" Olcay yelped.

"We? We won't get caught if you can keep up. Also, if we get caught it will be no fun anymore. So don't ruin this for me" Lua tied a cloth around Olcay's head to keep the hair out of his eyes. "Just keep up and don't get caught."

Before Olcay could argue the plan, Lua had already seized a moment to open the trapdoor and hide behind a barrel of apples. Olcay kept low to the ground and went to a crate next to her. Olcay's eyes had to adjust to the lighting. The well-lit hall was much brighter than the kitchen. Olcay took a few seconds to make out that the kitchen staff was making various meals. It was quite late, so it must have been food for the night shift guards and working staff. Olcay remembered their target was fairy cakes, and they had to be near a large oven. Cakes made from flower petal flour with various spices giving them an enticing fragrance, then glazed with nectar and topped with honey frosting.

Once Olcay's eyes adjusted he looked over to see Lua had waited for him and motioned him over. Olcay came over and could see she had a serious look on her face. Olcay looked over and could see one of the bakers was putting the finishing touches on a pan of fairy cakes. Olcay knew he was going to have to work with Lua to get the cakes. Besides, he did not know how to get back. To Lua's surprise, he decided to move to the far left of the room. He stood up and grabbed one of the crates, walked over and grabbed used dishes and pots, then placed them in the crate. He made his way over to the washing station.

"Hey, you! What are you doing?" A large, bearded man roared from behind Olcay. A hand grasped his shoulder and Olcay knew he was done. Olcay turned to find himself facing a chef with a build of a legendary barbarian. Olcay felt if he ran, he might make it a few feet before being tossed into a pie. "I need you to get the pans cleared off and scrubbed. Hurry it up, I want to get out early today!"

Olcay stared at him in a daze still waiting for death to happen. "Look whatever your name is, I do not have time to deal with the new apprentices. Get with the baker and plate the cakes!" He smacks Olcay in the back of the head and he stumbles and runs over to the baker's oven.

"Boy, where have you been? These cakes must be moved to the table so the frosting can be set. Get a move on."

Olcay figured with the room dimly lit, steamy, and all the staff was mistaking him for one of the other apprentices, he decided to blend in. Olcay grabbed a few leather holders and moved the pan over to the table to cool. Olcay was able to grab a smaller pan and transfer a dozen of the cakes, covering them with a top. He moved back to the crate where he started.

"Psst, Lua where are you?" Olcay pleaded to the dark corner. A small crack in the wall appeared and he saw Lua was waiting and he ran in. She shut the door behind him and then started to laugh.

"You are crazier than I am." Lua laughed and giggled at Olcay. He was covered in flour and sweat. He was visibly not happy.

"Well, you left me no choice. How was I going to get back to my room without you guiding me? What were you doing?" Olcay's voice was raspy and hyperventilating.

Lua moved over and showcased a crate of pastries, cakes, and tarts. She managed to grab a cart to pull it all down the hallway.

"I knew you had the fairy cakes handled so I went for the other stuff. A nice haul for your first time." Lua wiped a bit of flour off Olcay's nose. He was all but spent, but he realized he made a new friend at least, all be it one that will give him trouble someday. He finally cracked a smile. Their laughter was short as they could hear from the kitchen. "WHERE ARE THE DESERTS FOR THE PRINCESS'S BREAKFAST?!"

Olcay looked at the princess. "You stole your own food?"

"Well then, it's not stealing then is it Olcay?"

They both laughed together as they started the long trek back through the hallways in the walls. As they passed the gnome they saw earlier, Lua wrapped a few of the treats and handed them to him. He gave her a nod and thanked her and Olcay. "Guess this one was fast enough?" he chuckled as the two continued to run down the hall with their spoils.

They made their way back to the library where they first met each other. Lua had a small spot in the corner already set up for a picnic for two, as if she planned for him to be there. The two indulged in the desserts well into the evening. Olcay looked around when his eyes adjusted to the dim lighting. Olcay still felt something was afoot with the princess and inquired, "Why is a princess gallivanting with a commoner like me? I am sure there is a reason."

Lua was taken back by the comment and signed. "Olcay, you are forgetting your station. You are the son of the Oracle Fenya and the Master Smith Demir, with titles that far exceed the station of most nobles. Let us not forget you survived a judgment from the king, your title is all but a formality." Lua could see that none of this was getting through to him. "We all need allies, Olcay. I need someone who is not from the palace to support me. Especially on dessert runs." She smiled and Olcay was at ease.

Olcay, now more comfortable, looked around the room and spotted the statue he saw earlier and asked, "What is the 'Final Betrayal'?" as he looked back on its ominous presence.

Lua rose from her spot and picked up a lantern. She brought it close to her face; it was storytime, "The Immortal King ruled for almost an eternity before he was betrayed by his queen and council." Olcay was intrigued. "My father commissioned this piece as a reminder of what happens to even the most powerful of beings." Lua walked around the room, moving her hands as if she were telling a grand bardic story.

"They plotted for decades to kill him, and nothing worked." She looked at the statue almost emotionally. "In the end, they could only seal him away." She was almost choked up about it as she turned back to Olcay.

Olcay's interest was perked. "How did they do it?"

"They convinced him to wear the most expensive suit of armor ever made, they commissioned blacksmiths from every continent to make one of the pieces; it was eccentric and overly detailed. After a major battle, he was given it as a present." Lua started to mimic someone putting on armor with excitement. "The armor was cursed in every way imaginable, then each of them surrounded him and stabbed through each of the body segments to seal him in."

Olcay was excited to hear this version of the tale and leaned in as he sat on a chair to hear more. "Ebedi's face was unfazed, as if he were waiting for it, in my opinion. If anything, he was hoping something would happen." Lua gave a small sigh as she finished her tale.

Olcay had heard many of the stories of the Immortal king, but this was the first time he heard this version. She continued to bring a lantern close to her chin to darken her face. "The King cursed each of them with tragedy and the result was the Heartless Council."

Olcay felt a chill down his spine.

Lua smiled at him, "Wanna watch it?"

Olcay was taken back and was curious. "Why not, I guess."

She placed her hand on the statue and her eyes turned soulless and black as her father's did in the throne room. "Take my hand." Olcay reached for her fingertips.

"Lua what are you doing!?" The king's royal guard appeared from the empty hallway.

"Pasha? We were just talking." Lua pouted and pulled her hand back.

"If that was the case why are your eyes so dark?" She reluctantly released the statue, then he turned to Olcay. "Olcay, I will not discipline you for this. You survived the King's judgment today, so I know you are not to blame."

"Lua peering into the past is just as dangerous as the future. You know how your father feels about it." Pasha cautioned.

"How about an apology and then you forget what happened? "Hmm." Lua produced a plate of sweet treats they had procured from the kitchen. You could feel how frustrated Pasha was to see those cakes. He knew he just had a call about another kitchen theft … the 'Sweet Thief' had struck again. He placed the contents of the plate into a small pouch and then attached it to his side.

"Off to your chambers princess, my guards will escort you." Another plated knight that made no sound appeared behind her. "Goodnight Olcay, I will see you for breakfast then." She gave him a wink.

Olcay smiled back embarrassed. Pasha smacks him in the back of the head. "Best be wise and observe a shadow before you look at what is casting it. It is late and you should return to your chamber as well." Olcay took the moment in and walked back to his room. He did not sleep that night.

Chapter 5

The family awoke the next morning to find Pasha waiting outside their door. "I am under orders to bring you all to breakfast, then prepare you for your trip home." Olcay's parents were taken back by the royal escort for breakfast. Pasha continued, "You will be eating with Princess Lua this morning." They both only remember her as a child and did not realize she had remembered them. "Your son managed to meet her last night and received the invitation." Demir smacked Olcay in the back of the head. Olcay held the back of his head and rubbed the now very tender area. Oriel managed to let out a giggle at the display.

Breakfast was held in a room not far down the hallway. The aroma of fresh fruit, sizzling meats, and fragrant pastries filled the senses even before they entered the room. Princess Lua greeted them personally as they entered.

"On behalf of my father, I greet you as a friend." Lua gave a slight nod. Olcay could see her better than the night before. Her figure was well pronounced and fit; she wore a silver dress with red adornments. Her necklace was of the oracle guild, a dark eye with silver and gold. She walked over to his mother. "The past greets the future in the present."

Fenya responded, "The future looks to the past because they are the same." She gave an ever so slight bow.

"Ok formalities are over, Olcay and Oriel come sit next to me." She grabbed their hands and whisked them to the end of the long table. Pasha palmed his helmet in disbelief and their parents could only smile. They took their seats and began to enjoy their meal. The long table was a smorgasbord of earthly and heavenly delights.

"She is still the young girl we remember running around the castle causing Pasha trouble," Demir said.

"That she does," Pasha replied. Pasha walked over to his station near the princess. He was there mostly to keep her in line rather than for her protection.

Lua turned to Pasha standing behind her. "Do you want a pastry, Sir Pasha?" "I should not right now princess," Pasha replied with a bow but not without hesitation.

"Nonsense, you never eat when you should." Lua took out a small handkerchief and wrapped a few sweet items from the table and handed it to Pasha. He took the wrapped meal and placed it behind his back out of sight.

"Thank you. "I'll have these later," he coughed and cleared his throat.

Lua returned to her seat and giggled ever so slightly with glee. She turned to her guests. "Oriel, I have heard you are following in the footsteps of your father; do you plan to follow your father's career and work here in the capital?"

Oriel's eyes lit up with excitement. "Yes, I am hoping to take my final test soon, I am starting to work with fairies now." Oriel felt at ease with the princess. Lua came close to her and held Oriel's hand like family would.

"Fairies, that is so exotic. That would put you just at mid-tier smithing right now. Have you worked with a fire spider yet?" Her silver eyes shined of childlike energy.

Oriel frowned "Sadly no, father is negotiating for me with the blacksmith guild in the north for some time with one." She pouted as she turned to play with her pastry on the plate.

Demir interjected "Unfortunately, they are extremely rare and not easily tamed. Even then finding one that will do a contract with a smith is almost impossible. I was lucky to get training with one as a young smith, even then it was short-lived."

Lua smiled and motioned for one of the maids to come over. "Then I have a surprise for you." One of the maids from the corner walked over wearing a leather blacksmith apron and gloves over her normal outfit and producing a small fire spider from behind her back. The tiny creature was slightly larger than her two hands. It was bright red, and the flame it produced gave it a hairy look. Its eyes were large and captivating. It hopped onto a pan in front of the princess and gave her a small bow. Lua out of formality or even instinct gave a small curtsy to the creature. Oriel could not contain her excitement. Demir was in awe as it had been decades since he had seen one. Fenya took it in as she did not need her foresight to know what was going to happen next.

Oriel got up from her chair and took in the color of the flames. "Princess, may I hold her?" Lua motioned for her to approach. The spider turned to Oriel and backed up slightly. Oriel placed her hands together and activated her arm runes and glyphs. She then opened her hands towards the spider at the edge of the table. The spider became excited and scurried across the table lighting a table napkin and a few decorations on fire, before jumping into her hands. She embraced the happy creature as a mother to a child. Lua asked, "How do you like Racheed?"

Oriel smiled, "She is adorable I love the color of her flame coat." "Good then, she will be yours." Lua proclaimed.

Demir stood from the table. "Princess are you sure?! The gift is beyond priceless. Does the guild know about her?" He hesitated to even ask as his excitement was not easily hidden.

Lua turned to Demir, "Racheed needs a home, the smiths and weavers here cannot handle her power, and as you can see, she likes being held." She took a sip of her tea "I cannot tell you how hard it is to pet an overly affectionate flame spider. When she was found, her manner was considered aggressive in nature, and she was isolated for a long time. I was able to deduce she simply wanted to be held." Lua sighed. "I even took up temporary runes to be able to hold her till we found her a home. I lost three dresses to the flames; one was burned at a diplomatic meeting. So, if not as a gift, will you please take her home as an act of compassion?"

Oriel turned to her parents with eyes sparkling with childish bliss. It was one of those moments when protocol needed to be broken, and she did not know how to react.

Fenya stood. "I will accept this gift on their behalf, seeing as my husband is not willing to show the happiness he is hiding, and my daughter is too caught up in the moment as well."

Olcay spoke up, "What would the Princess ask in return?" His family was surprised at his question and Demir wished he was within striking distance. Lua tried to remain poised while drinking her tea but could not contain her excitement.

"I did have two requests if possible?" she got up from her chair and walked over to Oriel still holding Racheed. "I wish to have your first blade made from Racheed."

"The first blade?" Oriel said taking in the information with hesitation and awkwardness.

"Yes," Lua said with confidence. It was as if she had her mind made up and knew how this all would play out.

"Princess the first blade is always the worst. I would have to learn how to handle Racheed first, I could never do that to you. Let me honor you with a proper gift"

"No, I wish to have the first blade from Master Oriel." She smiled in reply. "Princess, it shall be yours." She bowed in response. "And your second favor?" Oriel asked with curiosity.

"It is a strange request. Can I watch a forging bond with you two?" The princess asked reluctantly while playing with a small strand of her hair. Most smiths were remote and secretive with their ceremonies.

Oriel looked at her father as if she needed guidance on this question. Demir stood up from his chair and knelt in front of the princess. "It would be an honor for us to have you bear witness to a forging bond." As a grand master, he could give permission and had no issue with this type of bonding.

Lua's eyes began to shine, and she leaned over and hugged the large Demir. He took in the initial shock and then she reasserted herself. Pasha and the maids could only sit back and watch as she continued to break protocol, which at the same time did not surprise them at all.

Olcay was excited as well, since it had been some time since he saw a forging bond up close. "With your permission, we cannot do it here. We would need a forge room prepared." Demir informed her. Lua smiled, then started walking to the back of the room, towards the adjacent door.

She motioned for them to come to her side as she opened the door. Behind the door was Demir's old forge from his time as Master Smith to the King. Demir got a little choked up in the moment. Fenya looked to the princess and asked, "Are you sure you do not see the future?" They both smiled at each other.

"You have gone and done it haven't you princess? This whole shop was clear across the city and was given to the guild. You must have pulled a few favors to get this all here." Demir looked around and felt some nostalgia with it all. Most forges are nowhere near the main structure to protect them from possible fires.

"Oriel, you go prepare yourself, I will hold Racheed for you." The spider looked at Demir from Oriel's bosom and did not want to leave her new friend. Demir placed his hands together opening his glyphs and runes. The spectacle ignited the room with a wave of light and heat. Racheed was excited and jumped to his open hands then scurried underneath his full beard. Oriel went and changed and returned to the forge posthaste.

"Are you ready for this?" Demir asked Oriel. Trying to be serious for the moment Oriel captured her composure… she nodded.

Olcay and Fenya guided the princess to a better viewing point a safe distance outside the forging circle.

"Olcay what is happening?" The princess asked in excitement.

"Forging a bond is different with each creature or being depending on the requirements. "Some are with contracts, blood oaths, and trials; others are simply a handshake. "Olcay stopped as he saw Lua was taken in by the show.

"Go on, please, I am listening; I just don't want to miss this. How does it work with flame spiders? Lua's voice showed she was beyond intrigued.

"Flame spiders are rare, so I do not know how this will work out. Not too many documents on them." Olcay never got the chance to witness many bonding ceremonies since some could not be observed.

"It is with silk and a bite," Demir announced from inside the forge. "First, we will showcase our runes in our hands to Racheed so she can see we are willing to do the bond. For creatures that we cannot communicate with verbally, our actions will make them instinctively understand our willingness." They placed their right hands out in the middle of the room and glowing red sigils appeared in their palms. Racheed peered out from the inside of Demir's beard and walked from his arm to their hands.

Racheed stood for a few minutes as the room began to emit heat and started to smolder. The fiery creature turned around in their hands a few times laying down golden silk in their hands. After this dance, a golden ring appeared around each of their pinkies. Demir looked into Oriel's eyes with excitement and then courage with what was to happen next. "Brace for it, sweetheart." Racheed reared up with her fangs and buried one into each of their open hands. A fiery venom rushed into their hands, and they stood firm as she released her bite. Their veins in their hands were lit up by the fiery venom. The display was short as Racheed jumped to Demir's shoulder and the room instantly went back to normal and cooled down.

Demir caught Oriel as she became light-headed from the experience. Olcay rushed in with a drink for his sister and a pastry. She arose to her feet, dazed but without any lingering problem. Demir chuckled as he made eye contact with Oriel again. "I am proud of you, didn't expect you to take the bite." They all turned around to see the now bewildered princess in awe.

Her silence was short-lived as she rushed over to see them up close. She asked them question after question. Even though they were both exhausted from the experience, they entertained her questions.

Her handmaiden interrupted "Princess, they are scheduled to depart soon, and you have lessons you are also avoiding."

Lua rolled her eyes and scoffed, then returned to her poise. "Thank you for indulging me; I wish you safe travels. Olcay, I will see you when you return." She gave him a small wave and a wink as she exited.

She departed from them and her staff. Pasha remained, "Your cart has been prepared for departure, and has been fully loaded with provisions and a few gifts.

The king will send an escort in a week to retrieve young Olcay." The joyful moment was humbled at the reality of the news.

Pasha placed his arm on Olcay's shoulder "Olcay, per the king's command you are to become my steward."

Olcay bowed to Pasha, "I am honored." His family takes in the news with continued hesitation. The last few days had been filled with extremes of emotion, which they decided to handle when they got home.

They followed the guards to their rooms to collect their belongings and walk outside to the courtyard. The squires were just finishing loading their cart with boxes adorned with the king's crest. As they tightened their frugal departure sacks into the cart, they recognized how the King was still generous with their family—his generosity knew no bounds. The cart was overfilled with food, wine, and alchemist metals. They were barely able to pile in. The outside of the castle gates was buzzing with activity. The business of the market was in full swing, and they picked up a few things along the way. After they made it to the final gate, a second cart was waiting for them, filled with provisions, materials for the shop, silken cloth, three fatted cows, and so much more.

Pasha gave them a quick message from the king. "The royal guards are stationed outside your land right now and will remain there till the King feels you and your family are safe. Also please register the dragon with the guild as soon as possible."

"Please thank the King on our behalf." Demir passes back to his old friend and ally.

Olcay and his family jumped into the cart and took the road home.

Chapter 6

The journey lasted all night and into the next morning. The military escort made the trip easier, and they did not need to worry about the roads. They came back to familiar sites, and eventually their home was within sight. The guards were stationed at each point outside the barrier, just as they were told. They also built a small dormitory area down the road to house the guards, complete with a kitchen, stables, and armory.

Demir spoke with them as they approached the house. Nothing was new since they left. The guards were told to remain outside the barrier unless summoned to allow his family their privacy. The family was happy to hear that bit of news. There were a few magical users as well patrolling the edge of the barrier and testing it.

Orion was at the front door of the home waiting to greet them. Orion embraced Oriel as she jumped off the cart "I see you are cured; the Gods be praised this day." He was choked up as he had no news since they left.

"Orion, help your brother unload the cart, feed the animals, and wash for supper." Demir was back to business, as he was looking to lay down from the ride. Sitting in a cart all night was hard on his back.

"What happened at the castle?" Orion asked.

"Olcay got a job, and I got a flame spider," Oriel said excitedly. "Where is Fico? I need to speak to him."

"I am here." Fico descended from the top of the house. "I am beyond happy to see you are alive. I guess the judgment went well?" Fico's voice was filled with relief at seeing his family okay. Fico saw that Oriel's shoulder gave off a light glow. "I see you have collected a new member of the family."

Oriel smiled like a small child with a new gift. "Her name is Racheed." Oriel reached back and presented the flaming red spider to Fico. Racheed looked at Fico's blue plumage and glowing aura; she began to dance in Oriel's hand. After a few moments, she became blue and gave a small bow to Fico. Fico was excited and did the same. "It is a pleasure to meet you as well. We have much to talk about."

"You understand her Fico?" Oriel asked.

"My, my… no I cannot translate. She is just happy to be here and liked my color." Fico replied.

Demir went to check the state of the forge, it looked like his fellow blacksmiths had put the place back into working order. He inspected the writing on the wall and knew he may need to rearrange a few things. At least he would not lose any days working. Fenya was able to put together a meal with some of the items the king had packed in their cart. They all gathered at the dining table, eating supper and debriefing what transpired. The moments were both cheerful and somber.

"Now the big question, who is the big fiery family member below our house?" Oriel asked her father.

"Yes, who is the dragon you keep?" Fenya stared down at her husband. He did not want to see the future on what was going to happen next.

Demir smiled under his beard as wide as possible. "Her name…" Demir mumbled quietly.

"Her?!" They said together.

"Yes, her name is Ejder… and she is." Demir was interrupted.

"Here." A sensual voice came from the corner of the room. All eyes looked and barely could make out who spoke out. A dark-skinned female figure in a black dress descended from the rafters. In the light, her skin glistened and the outline of scales covered her body and clothing. She moved with grace and intent towards the family.

"I hope you do not mind; the cavern was getting lonely, and since everyone knows I am here, I decided to say hi." Ejder's presence showcased her sheer pressure and power. Looking closer, her aura was emanating from below her scales, giving her the appearance of a long black dress. Her face was not quite human but was arousing to the eye.

She walked over to Fenya and gave a graceful bow. "I told your husband to introduce us. Please know, it was never my intention to be hidden." Fenya took in the information and calmed her nerves.

"Your husband and I created many weapons during our time together and made many enemies during the great war. I was the target of the Heartless Council while working with an eastern smith this past winter and I sought refuge with the only ally I could trust." She kept her hands together as if in prayer and was scared to be in this situation.

"Why was there a pact then?" Fenya asked.

"It was our old pact that was still active from the war. I had to do a lot of hiding in those days. He never released or changed it so nor could I." Ejder was visually shaken at this point.

Fenya softened her face, she no longer felt the need to hold a front and embraced Ejder.

"Please stay as long as you need," Fenya whispered to her. Demir began to relax and then met eyes with Fenya's… he knew he was going to get an earful later. Fenya also looked at Fico who then avoided her gaze.

"I guess some introductions are in order," Fenya announced.

Demir and Fenya never noticed the children were in a state of shock the whole time. Orion and Olcay were taken in by a near-naked form of a woman in their presence. "I'm a little old for you boys, maybe after your beards come in." She gave a wink to them both. She turned to Oriel who was speechless. "I hope to work with you someday young master."

"Thank you, I hope to someday be worthy," Oriel replied with a small curtsy.

As a little bit of a surprise, Racheed jumped from nowhere onto a small metal plate on the table near Ejder. Racheed began to dance, and her flame became black as night and bowed to Ejder. Ejder returned the bow then turned to Fico and they exchanged a smile.

"You are the little charmer, aren't you?" Ejder reached out as Racheed moved to her hand the flames gave a moment of heat then Racheed returned to a small metal plate on the table.

"Do you know each other?" Oriel asked.

"No, you would think we would have; being as old as we are. She just liked the feeling of my flame." Ejder replied. "I need to return to my cavern for the night. This form makes me feel tight and constricted." She rose from the floor and moved towards the door. "Oriel, please come to visit me sometime." The door flew open, and she took off into the sky behind the mountain.

"Now my dear husband, how did you keep her from my sight all this time?" Fenya was irritated, as there are few ways to hide from an oracle's sight.

The kids and Fico noticed the discussion was going to be intense and decided to leave for the next room. Fenya felt almost betrayed, yet understood the situation. She was going to forgive him, but Demir noticed it was going to cost him.

Chapter 7

It had been a few days since they returned home. Demir worked well into the nights catching up on his work. Oriel completed the smaller projects to help relieve her father's requests. She could only think of all the new faces she met in just a few days. She looked out the shop window and could see her brother, Orion, cleaning and doing chores. Her mother was making supper now that she had forgiven Demir, after much groveling. Olcay was in the corner of the shop, organizing the different metals. She could only think now he would be leaving soon because of her.

Oriel investigated the corner of the forge and could see a little golden nest Racheed had built. She could see her dancing playfully in the forge in her new home. She was in awe, seeing how adorable her new friend was doing her little dance of joy.

"Olcay?" She signaled to her brother. Olcay stopped doing his work as he turned to her. "Yeah, sis?" His thoughts had to shift from working to giving her his attention.

"I never really got a chance to thank you for helping me. I want to make something for you before you leave, a gift for your new job and status." Oriel could only smile as she still felt some regret.

Olcay smiled, he would have declined out of modesty, but he loved her work and could not resist. Even though his father and sister were smiths, he never really asked anything from them over the years.

"A writing quill with our shop's crest would be nice so I will have something always nearby to remind me of you all." He was referring to a hammer making two golden rings crudely drawn outside the shop in town.

Oriel accepted his choice. "Who do you want me to choose to forge it with?" "You can decide, I know you can't do it with Fico or Ejder yet and you need practice with Racheed still. Whoever you are most comfortable with." Olcay responded.

"I am hurt Olcay, I thought you were my little brother." Fico interrupted from his perch in the rafters. "We may never be able to forge in the fire, but you are bonded to me as my family." Fico came down and hugged Olcay with his great wings. Their warmth enveloped him and gave him comfort.

Racheed stopped her little dance for a moment and began to glow bright blue. "Are you planning something without me?" Ejder appeared from the darkest corner of the room. "Darling it would be fun to try something new." Racheed's excitement grew as he quickly changed from blue and black flames. "See even Racheed is down for some fun." Ejder pointed out.

"So, as a gift, we will make what you asked, a tri-flamed quill." Fico proclaimed as he dramatically spread his wings.

Oriel whispered forcibly. "What are you crazy?! I have no contract with you or Ejder, I can barely work with fairies, and what about father?"

"What about father?" Demir announced from the door of the forge. Everyone was taken back as if they had been caught. "I knew this would happen sooner than later." Demir approached them, saying, "Don't think I didn't notice Racheed's flame changes either, it was more than just mimicry." He slams his fist on the table. "Dam that king, he knew I would get caught up in that cute spider and not resist."

"Father, what are you saying?" Olcay asked.

"Racheed is on par with any ancient fire beast. After the bond I noticed the power coursing through me, it was already done. I did not expect yours would take and it would have just rejected you" Demir looks to Oriel.

"It was the King's Judgment on me that I was holding you back too much and that was my real crime." He placed his hands on her shoulders. "You survived the judgment from the king, and Racheed's bite told me you have the reserves necessary...I have been overprotective as a father and prevented you from growing." Demir's thick beard could no longer hide his emotional expression. "Tell me, my ancient friends, what I am I supposed to do." He turned to Fico and Ejder, he became choked up.

"The flame will burn long after the steel is removed." Ejder replied, "and be there long after it returns." Fico finished.

Orion and Fenya stepped into the forge after hearing the commotion and they stood in the corner.

"I was afraid you would grow up too fast and no longer look up to your father, all of you." Demir held it in as best he could, his eyes watered. "Orion is already not here as it is, and Olcay is now going to the kingdom as a steward." He pulled a dirty rag from his pocket and wiped his nose. "When did you kids grow up? When did you stop playing in the forge and making such a mess?"

Fenya placed her hand on his back, and he composed himself. He took a breath as he righted himself with determination and vigor. He stood before his daughter and placed his fists together.

"So, you want to do some multi-flame forging with higher-level beasts like your father now? You know what that requires, Oriel?" Demir looked into his daughter's eyes, and things became clear. It took everything he had to speak.

"Oriel, as a Former Grand Master of the guild, I grant you the title of Master Smith with all the privileges and honors it bestows." Demir ignited his right arm completely. The flesh under his skin could be seen and a secondary layer of writing revealed itself. More layers appeared, as if lettering was written on his bones.

Oriel acted on almost instinct alone and could not process the information fully. She took a knee before him. "I accept and swear by the blood my forge will spill and save."

He placed his palm on her forehead, an open space that was once blank on her shoulder filled with the family crest. It began to sear into her flesh. She did not flinch with the pain and kept eye contact with her father. An exchange of smiles between them and she hugged each member of her family. Then they all retreated to the far corner of the room.

"Are you ready for a contract with us Oriel?" Fico asked.

"I would be honored." She responded with a smile and a tear in her eye. She placed her palms together and her entire body ignited in anticipation. They stood in the middle of the forge and the room turned blue with their aura. Racheed jumped to Oriel's shoulder to enjoy the warmth. They spoke about their contract and terms; they reached an agreement. Fico shed a single tear and placed it into her hand.

The family cheered from the corner and stopped as Ejder approached. Her shiny body began to glow, her dress was replaced with a black flame, and her naked flesh was exposed.

"It has been some time since I made a contract with a woman. Are you ready young Master Smith?" Ejder purred. Oriel mildly blushed and nodded her head as she did not know what to expect from her studies. Ejder became close to Oriel's face she could see into her eyes as they changed into slits. She could see darkness and the full form of Ejder in her mind. She was magnificent, a black dragon of immeasurable size, her scales glistened in the shadows of their thoughts. Racheed still on Oriel's shoulder started to emit black flames and danced with delight.

"Do you accept the deeds of your creations as your own?" Ejder asked.

Oriel answered, "With all my heart." Ejder placed her lips to Oriel's as a dark flame enveloped them and dissipated. The family in shock turned to Demir.

Demir looked at them, "I swear she did not do that with me." His eyes were wide as he anticipated needing to explain himself again or sleep in the barn.

Olcay took in the entire theatrical event that unfolded before him. His sister had finally grown up. He could only think of what was to come for himself. He did not feel worthy of the moment, as he did not know what to do.

Oriel turned to Olcay and could see he was in a fog of the moment. She walked over to him and hugged him. "You are the main reason I am here now; you will make a great steward and make your moments to share as well." She returned his smile with a small smirk. "So, do you want anything special with the quill?"

Olcay's eyes grew, and he realized he was getting a truly rare gift. He paused to think, "A light to see at night, also to keep my hands warm, and have it open so I can add ink to it." His choices were practical and could be concealed because he did not want such a valuable gift to be stolen from him when he moved to the kingdom.

The final act of the play was now commencing. Demir prepared two pieces of steel on the workbench. One was for Olcay's quill and the other was for the princess's blade request.

Oriel had returned from changing into her work clothes, Orion and Olcay did the same. Oriel tried to remain professional with this monumental occasion for herself and just began to giggle. Oriel nodded to Fico and Ejder to begin. Fico's plumage ignited into a brilliant blue aura and hovered over the ground. The blue mass flew into the heart of the forge and the room sweltered. Ejder stood back as her black wings sprouted from her back. She inhaled and breathed a coal black flame into the forge from a small opening in the side. Racheed was in the midst of it all and continued to move about the interior of the forge unfazed by the power of her counterparts.

Oriel ignited the full force of her bodily tattoos, and they glowed through her leather garb. Her hair began to give off shades and hues of flame as well. Demir handed Oriel the first piece of steel, which she placed in the flames with her bare hand. The intense flames usually would cause some problems the first time. Her new master level markings made the difference. She could feel the heat being directed through her leg tattoos and into the floor. Oriel remained focused even as her garb started to catch fire as well. Racheed saw the steel placed next to her and began to collect the elements of the blue and black flame and webbed them directly into the steel. Oriel pulled the hot steel from the forge and began pounding it into the shape of a blade. She continued this for some time until she was satisfied. She then turned to the second piece of steel and continued the process. She worked in the heat for several hours with her family. At the end, two items were placed before her father on a red cloth. The dagger was flawless and brilliant and took on hints of crystal structures of blue and black. The hilt was wrapped in Racheed's silk and gave off a golden sheen. The quill was small yet not any less brilliant giving off the same sparkle of life; silk was braided to make a grip around the shaft, so it was easier to hold.

Demir inspected them and chuckled. Everyone was exhausted, except Racheed who was still enjoying the warmth of the forge. Fico had returned to his perch and was already fast asleep. Ejder had left for the night explaining something about wanting a barrel of beer.

Oriel placed the quill into Olcay's hand, it gave off the love and warmth that was put into it. The moment was only overtaken by Fenya yelling from the house "time for dinner".

That night Olcay took in the entire moment and ingrained it in himself. He played with his quill in his hand till he fell asleep.

Chapter 8

The family held a celebration the next day and invited some of the townsfolk and the soldiers to the festivities. Even a few wondering merchants set up shop and started to sell food and drink. It was a wonderful time, which helped them forget about what happened the week before. Ejder made an appearance sitting upon one of the barrels of mead she brought from her underground cave. Much of the town was there to see the new Master Smith's arms. It was a once-in-a-lifetime event. Usually, the event would have been held in the capital at the guild's tavern; Oriel requested to have it at home with people she knew.

Oriel knew she would have to eventually register with the guild to be able to practice on her own. Demir's rank allowed him to perform the ceremony on his own. Usually, only the masters of the forge, hammer, anvil, and the Head Grand Master of the guild can perform an anointing in the field. Demir was a special exception because of his status. Oriel knew being a master smith was only a small step and her arms had plenty of room for the road ahead.

Oriel's concentration was broken by the crowd when they all started to break out in song and dance. The extra people around made it difficult for the king's guard to keep track of everyone. Demir did not worry about it now that Ejder was out of her cavern watching the crowd. Any troublemakers would be roasted on the spot without mercy.

The event was also to celebrate Olcay's stewardship, but from the way people were gathered, you would not have thought so. Olcay remembered that when his brother got his apprenticeship, the family celebrated just as much. Deep down, he kind of hoped his stewardship would have warranted a spectacle as well.

"Why so glum my young darling?" Ejder appeared next to Olcay holding a wooden mug of mead. She leaned into him tightly. She realized her size was a bit much and adjusted to about Olcay's height and then placed her arm around his shoulder like an old friend. Olcay was surprised at first, took in the sudden arrival and smiled. "I kind of feel like the last story from the tavern bard after everyone has gone home."

She hands him the flagon of mead; he at first refuses, then looks around for his mother and takes a quick swig. He gave a small cough and gave it back to Ejder. She looked up into the night's sky and knew she would have to be serious for the moment.

"Well, her story you already knew the ending to. We didn't need your mother's foresight to know what she was going to do with her life." Ejder said calmly. "Your brother, as the oldest, picked up his trade quickly and had your parents as backers."

Olcay chuckled at the notion and took another swig as they both looked on. "So, what do you think will happen from here?" He asked as he looked at the ground and kicked over a few rocks.

"For them or for you?" Ejder asked and started to pour another flagon from her barrel.

Olcay looked up at her looking for answers "I guess for me?"

"You never asked your mother?"

"She never allowed herself to look into my future."

"Why is that?"

"I would have said yesterday because she never cared to. Now today…"

"Today?"

"Today, like you just said I can do what I want… but I do not know what that is."

"Well, you best gather an idea before the world decides it for you." She stood and grabbed his hand; he looks at her and blushed. "Oh… don't worry honey you are way too young for me, and you still need a beard before we can do something like that."

Olcay was mildly disappointed at what she said to him. He followed her to the cliffs behind the house.

"You ready?" Ejder gave a wide grin as her face started to change shape.

"Ready for what?"

She grabbed him by the arm and flung him into the air over the cliff. His descent and fear were short-lived as he landed on a black scaly mass before he could close his eyes. Olcay had landed on Ejder's back in her dragon form. The scales he landed on formed into a makeshift saddle and he held on as she glided around the valley. Ejder was quite beautiful in this form, her scales reflected like glass in the sunlight. He could feel they were hard and nearly unbreakable, yet her hide underneath had some give allowing her to move effortlessly. Her outstretched wings moved with grace and power.

He felt the air in his hair and could see the bottom of the valley below his home for the first time in ages. The valley provided Ejder's wings with plenty of updrafts to keep them aloft without any need to flap under her own power. After a few rounds around the valley, the river, and the mountain lakes, they returned to the cliffs of their home. She settled around a cliff on the far side of the home. An open cave, hidden from view from all directions by trees outstretched from the cliff face.

Olcay felt the trip had ended and dismounted from Ejder's back. He looked on as Ejder returned to her human form. He looked away as her body became more feminine and her clothed aura formed. Ejder increased the aura clothing so she would not strain the young man's heart.

"Welcome Olcay, to my home." They both walked into the cave entrance, shortly after the cavern opened up and it was well illuminated. He could see it was quite spacious and large enough for Ejder's full form to move around freely.

The cave had been constructed with purpose at one point and did not feel too hot or cold and the air was fresh to take in. The entire cavern was lit with luminescent crystals around the cave wall. Small rooms were also carved into the side of the main chamber. A bath made from an underground hot spring, a bedroom, a kitchen area, and a library were among the many rooms. In the middle of the main room was a large hole pointing upward with scorch marks around it.

"I guess that is where you send up your fire to the forge?" Olcay's voice echoed in the massive cave system.

"Indeed. What do you think of my home young Olcay?"

"I am fascinated. I don't think I expected so many smaller rooms." He was taking in the sight. Not many get to see a dragon's lair up close.

"At one point or another, I have entertained guests over the centuries here. Plus, some activities are just easier to do in human form." She held her hand to her cheek, and you could almost think she was blushing. "Like reading!" she interjected to herself. Olcay was still in awe and missed the comment.

"I am surprised not to see a horde of treasure everywhere for you to sleep on," Olcay commented.

"Most dragons sleep on the gold in their younger years before they can learn to change forms. It is soft to sleep on and does not catch fire. The downside is keeping it free of dirt and rot. Also, our main form can easily get dirt trapped between scales and can become uncomfortable. In our later years trying to spend dirty money from a horde can also attract unwanted attention.

"So, how long have you been down here?"

"You have always been the smart one since you were young. How long do you think?"

"You have always had a home here long before the town and the kingdoms were even here. I can remember stories told in the town of a dark shadow in the forest or behind the mountains, adventurers fighting to slay a fearsome beast. Then there were the incidents around the house of animals going missing, or bandits disappearing."

"So, do you remember being here before?" Ejder was excited at what she was hearing.

"It is a dream to me now and might as well be, I was so young. I guess you had your reasons to remain hidden for so long."

"I would say you three stumbled down here a few times, I don't handle younger children much and had to bring you to the surface a few times. I had to tell your father to keep you out of my cave. You could have gotten lost in here or stepped on, or worse." She blushed again and continued, "I was kept a secret to protect your family from attacks; however, knowing I am here may prevent them instead." Ejder said with some regret in her voice.

"So, the story of you being attacked by the Council and coming here for refuge?" Olcay questioned.

"Very much true; this cave is one of many residences within my territory. I left your father's service shortly after your family settled here to work with a blacksmith in another region. I returned here after the attack and when I found most of the other locations were vandalized."

"What is their obsession with you then?" Olcay continued to inquire.

"The Heartless council dared to challenge the Immortal King Ebedi and were cursed for their arrogance. As such the council and King Hakim wish to keep Ebedi imprisoned to protect the world. The belief that ancient creatures like myself and skilled smiths like your father can be used to free Ebedi."

"Have you ever met Ebedi? "Olcay asked quietly.

Ejder was taken back by the question as if she remembered something frightening.

"Yes. Over the eons, my nest mates and brethren have met him multiple times. Even as old as I am his legend has outlasted paper and the stones his name was inscribed on."

"What was he like?" Olcay was captivated with the story.

"He was quite charming, to be honest." Ejder gave a hint of a smile and turned her head. "He was also highly intelligent and had major plans for this world. He advanced all of us quickly almost if by design." She looked up as if she was remembering something.

"Then why would anyone want to stop him?" Olcay's curiosity was perked.

"His other passion was to end his own life, which led to wars, and destruction. To advance his cause; he created new magic, weapons, and technology only to cease his endless life. His delusional ambition attracted people that despised him and envy from others. The entire dragon race decided out of empathy or fear to help burn him away." Ejder's form changed slowly as she spoke out of instinctual memory from that day. "The dragon race set up a magic circle the size of a great city to protect the surrounding land. Dragon kin and heralds participated; it was a call of nature itself to obliterate him. The day came, Ebedi sat upon a simple stone seat surrounded by the elders of my race. Out of respect they wished to have some sort of somber moment for him. A final meal, a moment of prayer, and even vices. Ebedi only wished to get on with it." Ejder was acting out the historical moment at almost her full size. "The first dragon blasted Ebedi and expected the stories were fantasy. Ebedi sat upon the molten ground where his chair once was and smiled. I don't know how it happened, whether through primal instinct or the pride of the dragon race. The army pelted everything upon that spot for seven days and nights. The light from the melted ground could be seen beyond the horizon. When it ended; a lake of liquefied rock had one castaway floating in the middle.

He spent a week in the molten lake and cursed the universe in madness and anguish." She shed a tear for him and wiped it away with her tail. Ejder noticed her emotional tale expanded her to her true form. Ejder needed to calm herself a moment and then she returned to her smaller form.

Olcay sympathized with her and decided not to pry much more into the subject. Olcay cleared his throat. "What brings us down here then?"

"I mostly needed to stretch my wings for a bit and grab another barrel of wine to take to the party for myself. Also, you looked like you needed some air as well." She replied.

"Can I have a look around then?" Olcay was still energized from the story and was needing to run around a little to bring himself down.

"Of course, just stay out of my bedroom I have not cleaned up…" she then turned away "and I have no desire to explain anything." Ejder mumbled quietly.

Olcay went over to the library on the far end of the room as Ejder went down another hallway to the winery. The air in the library was stale with the scent of ancient books and scrolls. Some he saw were bound in chains and cages; others were laid out on a desk with scattered notes. He recognized a few of the books as standard fare, and some were in languages he could not even understand.

Mounted on a few of the walls were old maps of the kingdom and far-off continents. Some areas were missing or tattered. Olcay knew Ejder was ancient, and her collection showed she was intelligent. He skimmed through a few on folklore and heroes as she returned to him with a massive barrel of wine on her shoulder.

"I guess we should get going before anyone gets worried," Ejder said to Olcay.

"You have quite a collection."

"Books are my passion between mating cycles." Olcay turned out of embarrassment, as Ejder laughed at the cute face he made. "Guess we can use the stairs."

"Stairs?"

"How else do you think I could sneak up to the surface and get supplies? Can't be flying around the valley all the time with a cow in my grip."

"How did you stay hidden so well? Without suspicion?"

"I am ancient young Olcay and have been hiding longer than you can imagine."

They made their way up the stairs, and he found the hidden door that led out behind the rock face near the house. There was a barrier in place keeping it well camouflaged. Ejder said to Olcay, "Now I expect you to keep a girl's secrets; also, don't wander down the stairs without letting me know. I would hate for you to see something you may not want to see." She gave him a quick peck on the cheek. Her wings sprouted and she flew to her seat above the barn next to Fico.

Olcay was mindful of what Ejder said and decided to deal with his thoughts in the morning and rushed into the party in full swing.

Chapter 9

Olcay spent the week getting his things together for the move to the capital. He said goodbye to many of his friends in the village. The final day came, and the family waited for Olcay's escort to arrive. They could see in the distance the guards opening the barriers.

Towering in the distance they saw several figures; one was a large plated knight in dark armor riding an equally massive fire mare. Beside him were several escorts and a carriage barring the King's seal. The family was at a loss as to why a carriage would be coming down their road. The carriage stopped in front of them, and they all took a knee as Pasha dismounted to open the door. A disgruntled voice from the carriage said, "Please don't, I get enough of that at the castle." Lua was tired from the ride and was quite moody. The family raised their heads to see Princess Lua before them.

"Princess, would you at least follow the protocol till we get inside? At least not in front of the regular military soldiers." Pasha requested in a low tone and a sigh.

Fenya stood to get the protocol moving for Pasha. "Princess, we welcome you to our humble home, we are honored that you would travel so far to visit us," Fenya commented.

"Thank you, I am here on behalf of my father to inspect the Grand Master and his family's safety; he is upset that the royal barrier was breached." She descended to the ground from her high position. "I am also here to discuss this matter on his behalf, may I come inside." Her tone was posh, but you could see she was holding back immaturity.

"Of course, we would be honored," Demir replied.

The family, Lua, and Pasha entered the home as the guards surrounded the grounds in a defensive formation.

They all sat as Pasha stood behind the Princess. "Continuing the outdated formalities, my father wishes to offer you a safe place in the kingdom if you choose to return."

Demir responded, "Please thank his highness for the offer…"

"I understand and expected it," Lua responded.

Pasha readjusted himself to the side of the princess, "The next matter is the attack itself; fragments of the blade were taken to our wizard guild and found the original creator of the blade. It was commissioned recently by a blacksmith in the south. The king has commanded that I inspect this matter personally. I am to be attended by my new steward Olcay as his first mission." Pasha's voice was stern and commanding.

The family was in shock; Pasha was one of the greatest warriors in the King's army. Ascending to the royal guard after the war and then to the personal guard of the king. The task almost seemed too low for his status.

Olcay was eager to be on his first mission, he spent the week trying to be positive about his situation. "Sir Pasha, would it be excessive to send you on such a small mission?"

"After seeing the king up close, do you really believe he needs a guard?" Pasha paused and then continued. "The king wishes that this matter be resolved quickly, and we are to proceed from here south to finish the investigation."

Lua's face was irritated as she wished to move on from the business at hand. Pasha returned behind the princess. "Master Demir, I believe you sent a request this week to the guild to register the new Master Oriel?" Lua inquired

"Yes, I gave her the rank when we returned. I guess news travels fast." Demir responded proudly.

Lua stood from her seat. "When a new master is promoted, even the king takes notice." She walked over to Oriel and looked into her eye like a child would ask for candy or a new toy. "Master Oriel, did you fulfill my order then?"

Oriel could only smile. "Yes Princess, I finished it shortly after my quenching." "Can you please show me?" The anticipation was almost too much for her.

"Yes, I will go get it." Oriel went to her room and returned with a blue silk handkerchief tied with a black string. She placed the blade in front of the princess, and she removed it from the silk. It began to glow and gave off hints of blue and black.

"Let's have a look shall we." Lua's eyes went dark as she held the blade the family was taken back remembering the king's judgment. After a moment they cleared back to their silver shine. She smiled and then began to tear up. "That was a beautiful moment for me, thank you. I will treasure this forever."

The meeting ended as Lua wished to see the forge and touch the various items around the shop. Everything gave her a story that brought her feelings of joy and happiness. She met with Fico and was completely enthralled; she thanked him for his contribution to the knife.

Pasha gathered her back to the carriage, as he needed to get started on his mission. The guards left with the carriage and drove it down and back up the path. "Olcay, say goodbye to your family, we must be off." Olcay proceeded to hug each of them, the moments were somber as the sky turned from day to pitch black. A massive form descended from the sky. The form condensed into a single point next to Fico. The black mass reshaped itself into the sensual form of Ejder.

""Are you leaving without saying goodbye, young one?" Olcay was taken back by the sight and was blushing as she approached him. She looks down, "Sorry, I forgot to form the dress." She grabbed his face and kissed his cheek, then whispered in his ear. "You go choose your own path. You will do great things. Maybe grow a beard out before I see you again." A final hug as her aura enveloped them both. She then faced Pasha, her aura darkened the air around them and you could almost see her full monstrous form. "I have contracts with this family Sir Pasha, under which his mother wants him returned in one piece. I hold you responsible little one for his safety or I will bake you in your suit."

Pasha would not normally back down from a threat of any kind, yet he knew better than to mess with a dragon. He nodded his head. "Olcay we must get going then." Olcay brushed off the moment and mounted the extra fire mare Pasha brought with him for the journey. The two set off south of the village on a well-traveled road towards Harthen. Olcay could see his family and home getting smaller in the distance. Olcay and Pasha continued down to the crossroads before the forest near the village. The carriage and guards were there to meet them, and Princess Lua peaked out of the carriage curtain.

"I will wish you both safe travels. Return quickly or send a message when you find something. Olcay you may feel unfit for this task, but your blacksmithing knowledge will be needed for this trip." Lua smiled and motioned for Olcay to come closer. "Sir Pasha likes sweets if you want to get on his good side." Lua gave a small wink. Olcay gave a small nod in thanks, and they were off.

Olcay remembered the road when he went with his family for shopping and Oriel's training on a dwarven forge. They passed many farms that stretched far into the horizon. The smell of newly tilled earth filled the air. Olcay could only stare as his fellow rider was not much of a conversationalist. Olcay only knew of Pasha from reading and the occasional bard singing his tales. Before the war, there is not much known about him. His massive size was imposing and was enhanced by his impressive armor. Olcay recognized the armor was forged with a great beast, it gave off a red glow, common for knights of his rank and stature. Olcay did notice Pasha's sword was one of his father's early blades. It gave Olcay comfort to know that another piece of his family was with him on his journey. Their late departure did not allow them to get very far, and they had to settle for the night.

"We will stop here for tonight. Go talk with the farmer and ask for use of his loft and stable for us." Pasha tossed a bag of coins to Olcay. "As my steward, you will need to take care of our boarding and dinner." Olcay dismounted, then went into the farm house and arranged it. Olcay came back out after a few minutes. "We are good, sir; they have a few cots in the barn as well that we can use for the night. The farmer's wife also has a modest meal for us if we want to join them."

"Good, Olcay you join them and just collect something sweet for me when you come to the barn." Olcay enjoyed the company of the farmer's family; it brought him some comfort for the road ahead.

He returned to the barn to find Pasha had settled the horses and was sleeping in a pile of straw. The bed was too small for his large frame. When Olcay approached he could see he was still fully armored with his sword at the ready. Demir told Olcay that many knights from the war were always battle-ready. Olcay left a cloth next to him with sweet cakes and went to sleep as well. In the night a cold chill covered him, and then the warmth from the quill in his hand gave him ease.

Olcay looked through the window and could see the night sky. He began to think of his place in the world. The voice from the judgment came to him as well: "Free me Olcay." He tried not to think of it. He decided to doodle on a piece of paper to move his thoughts around until he could manage to go to sleep.

Chapter 10

In the morning, Olcay woke to the clanging sound of metal. Pasha had resaddled the horses and mounted their gear. "Olcay, you need to be more prompt in the mornings. Go grab us something for the road, just bag me something sweet. We need to get a move on." Pasha's voice was commanding and abrupt.

Olcay got dressed and proceeded with getting their meals for the road. Olcay returned, and they began their journey down the road. Olcay started to keep mental notes of Pasha's needs so far. He likes sweets, just as Lua said, and never takes off his armor. As they made their way down the road, Olcay continued to feel uneasy with such a quiet companion.

"Olcay, I guess we can get the formalities out of the way." Pasha reaches for a pouch on his belt and pulls out a scroll with the king's seal. "You are now my steward, 1st class, of his majesty's court to act in his interest. For now, your duties are something we will discuss when we return home. Till then, you will act as my assistant on this trip and my adviser, then in turn report to the king on these matters. You are charged with educating yourself on the matter of becoming a proper lord steward. You will be expected to also learn combat training from me until you can fulfill the role of your title. Do you have any questions?" Pasha was informal but to the point.

Olcay only nodded in understanding.

"I will have to guess your sword skill is that of a small child playing in a forge with weapons?" Pasha generalized. Looking Olcay over, "You have decent strength from working your farm and forge. It's not easy work, so we only need to work in drills. We will practice during the horses' rest periods."

Olcay excitedly nodded but remained quiet. Every imaginary battle as a child came through his mind. He calmed down as they rode on, then turned to Pasha. "Sir Pasha what can you tell us about our mission, if you would please," Olcay asked.

"I guess now is as good a time as any, the guild found the fragments to be made from a salamander and a demon forging from a blacksmith in the south. The only blacksmith that is registered with the guild that does both of those is a Master Smith named Yot," Pasha explained.

"Salamanders and Demons are hard to forge with especially together. We have a Salamander at home that has been serving in our family for a generation." Olcay replied.

"That is another reason I brought you, your knowledge on this matter will be most helpful. Can you tell me why they do not get along?" Pasha gave a slight turn of acknowledgment to Olcay to listen.

"Demons equate salamanders with pests." Since they inhabit the same areas, they tend to have a natural hatred for each other. We had a half-demon stop by wanting to work once and our salamander went crazy."

Olcay went on to explain the many combinations of steel that are possible and what makes for good steel. Demir knew Olcay would never work at the forge as a career, but he didn't want him to be excluded. Pasha listened intently and the time passed quickly for them both. Olcay felt the road was a little straighter from then on.

As promised Pasha drilled in combat practice, etiquette, and procedures into Olcay to prepare him for life at the palace. It took eight days for the mismatched pair to arrive in the southern town. It was some relief for Olcay, as the combat practice was taking a small toll on him.

Olcay was reminded of home, the cobblestone streets, the vendors selling their wares, and the smell of the countryside food stalls. Pasha's size and form were massive and drew many stares. The royal coat of arms on his chest, a black ax over a book representing the law, caused the crowd to part in the streets. Pasha saw a pastry vendor and dismounted from his fire mare, Olcay did the same and tied both steeds to a post.

"Master Baker, we are looking for your blacksmith; I am needing repairs to my equipment." Pasha inquired.

"He is down the street at the back of the town to the right Sir. Can I interest you in fairy cakes, or other sweets today?" The baker was a cheerful-looking man, his clothes and beard were covered in flour and frosting giving him a colorful look.

"Yes, I will take three of the fruit pastries, one cake, and whatever my young steward would like." Olcay excitedly took a cake as well and Pasha paid. Pasha always placed his treats in a small sack on his side.

The two set off to the end of town to find it quieter than most of the town. Blacksmiths typically were outside of towns in case of magical mishaps. As they approached, they found the forge was dark and the shop closed.

"Olcay tie the horses to the post there. Then go into my pouch and take out the short sword."

"Sir, what's wrong?" Olcay whispered

"I smell blood." Pasha drew his sword, and it gave off a mild spark in the air as if it was ready for battle.

Olcay did as he was told and returned with a sword in hand. Pasha signaled to Olcay to stay put and proceeded to the front door. Pasha knocked, but there was no answer.

"Master Smith Yot, are you home? I wish to discuss purchasing something," Pasha yelled. The smell was overwhelming. He tried the door and found it unlocked. Then he placed his main weapon against the wall near the door and drew his short blade for a close-quarters fight. Opening the door to a darkened room, the light from outside did not provide much assistance. The cold forge was rather big for making larger weapons and armor. On the left, he could see the remains of a gutted salamander; the insects have not come, so it is newly dead. As he rounded the table, he found the skeletal remains of a man, a faint light gave off a cursed fiery residue.

"Olcay it is safe; come in and tell me what you see." Pasha motioned to Olcay to enter.

Olcay was shocked and then nauseated by the smell of the dead salamander. After gaining his reserve back he stood up and had a look around the room.

"What can you tell me of this Olcay?" Pasha asked firmly.

Olcay came around the bench and saw the body of the man, it immediately gave him queasiness and the urge to throw up. He held it in as best he could till, he found a bucket in the corner. Pasha had to take a moment to realize this was Olcay's first dead body and needed a minute to regain his composure.

"Take a minute Olcay but I am going to need you to temper that stomach for now," Pasha said as he covered up the body's head with a rag he found.

Olcay is still woozy from the ordeal, so he had to look around the room. "It does not look like an accident. His arm and the room's runes should have prevented a curse from activating in here."

"Your sister was taken in by a curse in her forge. How can you tell?" Pasha remarked.

"Magic systems in general are not infallible. However, in the case of my sister, the curse was rapidly released by dragon fire and had no way of containment. Here, the room is intact except for the gutted salamander. Even the other magic items on the table are inert so the seals are working." Olcay felt some accomplishment.

Pasha nodded in agreement. Olcay continued. "His death would have upset the salamander, and I would expect it would have attacked the killer. I would think whoever tried to burn the salamander's body; but left it only gutted once they realized salamanders don't burn."

"What can you tell me about the thing on his arm?" Pasha asked.

"I do not know sir I have never seen someone use metal augmentations on their arm for forging. Blacksmiths do not need them in the forge since they would be immune to the fire."

"Our mystery is becoming cumbersome. The initial report for Master Yot stated he used demon fire for the blade used to attack your family." Pasha started to scan the room. "We are still missing our demon," Pasha whispered. Pasha lunged back from a faint sound heard from the right side of the forge. "Identify yourself or remain nameless in death!" Pasha commanded.

Both remained at the ready as nothing moved or made a sound. Pasha looked at the right side of the forge and could make out the faint outline of a door. "Olcay, do forges normally have doors?"

"Depends on the creature you are forging with. Some cannot shrink or take on a fire-based form, so they need a way in to contain their fire."

"Assist me," Pasha said as he walked over to the side of the forge. Pasha did not need assistance, as he found the handle concealed on the back of the forge and flung the stone door open.

They both peered into the darkness and could see the faint, red glowing outline of a female figure. "Please don't kill me. I saw nothing, I swear." A crying voice said in the darkness as the figure shook in the corner of the small room. As the tears fell, they caught fire, flashed, and dissipated.

"You have nothing to fear now, we are here to help," Olcay responded. The yellow eyes peered from the corner and glazed over in fear. The red-skinned body jumped into Olcay's arms and hugged him. Both were in shock at the speed she came out of the forge. Pasha sheathed his blade and went to the front of the room.

Olcay allowed the uncomfortable moment to pass as the young lady cried against his chest. The tiny sparks flew from her eyes. Her hair was black, and she was about Olcay's height. Her horns were less noticeable indicating she was only half-demon. The moment came to an end when Pasha returned with her clothes, which he found on a corner chair.

"Please wear this young lady, the lad's heart was not prepared for your figure." She took her clothes and dressed as they turned around. Pasha gave Olcay his seal and sent him to get the town guards and undertaker. As the crowd gathered, Pasha hid the demon girl behind his cloak to protect her identity and prevent a misunderstanding mob from forming. At Pasha's request, Olcay also secured a room at the inn to finish the investigation. It was almost nightfall before they could settle in the room and talk with the young lady.

"I was so scared; we were working on a spearhead for a client when someone came into the room. I didn't think of it at the time and kept heating."

"I heard the struggle outside, and after I felt my contract lifted, I stopped heating the forge. The killer must have thought the salamander was the only one heating the forge and did not notice me."

"Why were you locked in the separate chamber of the forge?" Pasha asked.

"Salamanders and demons don't get along, so I hid in the forge before he brought the beast in. We place herbs in the air so he cannot smell me and so we can forge without issues." She explained.

"Metal from difficult creatures or sources is highly prized, and can lead to new types of magical weapons," Olcay commented.

"Master Yot was my first contract since coming here, he was kind to me, like a father." Her tears came again as tiny flames.

"Do you remember forging a blade with a teleportation, berserker, and masking seal?" Pasha asked.

"Yes, it was last season, someone needed the handle to be reforged. He paid in old empire currency; it was still gold, so Yot did not care. He only needed the teleportation part added by us." She replied.

"We are at a dead end then," Olcay replied.

"We still have to wait for the body of Master Yot to be investigated at the capital." Pasha stood up from his seat "I will try the Drunken Head tavern in town. Someone may know something about our assailant or have seen something."

Olcay looks over at the demon girls and sees that she is frightened again. "We never got your name," Olcay casually mentioned. She looked up at him with some relief.

"My name can only be said when I have a contract with someone." She gave a sweet smile.

Olcay did remember that dealing with some fire-based beings', names were important.

"I will leave you two to talk," Pasha said as he approached the door.

"I should come with you," Olcay responded

"A tavern is no place for a young man without his beard, besides your mother and that cursed dragon would roast me if you were to come with me. I need you to watch her and guard this room." Pasha's voice was rough and stern.

"I do not think I could do anything if anyone came?" Olcay kind of felt he could not do much in a real fight yet.

"I will place guards downstairs if there's trouble. I will also leave this here for your protection; besides it draws too much attention."

He unsheathed his large blade from his back and placed its tip onto the floor and there it stood. It was perfectly balanced, did not lean or fall, and began to spin with a faint light.

"No one should be able to enter this room but me or if you need to in an emergency just grab the sword and let it take care of the rest. I will leave you be. Olcay, be sure to see if you can find out anything new from our guest." Pasha closed the door and left while the sword continued to spin and gave off a faint hum. Olcay seeing it up close and unsheathed for the first time, remembered its name from a ledger, "Fairies Guardian," which was made by his father during the war. He felt comforted by the fact that it was here.

Olcay and the nameless demon girl started to share a small meal that was brought to the room earlier. The demon girl turns to Olcay as they sat at the small table in the middle of the room. Both were exhausted by the day's ordeals to even talk but the awkward silence was not any comfort either. She caught a glimpse of his quill as he was taking down notes and her fiery glow returned.

"You're with the house of the Master Smith Demir?!" She squealed and moved closer to him. Her eyes lit up in flames and her skin gave off a red aura.

"My father is the Master Demir…" Olcay responded. He had never had a girl that close to him before.

"Please make a contract with me! To work in his house would be an honor." Her voice was high pitched and almost screaming with excitement.

"I am sorry, I cannot do that," Olcay responded sadly.

Her eyes faded and her aura dissipated. "Why not? Do you have a problem with demons? Is there something else you need?" She smiled and started to expose her shoulder as she crept up close to him.

Olcay panicked "No that will not be necessary, I am his son, but I am not even a blacksmith." Even with her reddish skin she blushed and recovered herself.

"Perhaps a small pact then." She played with her hair with her finger rolling it around.

"Is there a catch I am missing? Does it hurt?" Olcay inquired

"Since this is your first time, to get ahead of your questions, no one is losing their soul or life force. Contracts and pacts are just the way we do things and keeps people honest." Olcay gave some sigh of relief from the message. "I want to work under your house crest in the future and need introduction at some point. Now we just need what you want from all of this of equal value. So, what will it be?" Olcay still was over thinking the situation.

"You have to have something you want." She was becoming impatient.

"Sorry, this is all new to me. I was just living at home not too long ago and now I am a steward in the service of Sir Pasha, and I still don't have that figured out."

"Perfect then! I can be your assistant till you introduce me to you father."

"My assistant?"

"I can help you with errands, help with paperwork..."

"You can do all of that stuff?"

"Of course. Demons are merchants by nature, and it gets us both what we want."

Olcay was happy at the thought of not starting off alone with his stewardship. "What do we need to do?"

"A blood sacrifice under a full moon with our bodies entwined" she said with a straight face with her eyes burning red. Olcay was silent and was going to run for the door. She started to laugh and began to wheeze. Olcay was not amused. He turned around towards her and crossed his arms, humiliated.

"Seriously, you people and your wild fantasies about demons." She still had a few belly laughs left in her. "Our contract method is based on our goals. War contracts would be made with blood, love contracts have their method, and business contracts only need a signature. She grabbed Olcay's quill from the table and started to write the contract in the air. The letters were suspended in front of him as if they were on invisible paper. She handed the quill to Olcay. "Will this work for you?" Olcay looked it over carefully, then signed the contract, and it dissipated into a string of lights that attached to her skin and vanished.

"I guess I can introduce myself now, I am Azarla. I look forward to working with you." Azarla gave a small curtsy.

Olcay was able to smile. "I am glad to meet you, Azarla." Olcay, needing to learn more forgot about his mission and began to ask more about demon culture and writing craft she just demonstrated. The new conversation was a relief to them both and they talked well into the night.

Chapter 11

Pasha entered the rowdy doors of the Drunken Head. From the street it was one of the larger buildings in town. It served as a place for merriment as well as business. A perfect place for Pasha to get information. A neutral establishment that catered to all sorts of creatures and races. The wooden and stone structure was well kept. The rafters overhead doubled as a second hall for the smaller races. A few minstrels were in the corner playing as the bards told stories near a crackling fire. The smell of spilled mead and pipe smoke fumigated the air. Pasha's presence did not go unnoticed as the tavern was filled with many veterans from the last great war.

"Pasha, is that you?! My old friend." A small gnome sat on top of the bar counter, bearded, with a small lute in hand, a bright red kilt, and a red cone hat. "What will it be my friend, a distilled drink of fairy nectar?"

"Killion! I was unaware you were in charge here. What happened to Barduk?"

"I had to take over the place last season after Barduk drank his warehouse dry. We tried to take his drink, but he ran off… and there was an accident. He is in the corner with Grogg drinking." Killion pointed to a far corner of the bar. The crowd seemed to avoid that corner of the room.

"Pasha, I don't think I need to remind you that Grogg is a cleric and likes to preach his gospel," Killion warned.

"Still praising his blood god? Some things never change." Pasha almost seemed more relaxed and in his element. As he walked by a few of the warriors raised their mugs in respect to Pasha.

Pasha walked to the corner and saw Grogg, a large half-orc, immersed in a sermon with someone across from him. He wore a leather garb and the same bright red kilt as Killion. The red kilts of the old guard were the first on the front line during any battle. Pasha had to hold in the laughter as he remembered that during one battle the red kilts were staggering drunk. The enemy did not know what to make of the riled mess and left thinking it was a cunning trick.

The three settled here after the war and opened the tavern together. Barduk was the commander of the division and took his losses to heart. Drank himself into a depression deeper than most after the war.

Pasha drank his fairy nectar with his visor closed and walked over to Grogg's table. "Grogg, it has been some time, how have you been?"

Grogg closed his book and stood in front of Pasha, grabbed him by the shoulders, and head-butted his helmet. The noise rang out throughout the tavern as the crowd stopped to see the result of the impact. "Pasha you sweet-toothed bastard, what brings you here?" Grogg's voice was loud and so massively deep that it shook the windows.

Pasha unfazed said, "I am good my old comrade. I came to see Barduk; I was told he was here with you."

"He is. I was giving him a sermon of my…"Grogg was interrupted.

"Please make him stop. I cannot stand it anymore." A small voice replied from the table.

Pasha looked down to see a single wooden mug. The mug's front had the face of an old man, whose eyebrows and beard were replaced with burly weathered branches. A long wooden pipe protruded from the face.

"Barduk? What happened to you?" Pasha's voice was one of concern and mild laughter.

"I got drunk with some dryads drinking the flux from their sacred trees', fell asleep in some sacred circle, and this was the result. I am not in any pain, but the effect is only around a hundred years." Barduk said with a laugh. "My only real curse is Grogg here lecturing me on his god, of which I listen to every damn night."

"He needs to use this time to reflect and maybe grow from this." Grogg bantered on and Barduk became increasingly angry. His wooden head danced on the table as the liquid ale he held spilled out.

Pasha interrupted. "I am sorry for your situation, but I am here on business my old friends. Can you tell me anything you know about the late Master Smith Yot? Or anything else that may be out of sorts."

"Yot? It was a shame to hear of his passing, we will need to call the guild soon to get a new replacement." Grogg commented.

"I have only been in the tavern and many strange characters do come through here. Could have been anyone." Barduk's furrowed eyes were troubled.

"Did anyone come in spending old currency, perhaps?" Pasha inquired

"Yes, we had one creepy-looking fella, in a cloak, no coat of arms, just came in for a drink and left. Headed eastwards." Barduk responded.

"Would you be able to know him if you saw him?"

"Could not forget him, he was clearly wearing armor underneath that cloak, yet he made no noise and was quite light on his feet."

"Anything about the demon girl in his shop?"

"She came about a year ago, she was looking for work, and you know they don't like being unnamed. Yot took her in. She put in the work so you know she had no ill will." Grogg answered.

"I guess this mystery continues." Pasha went on to confide in his old battle mates about his mission and the search for those who attacked Demir's home. Grogg looked to his gear and felt like his own kin had been attacked.

"Pasha, you summon us to battle again when you find your answer," Grogg said. Pasha felt some nostalgia from being around everyone in the tavern and was getting comfortable for the evening.

The moment was then interrupted. A flash of light illuminated the bar, blinding everyone in the room. Pasha stood at the ready as his sword appeared in his hand along with the bodies of Olcay and the demon girl, phased beside him.

"Olcay what happened?!" Pasha shouted.

"We were sitting in the room and three people burst through the door and barrier as if it was nothing. I went for the sword as you instructed and now, we are here somehow; it all happened so fast!"

Pasha yelled out. "Grogg, Killion, my fellow warriors, we are about to have unwelcome guests. I will need your assistance to minimize causalities." Grogg pulled an ax from behind his seat, dried blood had seeped into the cracks and gave a dark hue to the blade. Killion hopped onto Grogg's shoulder carrying a small rapier, it was not longer than a regular knife. The rest of the patrons brandished their arms, many of them veterans of the last war. Even the barmaids Pasha recognized as former soldiers were at the ready. Each paired up and tactically covered each part of the tavern. The instinct of combat sobered up the weary warriors. The bartender, a giant female who stood almost a full head above the rest of the bar, came from behind the counter with a giant hammer in her hand that she moved with ease. "Illa, my love please get back behind the counter," Killion yelled.

"Like hell, I will; no one is messing with my bar." His wife answered. "Yes, I am more worried about what you will do to the bar." Killion cringed

"Olcay, Demon Girl, get behind the table and barricade yourself." Pasha tossed Olcay his spare short sword, he then moved into the middle of the room to take on the front door. The two flipped the table and Barduk fell to the floor, his ale spilling everywhere.

"You owe me a drink." He yelled.

The patrons watched the doors and windows. The minstrels and bards hid behind some barrels. The bartender had her hammer ready to destroy anyone that came through. Only the noise of those with the ladies of the evening could be heard from upstairs, as they did not notice the commotion.

The front door shattered as three dark figures started running into the tavern. The first two were able to clear the door with ease. The third was caught in the downward swing of Illa's hammer. The force cracked the stone floor, the dark mass struggled and stopped.

One took to the ceiling to flank Pasha in the middle of the room. The other launched a direct assault on him. The one on direct assault maneuvered to the side, bypassing the swing of weapons from the tavern patrons. It headed towards where Olcay and Azarla were barricaded. Pasha deflected the attack from the ceiling, he caught a glimpse of the man underneath the dark gray cloak. His flesh was gray and lifeless, and his eyes were glazed. Pasha took advantage of the close moment inside his range, grabbed him, and tossed him to the ground. The body bounced and was followed by a sword through the shoulder. "Grogg! Killion! It's a Heartless!" Pasha yelled

Grogg had already run to intercept the one after Olcay and Azarla. Killion took to the air from his comrade's shoulder and took a second jump from the wall, attacking from the side. Killion was knocked out of the way with ease. The distraction allowed Grogg to come from the blind side with his ax, connecting with the assailant's face. The ax drove through the assassin's skull and then lodged him in place against a wooden beam in the wall.

"Like old times." Killion laughed as he pithed the back of the assailant's skull. Grogg rolled his eyes in laughter. "At least you still have your clothes on after this fight."

Pasha sees that the main assault is over and turns his attention to his pinned prey. He goes to release his sword with his right foot firmly on the thing's neck. As quickly as they appeared, the bodies of the three turned to ash, leaving only the gray cloaks in their place. Pasha took a stance at the ready and held his blade pointed at the door again, waiting for another wave. Instinct and a battle sense of decades surmised in a moment... he released his blade and it flew towards the ceiling. The blade held in the air for a moment... blood and entrails spilled from the air. The invisible master of their unwelcome guests appeared from around the blade. The twisted creature roared in pain as the blade turned around and returned to Pasha's hand. It incinerated into ash as the others did. The room was left with more questions than answers.

Chapter 12

Pasha and Olcay remained in town as they waited for word to come back from the kingdom on what they were to do. Master Yot's body was sent to the capital for study, along with a message of what had transpired with the Heartless they encountered. The veterans in the pub were excited by the adrenaline of battle, which was rekindled with song late into the nights at the tavern. Pasha continued spending the mornings training Olcay in combat with a sword and the afternoons on etiquette at the castle. Olcay was able to pick it up quickly. In the evenings, Pasha spent time in his room alone, ordering the occasional sweet buffet.

It had been more than ten days since Pasha sent his message to the kingdom. It was dawn when a rider appeared before them. He carried a message from the king.

Sir Pasha:
In the name of the King, you are to depart immediately to the border of the great citadel and find answers to why our borders have been violated under the treaty. You are to take your appointed steward and the demon girl with you.
This act of aggression within our borders must be answered. An escort will meet you at the border to provide safe passage. Your sword will remain sheathed and not be removed from your person.

The sigil of the king embossed the bottom of the letter, which was represented by a book and ax. There was a package with the message that carried the grand seal of the king and included a diplomatic decree. Pasha took a few of the sweet cakes that would make the journey and pouched them at his side. The last time he was in the citadel was with his blade, cutting down the Heartless army.

He readjusted himself in his armor and took in the last bit of relaxation he had seen in many years. He left the loft he rented and gave his regards to the master of the home. He found Olcay in the tavern, sitting with Barduk and the demon girl.

"Olcay, we are going to depart for the Heartless Empire. The king wants us to meet the council."

"Sir Pasha, that sounds almost suicidal to walk into enemy hands." Barduk interrupts.

"Don't worry. I was seeing if you could join us?" Pasha asked.

"Why would I go? I have a bar to run." Barduk answered confused.

"Well, I came here before for your council, and I will need you as a backup if everything goes wrong... or you can stay here and review Grogg's sermons for the next hundred years."

The small wooden branches for eyebrows closed over his eyes as the pain was all too real now. "Fine, I wish to be carried at least and not left in some bag, so I don't get motion sickness."

Pasha turned to the young demon girl. "You, young lady will also be joining us as well."

"It's Azarla." She said as she covered her cheeks and blushed.

"Azarla? Olcay, do you care to explain?"

"Sorry Sir, I found it rude not to use her name. I made a small pact with her."

"For what and what did you exchange, you know you have a dragon at home that would be upset if you came back soulless for a night of wiles." Pasha's voice was palpable and angry.

"I am not a whore or a succubus, you pervert! Olcay was a gentleman; even though I would have made him a man, but his beard is not in yet. For now, he needed help with his work in exchange he will introduce me to his father." She was redder than usual.

"Uh-huh, I will suggest in the future that you please discuss these actions with me first. I don't need to lose you on our first mission. I can't have another apprentice die on me." Pasha grumbled. Olcay's eyes widened in shock and could not give an answer.

The little band of four headed southeast along the main roads. Three days of travel were met with a small settlement along the border. In the distance, they could see the royal guards at the entrance to the village.

"Sir Pasha, we have been expecting you." The guard announced.

Pasha could see the crest of the king over a tent off to the side of the settlement. He shook his head as he approached. "I guess this is our envoy to the capital?" Olcay asked Pasha.

"Unfortunately, yes." Pasha was shaking in his armor.

"Unfortunately? Sir Pasha, I guess I should not have brought you any dessert from home then?" Lua came into view from their side. Pasha dismounted from his steed immediately and took a knee before her.

"Princess?! I spoke out of context my deepest apologies."

"Sir Pasha, please rise you know I hate that, and we have known each other forever now."

"Thank you, Princess." Pasha arose to his feet. Olcay and Azarla dismounted as well and gave a bow.

"Olcay! I am so happy to see you again. Who is your new fiery friend?"

"I am Azarla, former assistant to Yot." Azarla smiled and gave a small curtsy.

"Sorry for your loss. You are under my care here."

"Thank you for your kindness my lady" Azarla almost wanted to hold back tears.

"Pasha, we have much to do before we cross the border. I will need a quick briefing on this." Lua demanded.

She walks over to Pasha. "Please give me your sword." Pasha pulled his sword out and presented the handle to Lua. She grabbed the end; her silver eyes went black. Azarla stood back from the sight. Olcay already saw this and was less taken in by it. Her eyes went back to normal, and she sighed.

"That was quite a bit of fun you went through. We depart at once." Lua commanded.

"You heard the princess; break camp we leave immediately!" Pasha ordered.

Lua's playful demeanor was all but gone. The guards started to pack up their horses and their attendants broke up camp. They had no time to wait and needed to ride. Olcay taking the hint with the others offered help. Azarla was pulled to the side by the princess.

"Please stay close to me, you are our only witness, and I will see you safely returned to the kingdom." Lua's confident voice was wholesome and pure. "We are going into enemy territory but with Pasha and the guards here, we will be fine."

After the camp was taken down and packed, they rode through a great forest to the unmarked border. The attendants stayed with the carts with a few guards as Lua and the rest continued to ride towards the Heartless Capital.

"Pasha you have your orders from the king, please follow them. Olcay please refrain from speaking or you may end up like before. Azarla my dear please stay at my side and do not speak as well, I would have left you at camp, but you are needed as an eyewitness for these proceedings." Lua's commanding presence was something to behold.

The Citadel was not far from the border. The land itself was lush and green, wildlife could be seen in abundance, and it was all but a paradise. Nature itself thrived in the area and could be seen well beyond their destination. Olcay took in the spender of the area and felt almost whole.

"Olcay, beautiful isn't it," Lua asked him.

Olcay nodded in agreement. "I would not think such a place could exist."

"I am sorry Olcay, but this is a farce," Lua responded. Olcay was confused and thought to himself it did not appear to be magic. "Olcay, the people here do not need food to eat, wood to build or burn, and no reason to worry or even love. That has been taken from them." Olcay felt the cold now that the others felt. He could see no one, nor any settlements. He could sparsely see the remains of building hidden in the woods.

"Those who would dare enter these lands without permission would find themselves in a bit of trouble. If the curse of the land does not make you remove your heart, those who are cursed will remove it for you." Lua explained.

"Then how are we unaffected?" Azarla asked.

"The diplomatic seal with Pasha does provide us our pass; however, I still would not wander far from him," Lua warned. The group started to make a tighter formation around Pasha after hearing this.

The citadel itself came into view. The remnants of a great empire of the Immortal King. The surrounding city had been overtaken by nature and disappeared into the surrounding tree line. Only the central throne room of the main castle remained with a single tower. Townsfolk could be seen wandering through the city. With no need to eat… there wasn't a need for shops. With no love, there wasn't a need to speak to their fellow people.

Olcay could see they all had a distinct smile as they walked aimlessly into one another. But, as they approached, he saw some facial expressions change to lifeless, cold, and foreboding. Azarla was just as unsettled as he was. Deeper within the crowd, Olcay could see some had eyes with a shine and others were pale. The ones with eyes that shined knew they were there and followed their movements across the broken streets.

Pasha noticed Olcay was looking at them intently. "I see you've spotted the difference in their eyes Olcay?" Olcay nodded. "The shiny-eyed bastards are the ones that gave up their lives willingly. The pale eyes had it taken from them." Pasha's voice was somber. At this point, all the guards wanted to draw their weapons or flee, as the crowd began to follow them.

Outside the ruined structure, several men were waiting to accept them and hold their horses. They were covered in tattered armor, their eyes lifeless. One formed a few words of broken mumbling, indicating they would watch the horses as they dismounted. Olcay remembered his instructions to keep quiet and stood beside Azarla; he had seen she needed courage as much as he did. They were escorted from the outside and up the main steps to the main entrance door. The massive size reminded him of the king's door back home. The crumbling walls were also starting to be overrun with vines and plants, almost blending in with the dark forest growing in the side hallway.

The courtyard was falling apart as several trees started to displace the cobblestone. It was difficult terrain for the party to traverse. They came to the large entryway that was open with no guards in sight. As the sun set behind them, the various broken windows naturally illuminated the main hall. They could see seven elevated thrones, one large in the middle and three on each side. They were adorned with jewels and gold hidden in the vegetation surrounding the main hall.

Lua took the lead, followed by Pasha, Olcay, and Azarla, while the guards remained outside. Azarla took Olcay by the arm to steady herself on the uneven ground. They approached the center of the room and could see figures sitting upon the thrones. Olcay could remember the stories of the Seven Heartless thrones.

From the left he could see:

Lord Nefret of the Unfulfilled Heart was a young ruler, sitting tall with long blond hair that came to his shoulders.

The Lady Kirik of the Broken Heart, leaned to the side, paying no heed to the party's entrance. Her raven dark-haired covered her pointed ears, she wore black robes over her distinct voluptuous figure.

Lord Seket of the Shattered Heart covered his face and body completely in a white hooded robe. He leaned to the side, showing no interest in them.

On the right: Lord Groun of the Cold Heart wore a blue robe over a white tunic. He was poised with mild intrigue and was slouching towards his knees.

Lord Varish of the Stone Heart was dressed in full metal plate, similar to Sir Pasha's, but his height was above the chair.

Lady Tash of the Lost Heart wore a red dress, her legs barely touching the floor, and she firmly clutched a small book in her hand.

All of them had a small altar next to them with a heart placed upon it. The hearts were lifeless and covered in dust, untouched, and not beating.

In the middle was Queen Yulia of the Broken Heart, rising to meet her guests. She stood a full body length higher than the rest of them. She had a long, slender body that accentuated her height even more. Her long, elegant dress adorned with gold and silver gave a radiant glow.

A small guard to the corner slammed his spear end on the ground three times. "Your majesty, I present Princess Lua, daughter of King Hakim of the Uneven Throne, Sir Pasha, son of Savasci and personal knight of King Hakim, Olcay, son of Demir, and steward to Sir Pasha, and Azarla, daughter of unknown." The prenotion of hearing their names without ever giving them was chilling and unsettling.

Lua gave a small curtsy, Pasha took a knee and motioned the others to do the same,

"I greet the past, for I know it to be there," Yulia announced in the great hall. "The past accepts everyone, for that is where all futures reside," Lua answered. The queen sat back down and motioned, giving Lua the further right to speak.

"Thank you, your majesty, for greeting us in your home. I am here on behalf of my father to discuss matters of the treaty." Lua's voice was firm and unwavering.

"The matters of the treaty are not in question; you are here for harassment. The Council here has only one purpose; to maintain the seal on Ebedi. We do not care about the affairs of others. The pain of our losses was too much to bear that we removed our own hearts for it." Lady Tash bellowed.

Queen Yulia spoke. "That will be enough out of you. The eyes of the past are not clouded like those of the future. To answer your questions, we do maintain a spy network and were aware of the attack on Demir's family." The queen stood and began to walk toward them.

"We took it as a coincidence, thinking it was from someone jealous of his talent, as we were investigating former loyalists to Ebedi and tracked down a smith that was forging items to free him, I believe it was Master Yot." Her eyes fell upon Azarla and quickly returned to Lua. Azarla went to speak, and Olcay squeezed her hand; she understood and returned her bearing.

The queen continued. "The unknown here was targeted as a possible co-conspirator and Ebedi loyalist. However, looking at her now; she is too young to know Ebedi and her manner now tells me she is no threat." She leaned down to Lua's face and stared into her eyes. The queen's skin up close was like a smooth marble statue and flawless. Her eyes were blue as the sky yet lifeless as a stone.

Olcay began to think about Ejder on the run from the council. Why did Yot's weapon end up being used to attack his family? Why did Yot make the weapon to begin with? His eyes were averted, he held his tongue, and it did not go unnoticed. Yulia and Lua both looked his way.

"The young Olcay seems to have something to contribute to this matter." Lord Seket said

"I would avoid speaking young one it is not a pleasant experience to speak here. Even with permission, the task may not be to your liking," Lord Groun followed.

"You think you would have remembered your experience with your judgment." Lady Kirik continued.

Lua and Pasha started to feel the situation was about to get out of hand. An aura started to displace the room and their voices edged him on almost daring him to

76

speak. It was odd for him, as he mustered the courage to speak and not the will. He remembered the same feeling when he stood before the king and endured it.

"You! Murderous heartless scum, how could kill Master Yot?!" The crowd looked towards Azarla and then went silent.

Lord Seket stood as the queen sat back down in her seat. "Do you wish to speak to us on matters of the heart, you unknown?"

Lord Varish stood "Maybe she thinks she knows grief better than all of us. Come offer your heart weighed against mine."

Olcay could feel the room grow heavy and cold; it was purely nauseating. Time all but stopped as he could see that look of fear in Lua's eyes. Pasha was all but stopped reaching for his blade. He was reminded of the judgment he suffered before; yet this was filled with malice and death.

Azarla looked to be speaking and infuriated. She was in deep pain on more than just matters of Yot. He could see her words caused each of the Council to rise and draw in closer to her. Azarla's eyes were blank as the conversation ended and she fell down to her knees. She then uncovered the top of her dress and exposed her breasts to the court. Azarla grabbed and clawed at the middle of her chest. Her nails began to dig into her skin, blood began to trickle down as she started to remove bits of her flesh reaching for her heart.

Olcay's heart pounded as he could do nothing but watch. He began to cry as she reached further into herself and the blood began to pour. It was slow as she began to scream. She was very aware of the pain but unable to stop herself as she tried to get through her ribs.

Lady Tash jumped down from her throne and walked unhindered by the matters of time to Olcay. "I can sense you have lost hope; do you wish to save her life?" Tash's eyes were red and she stared deeply into his. Olcay could only nod. "Then you are going to need to offer us something better."

Olcay could feel that he could move again and ran past Lady Tash to Azarla. He tried to pull her hand away from her breast as she mutilated herself. For a young demon, she was strong, and it made matters difficult. He could hear them around him whispering and calling for him to speak as well. Olcay had to think quickly and pulled out his quill from his pocket and wrote into his book from his pouch. He placed the message before her eyes.

Olcay could see the faint writing on her chest underneath the blood start to glow and subsided. She stopped tearing into her chest and removed her hand. She could see clearly now and went to speak as Olcay covered her mouth. She bit down as she felt the pain in her chest.

Queen Yulia stood up again and approached them. "Impressive young one; not many could break our deliberation so easily. What did you write there?" Olcay reluctantly handed her the book page he wrote on, she almost had to kneel down completely to be able to reach him on the ground. She took it and it read: *You and I have a Contract!*

"I see, we may have had her heart, but you had her soul." The queen mildly amused almost let out a small laugh. "Had this been when I had a heart, I would have laughed at this for days." The Queen's voice was shrewd and mocking him. Something was still off about the room, and Olcay could only play along with what was happening. He bound up Azarla's wound the best he could as the council continued to look on. Her hands were mangled with bits of flesh and bone. Time was short to get her help, but he could see the room was hazy, like the air above the heated surface of a forge.

The queen walked back to her throne and the rest of the council reseated themselves. "Olcay, you may speak freely here without any effect. We have never failed to take a heart, we are intrigued." Lua and Pasha could now move and took in the new information and calmed themselves. Pasha never got a chance to take his sword out. His priority was Lua and could only fear he almost failed.

Lua returned her poise, as she regretted bringing them here. She looked at Olcay and gave him a quick nod and he understood he could speak.

Lady Tash stood down from her chair as Olcay approached the center of the council. "Words are important here; speaking is equal to life and death. You do not know how a single breath can befall an entire kingdom or capture a lover's heart." Olcay took in the warning.

"Your majesty, what is the council's interest in me?" Olcay asked.

"We don't get much in the way of topics here beyond a good book, but we heard of your judgment and wanted to see what kind of person can stare down a king. Apparently, now one that can also stare down a queen." Her voice simultaneously amused but significantly upset.

"Wouldn't this have ended badly? Killing an envoy under the protection of the princess, with Pasha here as well." Asked Olcay.

"If they could have seen what happened, it would have been bad, yet we are alone right now." The queen gave a deadly stare and an ear-to-ear smile. Olcay looked around and could see that the room was empty, no one was there. He felt the same feelings about his judgment before.

Olcay remembered everything that led him to this point, Ejder entered his thoughts and her being in hiding. "What is your purpose in hunting down Ejder?" Olcay asked.

The Queen settled her face. "We are only interested in the imprisonment of Ebedi, those who are deemed a threat to that are dealt with. Even your cruel king yields to our methods. For now, she is in the care of your household so we see no reason to continue." Olcay wanted to press the issue, but the Queen continued, "We can free you of your judgment if you wish; the king can be barbarously cruel placing such a thing on a child." Whispered the council in the back of Olcay's mind.

"It is a kind offer, but I will respectively refuse." Olcay gulped as he clinched his own chest. Part of a blade pierced through the air next to Olcay and started to cut reality next to him. Olcay could see that it was half of Pasha's sword blade, the air itself shattered as if glass window struck with a rock. The room reset itself and Olcay could see where they were in the middle of the throne room.

"I believe we are done here," Lua interjected. She took a defensive position in front of Olcay and motioned for him to get back further. Pasha was attending Azarla as his blade stood watch over them. Pasha was able to start pouring out healing potions on the wounds to close them up on Azarla chest and took her in his arm.

"We were under the understanding that we would be safe here; my father would not be happy with this." Lua's voice was stern and harsh.

"You know we cannot leave here; just as well as your father cannot leave his throne. All as part of the treaty." Lord Groun snakingly rebuffed.

"He would not go to war for an unknown. A lasting stalemate that keeps the world from imploding" Lady Kirik smirked.

"True, but you were looking at Olcay, and he's already sworn to the King," Lua replied, her tone reserved.

"We simply only had a curiosity; can you blame us?" The Queen stood again amidst the thrones. "If you have nothing else to discuss, you have nothing for us; we have nothing for you and your king. Please leave by nightfall across the border." The queen sat down and shooed them away. Lua felt the need to speak more but knew that there was nothing more to be gained from talking. She gave a forced bow and motioned to her party they were departing.

What could really be done? Justice would have to wait. Azarla needed their attention, and the smug council was not going to be swayed by empty words or unstructured threats. Nothing was going to be accomplished today.

After leaving the entrance to the throne room, they made it to the outskirts of the castle. The knights they left were still waiting across from the glazy-eyed heartless guards... watching. Pasha had one of the knights start with healing and tend to Azarla. They mounted her on a saddle with one of the knights to keep her stable till they could make it to the border. Olcay wanted to scream, yet the fear of what might happen kept him from doing anything. The knights used hand signals to communicate; after such an ordeal, no one was speaking. They made it back across the border as the sun was setting and made camp in the forest.

"Olcay I will need to speak with you at the princess's tent please," Pasha said to Olcay sitting by the fire.

Olcay followed Pasha to Lua's tent, he opened the curtain, and his eyes readjusted to the light in the small room. On a cot on the right side of the room, he saw Azarla sleeping and well bandaged. Barduk was placed on a table next to her and was performing some healing magic.

"She is stable Olcay thanks to you. She was spared a fate worse than death. That should bring you some comfort." Lua stood by him as he looked at Azarla.

"What was that? Why were we attacked? Please explain it all to me? Olcay pleaded

"Before the great war this land was thriving under the rule of the Immortal King Ebedi. His life goes back further than any oracle could see and goes farther than anyone could foretell. His Council, wanting power or for other reasons, decided to imprison him." Lua walked back to her seat at a small table.

"Mind you, the plan was to kill him, yet he always showcased his immortality, nothing could harm him. It was said he had an open invitation to every elemental beast, magician, and assassin to kill him by any means." Lua drank from her glass on the table and held it in her hands. "It was said he even found death herself and tried to kiss her, but she resisted his advances, and this affair also infuriated the Queen." She walked over to Azarla and adjusted her hair away from her face.

"I told you before in the library that in secret the Council plotted to build for him royal armor, not that he needed it, and offer it to him as a gift for his victory over a rampaging horde, the armor turned out to be a prison that would keep him immobilized." She sat down on the bed and held Azarla's hand. "Seven blades were fashioned to act as keys to his armor. When he put on the armor, each of them stabbed into each lock. The blades passed through him, but they served their purpose by locking him in place." Lua continued to speak as she inspected Azarla's bandages.

"The blades themselves were heavily cursed and infused with every ritual that could fit into the blade to hold him in an eternal limbo. That night, the council celebrated their victory, dancing around the statue of Ebedi, mocking him. They even took turns fornicating in front of his open eyes and urinating on his prison." Lua looked up to Olcay. "He would go on and say: What is a prison to an immortal? As time goes by this will go from story to legend, and then be forgotten. Just as all of you are just a story to me, this prison will be forgotten and gone." Lua used a deep, dramatic voice for effect. "As time went on, each one of the Council members started to change and have a tragedy befall them. They removed their hearts to end their pain and ended up as the accursed creatures you saw today."

"That still does not answer the question what do they want with me? What was that they did to us?" Olcay was noticeably frustrated.

"You have several things they find fascinating; you are the son of two legends, you stared down a king, they went over that, and I believe they were telling the truth. What they did was similar to my father's judgment, it is known as the 'Deliberation'."

The princess continued to explain more, but Olcay felt it was starting to be too much for him. He thought of home and how he wished it was simpler. Then he remembered the attack on his family and remembered why he was there in the first place. He then looked at the bandaged body of Azarla and knew it would not end even if he went home.

"I know they are keeping secrets." Olcay interrupted.

"How do you know?" Lua asked

"They avoided the question about Ejder."

"What does Ejder have to do with this?"

"Ejder told me before she came to my father's home that she was attacked by the Council. They are getting rid of blacksmiths, witnesses, and fire beings for some reason."

"The Queen said they were getting rid of loyalist to Ebedi. They may have been suspicious of her without cause."

"It has to more than that; Ebedi's imprisonment is part of the reason for the treaty? Then why keep the loyalist a secret?" Barduk interjected. "It would be easier to report loyalist and prevent unnecessary treaty violations. I would surmise they are getting rid of those capable of freeing Ebedi."

"Then we have a problem." Pasha interrupted. "We will need to have prominent smiths in the kingdom put under observation, yet not in a way that draws suspicion from the Council."

"Agreed, I will have a message sent to my father on the issue at once." Lua's voice was concerned.

"The Council is not so easily unprepared. As the young man has said, there is more missing here." Barduk hopped over closer. "They have the right to be paranoid. Ebedi was fearsome, and his immortality only embellished his legends. He never needed to bring an army into battle since he did not need one. I once saw him run naked into the midst of a shower of arrows; then walked to the front of the archers' line unscathed. The entire regiment laid down their bows and walked off the battlefield."

Olcay could only imagine such a sight. A man that beckons death to the point of madness. Olcay sits at the table close to Barduk. The back of his trouser felt out of sorts and he reached into his pocket. He could feel an object in his back pocket that he had not noticed before. After a slight lean to give room for his leg, he pulled out a small red book.

The others did not notice as Olcay recognized it from the council room, Lady Tash was holding this book. She must have slipped it into his pocket at the moment he freed himself. He placed it in his front shirt pocket; none of them appeared to notice.

"Olcay it will be a long road home. Get some rest and we will talk more in the morning." Lua requested.

Olcay excused himself from them and went back to his tent for the night. He passed the guards by the fire cooking under the moonless sky. In his tent, he lit a small lantern and pulled the book from his pocket. It was small, leather-bound, and tattered from age. The pages were in a language he could not read. He noticed a large, old, faded crest on the front of the cover, he could make out the crown but could not tell what it was.

The whole time he felt as if he was only an observer to time as it passed him by. He has yet to fulfill his role as steward to Pasha, their investigation has produced nothing, Azarla is hurt; and the voice from his judgment is now bothering him at night.

"Are we going to talk about the book you left out of the meeting?" A voice said from the stand next to his cot. Olcay was completely startled and fell back from where he was sitting. Barduk had appeared on the table next to him.

"How did you make it in here?"

"We old folks have our secrets just like you are trying to keep right now."

"What am I supposed to do then? Everyone seems to have everything together on this journey." Olcay sat next to Barduk on the cot. "I want to help too."

"You are helping." Barduk exclaimed.

"How am I helping?" Olcay retorted.

"You are the steward of Sir Pasha and a representative of the King himself." Barduk tried to console Olcay as best he could.

"What does that even mean for me? Pasha is the most powerful knight ever to be born since the King himself, and the King has stewards and a full court. What is their need for a blacksmith's son?" Olcay's voice was distraught.

The grumbling voice of Pasha from outside the tent interrupted. "That is something you will have to figure out on your own. I can't hold your hand for you to temper your own metal."

Olcay fell silent as he contemplated his words.

"The princess has agreed with your concerns with the council and the possible future attacks on smiths in the kingdom."

Olcay reached into his pocket, pulled out the book he was hiding, then handed it over to Pasha. "This was hidden in my pocket by Lady Tash during the altercation with the council."

Pasha took the book and looked it over. "I expect you to be more open with us next time. We are working together on this…understand?" Olcay nodded in response.

"Good. We turn in for tonight we look this over in the morning. Get your rest."

Chapter 13

Oriel went back to her studies a few days after Olcay left. Fenya found herself alone and could no longer hold back her tears. She was very clingy to Oriel since the boys were now gone. The family was also trying to get used to the increase in guards around them. The king wanted increased protection until he was sure the family would be safe. All of it was becoming overwhelming. Father needed to go to town for work, but he mostly just wanted to make sure the twins were not destroying the shop. Fenya headed to town later to get food and supplies; generally, to see familiar faces. Oriel hid away in the workshop and turned up the heat to make it unbearable for the guards to be there with her. To clear her head, she went back through her metal collection for her guild exams to refresh herself. The metal itself was a lifeless shell and could only contain or act as a conduit. She laid them out in front of her. "Dragon, phoenix, spider, fairy, mare, salamander, wild, demon …" She paused as she noticed a piece of the cursed sword in her collection. It was lifeless now, but she still felt the pain of it. It ate through her protection, so it was not something that could have been easily done. The parties involved had to be willing to create such a weapon, and it was manufactured quickly, hence why it was very unstable. She learned from her father that it was the embodiment of the forge that laid down these rules. Fire being her source she did not want any harm to come to those who made the fire.

The forge inscriptions usually would contain a curse and the blacksmith would stabilize it when it was processed in the fire. Her father was one of the few who could do both. Oriel needed more practice to handle both processes. Oriel only inherited from her father the ability to hold fire but not the ability to manipulate it. That came with the training that she still needed.

Since the war, there has not been much demand for curses on weapons and armor. Oriel also did not want anything to do with them. Purification and disposal were more to her liking at this point. She tossed the broken piece of metal into the scrap pile. The metal sound woke up Racheed, who was sleeping in the forge. She scurried around, stretching her legs, and came out of the forge.

Racheed placed her two front feet in the air and started her little dance, then gave off a red flame to match Oriel's hair. Oriel smiled and placed her palm down, and Racheed climbed up onto her shoulder and continued to dance in enjoyment. The warm forge made the little spider livelier, and she shifted colors. Oriel felt warm on her shoulder but did not give off a flame that would burn.

Oriel thought to herself about where her brothers must be at the moment, and she started reminiscing. She went back to her workbench, looking at all of the open projects still being worked on. The lifeless steel was used mostly for smaller projects and tools. It was made to receive magic or be used as-is. The alchemic steels were sent by mages who had a specific request in mind for their projects. The steel had small incantations written on them or a spell that needed to be applied with inscriptions or a scroll. Most of these only need low heat from non magical sources since they only need to be shaped.

Magical creatures would be used to give the metal extra properties that could not normally be inscribed or imbued into it. The properties added depended on the personality of the creature itself, and some were more sought after than others. So, a scared, injured, or angry creature's personality would make the blade weak and brittle.

Oriel could see the excitedly happy spider wanted to make something, so she pulled out a bit of metal from her collection. Showing Racheed, she explained. "I have not played with wild metal in a while. This piece came from a volcano in the south during mating season for the salamanders, the heat they gave off imbued the metal with colorful properties." Wild metal was a guessing game; even at the open markets, much of it was slag being sold as wild metal.

Racheed felt Oriel's intentions, dismounted from her shoulder, ran back into the forge, and turned up the heat. Her colors started reflecting off the wall even in daylight. Oriel started to heat the metal and reminisced about the quill she made for Olcay. She knew he wanted something else but thought he was being too modest to ask for it. Multi-flamed items were highly desired but not easy to make. Most blacksmiths only dealt with two creatures at a time. Limiting factors are their fire affinity, contracted creatures, or skill level. Some creatures just can't stand being in the same room with another. It took Father decades to get this far with his creatures and training.

Oriel's mind wondered from one idea to the next. Oriel remembered the princess's offer to work in the capitol. What if she set out on her own? She would start a shop with Racheed; a salamander is easy to obtain and is useful for small work. Having a salamander did prevent her from getting a demon contract. Elementals were annoyingly high maintenance. Fire-based fae were also an option. She did desire to see the world.

So much went through her mind that she was only hitting cold metal at this point and forgot to reheat the billet. Oriel's heart wanted more. She received her final runes from her father but still needed the guild's license to practice outside her small village. Oriel wanted to try working with other creatures as well, so much was racing in her mind. The steel was cold again and needed to be reheated. It was all too much to handle.

Looking down at Racheed, Oriel took it all in with a smile. She worked well into the afternoon thinking about what she would do. The metal still rang cold. The wild metal remained untamed and folded with no rhyme or reason. Oriel just returned the metal to its box, where she found it. She did not notice that Fico had returned home and floated down next to her.

"That does not look like a proper blade," Fico said from behind her.

"AHHHH!" Oriel was startled, putting her hammer in the air and setting her runes to defend, and then was winded when she saw who it was. "Come on, Fico, you know better than to sneak up on me when I have a hammer in my hand." Oriel's voice went from scared to firm.

"Apologizes, usually hammering steel gets you more excited. I see you have too much on your mind." Fico stated with eloquence.

"I guess I expected to be doing more after I was given my Master Smith tattoo." Oriel started to sulk.

"You did get most of your runes fairly quickly. Most smiths spend decades getting theirs, and many never know this level of achievement." Fico tried to look positive at the situation.

"I was hoping to move to my own shop, but this isolation has us here till the kingdom lets us out." Oriel pounded the cold steel with anger.

"Have you heard the news about Olcay?"

"No. Has something happened?" Oriel's mood suddenly changed.

"Seemingly he has taken on the Queen of the Heartless Council. Stared her down unscathed." Fico was excited about the tale he was going to tell but was interrupted.

"What is he thinking?!" Oriel gave a voice of concern and fear.

"His job Oriel, he took it on to save you."

"Yes, but it sounds like he is being reckless."

"Apparently, he was saving a female demon in distress, his tenant."

"He has a tenant now?" Oriel's face was in shock. "Where did you hear all of this?" She asked.

"Your mother received a rider in town, with the message from the kingdom. I surmise she has a few friends keeping tabs on what is going on."

"Sounds like he's starting to grow up." A smooth female voice came from the roof. Ejder had been listening and reformed herself on the ground in front of them. "I do fear he is starting down a dangerous path for someone his age."

Oriel took in the moment to remember how they were all kids once. She knew that she would need to move on from this place as well. For now, she would need to see if she could help Olcay first. "Well, if Olcay keeps on getting into trouble, we are going to need to make sure he can get out of it." Oriel's enthusiasm was showcased by a quick glow from her markings. Fico and Ejder both gave a smile as they all heard the family cart pull up to the forge. Demir and Fenya had returned home after their errands, and Oriel saw they had the same idea.

Hix and Stix were with them, and it looked like it would be a long night. Demir had the same idea in mind after he heard what happened. He brought some metal for the project from his collection. He had been holding onto a piece of wild metal for some time, formed from cold fire found in the frozen waste. He could never use it because it would require too many creatures to even heat it and was not cost-effective. In the back of the wagon were a few barrels of ale to get them through the night. Fenya looked over to Oriel, "After I got the last courier, I talked it over with your father; Olcay is going to need our help."

"How do you suppose we start?" Oriel asked her father. Demir pondered it for a moment and then coaxed Racheed out of the forge with a small treat. She scurried to his hand and ate what looked like a small cookie. He then presented the steel piece to Racheed. She tapped on it with her legs, and her flame coat started to shift through different colors as if she were trying to make sense of it all. Her flame eventually changed to white; it was intense as the room itself lost color for a moment.

"Well, it looks like we start with her to allow us to make the steel workable, have the others keep it heated in the new stage, and then finish with Racheed again to stabilize it all," Demir suggested. The rest agreed to the new process. Demir placed Racheed back in the forge. She was still holding her cookie and taking small bites. She cast a small aura around the cookie so it would not burn as she consumed it. Oriel took the spot as assistant, but Demir then moved her back to the front. "You are taking the lead on this one." Demir smiled and said, "Don't worry, Hix and Stix are sober this time."

Oriel did not need to be told twice and took the cold fire steel from his hands. Oriel reiterated her father's suggestion. "We will start with Racheed, then Ejder and Fico, I will need you to help with impurities, and twins, I will need you to dance the incantations, they are on the wall in the forge."

Each one of them took their place. Racheed's color started to rapidly change with excitement. Hix and Stix disrobed and went into the forge as well. Racheed took a look at them both and gave her a small greeting dance and a small bow. They returned the favor. Oriel did not allow much for pleasantries as she activated her arms. Demir did the same and then reinforced the forge's circles with a bit of blood incantation. Oriel looked at each of them to make sure they were ready for the task ahead. The outside of the forge started to shake, the guards were in a panic, and Fenya had to run out and tell them everything was okay. A barrel just outside the barrier caught fire due to the heat. Demir noticed the accident and opened a box on the side wall. He pulled out a scroll and tossed it into the fire. Glowing writing started to flow out of the forge and onto the ground. It started to spread outside, to the walls, the house, the military encampment, and the rest of the grounds. The temperature dropped outside to a comfortable level, and the blaze was averted. Demir gave a thumbs up to Oriel to continue.

Oriel placed the steel into the forge, Racheed went over and started to play with it like before, and her coat went white. The light was extremely bright as the steel went from orange to a bright blue. The forge went cold, Fico moved to add his flame, and Ejder changed her form to give more heat to the process. Demir handed Oriel some darkened glasses to cover her eyes. It made the work easier as she started to shape the metal into a blade.

As Oriel cycled through heating and folding the metal, she moved on to the twins. She signaled them when she was ready and started to change the hammer strokes to a rhythm.

> *O living forge hear my call*
> *May the wielder never fall*
> *Protect him from evil's gall*
> *Keep him from the silver hall*

Racheed danced with the twins, and a beautiful, colorful display unfolded. Demir started to back away as Oriel had the project handled quite well. He went to work on selecting a pommel and guard. The crew worked well into the night crafting the piece. The light could be seen by every town around the mountain as if it were a sunrise. As the forge was closed for the night, there was a mild tired celebration.

"You don't think it will be a bit much?" Fico asked.

"No worries, the grip can only be held by someone of Olcay's kin," Demir answered.

"I understand, but do you think it's a bit over the top for Olcay? He may never want to touch it." Fico's words fell on deaf ears as the rest started to look over what they just made. Fico decided to leave it be. They were all exhausted and called it a night.

Chapter 14

Olcay spent the ride back to the kingdom contemplating everything that had happened to him. Barduk held onto the book for the trip. Pasha did not want the Princess to get too ambitious and attempt to peer into the book's past by using her oracle abilities. Barduk suggested locating scholars to investigate the mysteries of the book. They just passed the fork in the road that would have led back to Olcay's home. Pasha saw him looking at the sign. "If all goes well with our time back at the kingdom, we will be back this way again before the harvest festivals."

Olcay gave a hint of a smile and nodded to him in thanks. As the kingdom came into view, Lua sighed. "Guess we better prepare." She signaled to Pasha, and he nodded in understanding.

The guards surrounded her in a square formation, and Pasha started to move to the front. "Olcay, I am going to need you to come to the front with me. As my steward, I need you on my left." Pasha motioned him over.

"Yes sir!" Olcay started to move over and sat straight in his saddle.

Pasha handed Olcay a pin for his cloak to be worn on his right shoulder. It was Pasha's crest of gears and a fairy. He mentioned before that it was presented to him from a village he saved and became his symbol.

"I am honored sir, thank you." Olcay pinned it to his tunic.

"We have a few formalities when we get back to the castle to discuss. For now, just sit up straight and try to not say anything till we are back in the castle itself." Pasha's voice was serious.

The group stopped just before the clearing, and Lua dismounted from her horse and went into her carriage. She mumbled, "I hate this thing."

Pasha responded. "Princess, you know decorum requires these formalities."

"I know, it's just a major drain on me," she whined, kicking her feet like a small child who's not getting their way.

Azarla was already in the carriage and gave a small giggle. She was still bandaged and visibly weak. Lua turned to Azarla, "What can I give you to burn this carriage by 'accident'?" Azarla could only laugh slightly, as it hurt too much for her.

"Princess!" Pasha bellowed.

"Kidding Pasha! Kidding. Someone did not eat enough this morning." Lua mumbled under her breath.

She shut the door, and all that could be heard was the mumbled squeals of the young ladies talking. Pasha returned to the front of the procession. The princess bonded with Azarla on the trip back to the kingdom. The princess even gifted Azarla a dress to give her something more than bandages to wear as her main fire-resistant clothing was damaged from her encounter with the Queen. The dress was one the Princess used to handle Racheed.

"Not much on formalities, is she?" Olcay said.

"Neither of us are into it; I let her frolic around the rules outside of public. "The gods know she likes to press that line. The princess flirts with trouble at every opportunity." Pasha tried to calm himself in front of the others. "You must be aware her father sits on his throne and never leaves. The treaty with the Heartless Council forbids both the king and the queen from leaving their thrones. The war nearly tore the land apart. Just standing on the battlefield, those two started destroying reality." Pasha could see the front gate and stopped talking.

"Go on, what happened?" Olcay wanted to hear more.

"We will talk more later, right now we need to get through the gate."

As they approached, the guards lined up to greet them. The bazaar had already cleared a path for the group. The people had started lining up; small children were upfront, some little girls with small flowery crowns. As the procession moved, many chanted 'Princess Lua'. She opened her curtain and began to wave to the crowd. Olcay realized that Lua was extremely popular with the people. No one ever sees the king outside the castle, so she became the face of the kingdom. As they came closer to the gate of the inner wall, the crowd began to thin and disperse. The massive door shut behind them, and they all dismounted in the empty courtyard. Pasha dismissed the other guards. The carriage driver jumped down and opened the door.

Azarla jumped out of the carriage first, stood next to the driver, and gave a dignified curtsy. The Princess looked about the courtyard and saw they were alone, so she jumped down from the carriage.

"Praise the gods that is over with." The driver let out a small chuckle and then returned to his barring. "Father will want a briefing after dinner. Whose turn is it this time, Sir Pasha?"

"I believe my young steward will be the one briefing this time."

Olcay's eyes widened and he stared at the princess's face since Pasha's was behind his helmet. The seriousness on her face was palpable as the smile she was holding back revealed itself.

"Ok, this time I will report in with my father, but you will owe me one." The ladies went back into the main entrance of the castle. Azarla waved back to them both as the door closed.

"Olcay, you will come with me." Pasha turned his horse around and began to go through the side gate. Olcay remounted his horse and followed him. The castle grounds were massive, with a small town within the grounds. The staff, guards, and their families lived within the grounds. The gardens and ponds provided peaceful tranquility within the stone walls themselves. They were greeted kindly as they passed people on the street. Small children shouted "Pasha! It's Pasha". Some were brandishing small wooden swords, like a small honor guard. Pasha unsheathed his sword and tapped the children's makeshift weapons. A small amount of light enveloped their weapons, and they began to spark. "Go now, protect the kingdom!" Pasha then tapped the ground, and a small, lighted phantom of a monster appeared. Fairy magic, a type of harmless decoy to ward off intruders. It sparkled and popped. The children ran off with their shiny new weapons and started to fight the imaginary enemy. Their mothers were sitting nearby at a table, spinning wool. One of them spoke, "Thank you, Sir Pasha."

Olcay, having never seen the man's face, could see his heart was empathic and kind. At the end of the road, they found a white manor. A few guards were posted; the captain greeted them. "Sir Pasha, Steward Olcay, welcome home. Reports are on your desk in the study, and the staff has prepared a meal."

"Thank you, Captain, send your men home for the evening, there is no longer need for guards at this wall now that I have returned."

The captain saluted and went over to the guard shacks.

"Olcay, as my steward, you will be starting your actual work in the morning. For now, we will celebrate our return and feast on the meal the staff has prepared."

A couple of stable hands approached them and took the reins of their mares. They both dismounted and went to the door of the manor. The door was wooden and carved with various creatures from across the land. The steel on the door handle was Pasha's crest. The door opened to reveal three staff maids, all of whom gave a small curtsy as they went in. They were all dressed in black with white trim. They all seemed to be faerie or beast-like, with tails, wings, and even fur.

"Please not in my own home when I am tired," Pasha growled. Olcay understood that Pasha was not into propriety in private.

The head maid responded, "We were only greeting the young new steward of the house, Sir Pasha."

"I am new to this, and I do feel weird about my role here." Olcay extended his hand and said, "How about hello? And we work our way up from there?"

The maids each shook his hand. They noticed that his hands were those of a laborer and not those of a soft bureaucrat. They all smiled and disappeared into the back. Olcay could hear them talking with the other staff in the back, whispering, "He is cute." "He still needs a beard." "He is very young for a steward." "Do you think he is promised to someone?"

"Olcay, I will be going to my room to remove my armor, and I will join you for dinner." Pasha informed Olcay. Olcay felt a mild amount of excitement, for this would be his first time seeing Pasha's face since they met. Pasha was always alone while eating or sleeping. One of the maids appeared again from a side hallway.

"Sir, we have prepared the Steward's room." The young maid spoke.

"Good, Olcay please go with Rin and settle in," Pasha commanded

"Please, young Steward, come with me." Rin's voice was serious and stern. Olcay followed the young maid down the same hallway she came from. Olcay could see Rin was a mix of fae, or elf, and beast. He could not make out much under her hair. It was distracting as it changed color as they walked.

"Your belongings have already been moved to your room and put away." She looks back at him. "The staff who live here are located in the left hallways. Upstairs is exclusive to Sir Pasha; please avoid going up there unless for official business or when called. Your study, library, meeting room, and quarters are located down this hallway." Her voice was direct and exceedingly serious.

They passed each room as she showed them. The study was well-lit with windows, wood paneling, and a desk in the middle of the room that had papers and scrolls stacked on top. The library was walled completely with books and scrolls to the ceiling; it smelled of paper and ink. A small statue of a fairy stood in the middle of the room with a round table around it. The meeting room was long and had a massive table in the middle of the room. A map of the known world was carved into the table's top. More maps were hung along the wall at the entrance of the room. The room was only lit by light crystals along the wall and ceiling.

Finally, he was able to open the door to his room. The bed was covered in a large red blanket, with a canopy draped over the top of the bed. The entire room was lined with various artifacts in cases, artwork, and plants in the window. A small plate of pastries and hot tea had also been prepared and placed on a small table. The impressiveness of the room also made him feel like he was not at home.

"Please settle in. I will have one of the seamstresses come in for your fitting."

"Fitting?" Olcay inquired

"You are now the steward of Sir Pasha, the kingdom's greatest hero and head knight of the king's army. You will be needing to dress accordingly when you are out of these grounds."

"Understood." Olcay was feeling he needed to catch up on etiquette soon.

She shut the door behind her, and Olcay was finally alone. The journey had finally caught up to him. It had been a few months now of traveling, hanging out in faraway towns, facing the Heartless Council, and being away from home. Now he was in a massive manor and did not know what to do with all of this splendor. He could hear a small knock, but it was not at the door. He looked up as he heard more knocking. He spotted a smaller door above and left to the main door.

"Please come in." Olcay answered and looked upward in curiosity.

A small fairy opened the small door and entered the chamber. She fluttered down an arms distance to his face and gave a small curtsy while in flight.

"I am the seamstress Lin. I am here for your measurements for fitting your clothing and armor, Sir." Her voice was poised and fearful of the new steward.

She was quite cute, with long brown hair that had to be tied to prevent it from going down into her wings. She wore a small outfit similar to that of the other maids. Her wings were crystal clear and blue in hue. She had a shyness to her and was a little skittish.

"It is good to meet you Lin. I am Olcay, son of Demir." Olcay could see she was uncomfortable. "Would you like to have one of these sweets left here? I don't think I could eat them all." The young fairy's wings fluttered quickly for just a brief moment. Olcay reached over and took a cloth napkin from the table, wrapped one of them in it, and handed it to her. She was hesitant, initially backing away from the treat and then inching forward. "My family works with a couple of fire fairies, a couple of troublemakers, but good friends."

"What are their names?"

"Hix and Stix, twin brothers."

She took the cloth with the pastry in her hand and sat down on an upside-down cup on the table. "The chef wouldn't let us eat these today, he said Master Pasha was returning with his new steward and they were for you." She began to nibble at the tasty treat in her hands with delight. She gave off a cheerful smile and blushed ever so slightly.

"I am a simple smith's son and have made no mark to deserve such tribute."

"Oh, no Steward! You are the young man who took on the King's judgment, you stared down the Queen of the Heartless, and you saved a young fire demon's life… the manor is buzzing with your deeds!" Lin's voice recounted his deed with vigor and excitement.

"How could the manor know of any of the things I did while we were out of the kingdom?"

"Sir Pasha sent back with updates with message couriers. The manor has been curious of you and in some cases scared of what type of person you were."

Olcay was taken back again to that moment he first came into the room and had a realization of all he had done, and for him, it had been extraordinary. "I hope I made a good first impression."

She smiled at him and blushed again. "Well, most of the girls were hoping you had your beard growing in."

Olcay smiled, but now the joke had run its course with him, and his eye made a slight twitch. "I guess we should get the fitting done," Olcay said, wanting to change the conversation.

"I already did your fitting while we have been talking. Well, to be more accurate, the weaver spiders took your measurements."

"Weaver … spiders!?" Olcay's froze and his eyes started to pan the room. Olcay then began to sense small movements coming from the back of his shirt and pants.

"Best not to move too much before they are done," Lin advised him as she sipped some tea from a tiny cup. Olcay held still at her recommendation. He then slowly felt them start to disembark from his body. He spotted a few of them, they were smaller than buttons and gave off several different colors.

"I will work with them and the others to make your vestments. They should be completed and in your wardrobe in the morning. Your measurements will be given to our on-site blacksmith, who should have you something by your next outing with Sir Pasha." Lin dusted off her clothes and hid a couple of pastries in the cloth napkin. She flew up to her door and gave him a small curtsy and a wink. Lin closed the door, and the childlike banter started as she entered the hallway.

Olcay, again alone, decided to lay down on his new bed and stare at the red canopy over his bed, wanting to think about nothing. He closed his eyes for a small nap.

Olcay awoke after a couple of hours, well rested from the long trip. He could see the light in his room had shifted, and the light crystals in his room started to glow from his ceiling. He looked over to his dresser and noticed a long wooden box. He could see a small note addressed to him in his mother's handwriting.

My Son
It has not been long since you left us. Orion has gone back to his
merchant guild and is traveling north for the harvest season. We believe he

may have found himself a girl. I could look into it, but your father was not allowing me. Oriel is looking to travel as well to get experience with other fire creatures and people. She does not wish to embarrass herself. So, your father and I will have the house all to ourselves soon. Pasha was kind enough to send us updates by courier about what happened. Please be careful and don't do anything rash. As such, your father and sister enclosed a gift for you in honor of your stewardship. Please keep it with you at all times and be safe.

    Love from us All
    Mother

Olcay took a moment to read the parchment again, then rolled it back up and placed it on the stand. He felt a mild amount of relief and bereavement. He turned to the box and saw the seal of his father and sister on the latch. A dragon and phoenix graced the house crest. Over the latch, a lock was held in place with a spider. It would not open at his first attempt, and for a moment he was befuddled. Then, in a brief moment of inspiration, he pulled out his quill and tapped the front latch. The amount of detail that went into the box was incredible, and the internal workings of the box came to life as each part was unlocked. Olcay remembered his father having him work on these mechanics in his shop when he was younger. His smaller hands were an asset and made these projects easier.

He lifted the lid to reveal a golden, silk-lined box. He reached in to uncover the shape within the lining. The blade was a short sword of mirrored steel. He could see the hue changes in the blade where the different steels melded together. Ejder, Fico, Hix, Stix, Racheed, and some steel from his father's collection. Olcay picked it up from the box and felt no weight on the blade. The handle reacted to his hand; the guard gave off a red-colored glow. Olcay expected this as he knew the sword would mark him as the owner. A well of emotion enveloped him, and he placed the sword back in the box. A mild amount of anxiety took over him as well. "Are they crazy? This is a sword for a general or a King. It would cost a castle to make a blade of this caliber." He thought to himself.

It was a nice touch to have the blade only react to him; at least no one could steal it. Still, he felt out of place with the gift. A knock at his main door startled him, and a sweet voice could be heard. "Steward Olcay, dinner has been prepared."

He opened the door to see one of the maids he saw earlier. Olcay wanted to turn down the offer, but his stomach overruled him. "Lead the way."

Olcay was taken back to the main foyer, where he came in and took a right into the main dining room. The room was well lit, and a modest, personable table he would see at home was at the end of the room near the fireplace. A massive banquet's worth of food had been piled on the table and would have fit better on a dozen tables. The staff of the manor had gathered there. Were they attending Olcay? He already felt awkward and did not want to be surrounded by people watching him eat. There was too much food for just him and Pasha.

Olcay looked at the table as it would be set up at home. Standard wooden plates and a few metal utensils. The table was set for more than a dozen people. He realized he had not changed for guests and did not want to dishonor Pasha's home. Before he could react, the side door had swung open. Azarla and the Lua entered. A mild amount of relief at seeing familiar faces did fill him. Azarla came over to Olcay and gave him a quick kiss on the cheek. "This has been quite a trip for us both." Azarla placed her hands over her chest, remembering the moment. "We need to talk more later." The rest of the staff seemed familiar and relaxed, with the princess having just walked in as well.

The side chamber door also just opened, and in stepped a towering, slender man in a full-length blue robe. The shape of the man was masked by the flowing nature of the robe. The top part of his head was covered down to his nose with a metal plate and two small holes for his eyes. The jawline was covered in a massive black beard and mustache. The staff turned to him and gave a slight bow. Lin, the maid, announced, "Sir Pasha is here; please sit and eat." The staff turned to the chairs and benches and sat at the table. Olcay was brought over to the left side of the table, next to Sir Pasha. Azarla sat next to Olcay, and the Princess sat to Sir Pasha's right and across from Olcay. Olcay looked up to a small alcove above the fireplace, where a small table of fairies, gnomes, and other fey had gathered to eat as well. At that moment, he felt at home. The Princess and a Lord Knight sitting with commoners and staff for a meal was not what he expected. As they all started to eat their food, Olcay turned to look at Sir Pasha, and he noticed.

"I guess this is the first time we have actually been face to face," Pasha remarked.

"Yes, it is. I'll admit I made several assumptions about how you'd look and hoped one of them was correct. I think at least the massive beard was one I got right."

Lua laughed, "I swear he lives in that suit more than he should. He should get out and stretch more."

"Princess!" Pasha's voice was frustrated.

"Oh, come on, Pasha, let me have this, Olcay, what else did you expect?" Lua pleaded.

96

"As you please, Princess, respectfully, Sir Pasha, I did expect you to have more weight on you; with you eating only sweets and cakes our entire journey," Olcay replied.

Lua snickered and then began to laugh. The staff gave into her laughter as well.

Pasha, wanting to change the subject, turned to Lua and asked, "What happened when you delivered the message to the King?"

"As always, he was unmoved by the message. He did not expect a blatant attack on us with you there. He did have our doctors look over Azarla, and I left Barduk with father's advisers to look into the book." Lua replied.

Olcay turned to Azarla with concern. "I am fine, Olcay; besides a few scars, I will be good in a week or so." She grabbed his hand to alleviate his concern.

The night continued with the bards and musicians, and the staff started to liven the party throughout the night. A few began to dance as Pasha looked on. He would occasionally make a hand motion or tap his foot.

Olcay took in the rest of the night in his new environment of song, dance, and food.

Chapter 15

Olcay woke to find himself in his new bed and looked up to see the curtains above. He could hear the movement of fae in the walls and other staff in the hallways. The morning was lively, and Olcay did not want to miss out on his first day, so he went over to his wardrobe.

He remembered Lin said his clothes would be done in the morning by the weaver spiders and be in his wardrobe. As he opened the doors, the light from his window illuminated the inside of the wardrobe. Vests, jackets, pants, gloves, and even undergarments are all neatly hung or folded. He reached in to touch the silken sleeves of the jacket and could not remember seeing anything so well made. In the corner of his wardrobe, he saw a silken cocoon that reminded him of Racheed's. "It has to be where they sleep. Better not wake them." He quickly took out his day's clothes, a red vestment and pants. A jacket would be too much for the warm weather. He thought to himself that he should ask Lin later how to thank the spiders for their hard work.

He went over to the door and opened it to find Azarla standing there, waiting. "Breakfast is ready; we should go. You look nice, Olcay, I mean Steward." She gave a small curtsy in her red lace dress. They went to find the dining room empty and with only two place settings.

"The staff eats breakfast earlier so they can get started on the day," Azarla informed him. They both sat down together and started to eat. The sounds of them only eating echoed in the empty room, followed by silence.

"Where did the staff place you in the manor?" Olcay asked.

"I have been given a guest room down the hall from yours, it was a bit much for me. I guess Sir Pasha takes great care of his staff that lives here. Most are of mixed households or fae background." Azarla answered.

"I noticed that there must be a whole housing district in the walls." Olcay pointed to the small doors along the wall.

"Amazing, I have never heard of home design like this. Hollow walls like streets?" Azarla commented. Olcay remembered the walk in the castle through the walls and could see where the idea came from.

"So, what is the plan for you now, Azarla?" Olcay asked.

"I am still bound to you by our contract; I hope you don't intend to break it with me." She pouted.

"No, I mean, it may take time to find out what happened to Master Yot, and it may be a while before I introduce you to my father and sister. I also like having a friend around, as I am new to all of this."

"Good! I did not want to deal with being nameless and having no contact. It makes things inconvenient." Azarla happily exclaimed and returned to her meal.

"I guess we can continue the contract and have you assist me in my steward duties. If that is ok with you?" Olcay said.

They nodded in agreement and had just finished eating when one of the maids came in. "Pasha will meet you in the study, Steward."

They both got up and followed her to the study, where they found Pasha at a desk, drinking tea and reviewing some papers.

"I hope you both slept well." Pasha's voice seemed to be more proper this morning.

"Yes, Sir Pasha," Olcay answered

"Thank you for the lovely accommodations," Azarla replied as well.

"Good, I guess we will go over your duties as Steward of the House of Pasha." He motioned for them to sit in the two chairs in front of him.

"Olcay, as my steward, you will represent my interests in all public and private affairs. You will start by learning about your new family. You will need to meet all the staff and get to know them. You need to learn their jobs, pay, work schedules, and deal with all disputes. Later, you will learn about the staff at the palace. These are the people you will be interacting with. Finally, you will learn about the other stewards, viziers, and lords. Once you have adequately achieved the basics, I will start giving you more to do." Pasha took a breath to allow for questions, but Olcay had none. "You will still accompany me on missions, handling lodging, food, and other tasks. You will need to get fitted for light gear for our trips. Your family's gift will be needed someday, so always have it with you." Pasha looked again and waited for any questions. "You will receive more combat training with the soldiers between your duties." Pasha stopped to look over his notes. "Today you will follow me to the palace and observe. Please make yourself ready. I will have to assume your contract is still ongoing with Azarla?"

"Yes, Sir Pasha, the contract states I will help him as his assistant till I meet his family and apply for work there and to help out with the investigation of my late Master Yot."

Pasha took the information in and muddled over it. Pasha also felt, as he looked at her chest, that she needed protection until they could uncover what had happened. Pasha reached over with a pen and signed out a contract in front of Azarla, then handed it to her. "I have you appointed as Olcay's vice for the time being; that way we can have you officially in court and provide protection as well. It will also provide you a means to visit the Princess, she mentioned you developed a bond during the trip home. You are also entitled to a stipend from Olcay's accounts. Please try to keep him out of trouble."

Azarla was excited to read the contract, when she signed it the paper and ink converted to light like before and disappeared under her skin.

"Now that the formalities are over, Olcay, prepare yourself for court and make sure you have your family weapon on you."

Pasha got up, dismissed them, and went upstairs to put on his formal wear. Olcay went to his room, and Azarla followed. As he stepped into his room, she quietly let herself in behind him. "Azarla? I can change myself."

He turned to see Azarla in tears, holding her bosom. "Azarla? What happened?"

"I still feel it, it still hurts." She looks up into his eyes. "Why did you save me?"

He can see in her eyes years of neglect and dismissal. Dealing with hatred and prejudice, he saw that his act made her question many things.

"Nothing gets done by doing nothing. Up until that point, I had been waiting to see what life was going to do. I could not go through life knowing I could have done something."

"I do not know what I can do to repay you for all of this."

"For now, let's be friends, and you help me figure out this steward thing."

He wiped her tears, and she felt a warmth from his hand. She gave him a small peck on the cheek, turned to his wardrobe, and opened it up. Olcay was in shock for a brief moment and took it in as a memory.

"It's best we pick out something nice for your debut in court. Pasha's crest is red and gold." A few of the weaver spiders scurried around as she rummaged through the closet. A few fell down and were surprisingly upset about it. Azarla lit a small flame with her fingers, and they ran back into the nest.

"Azarla, don't do that." Olcay scolded.

"Sorry, sorry. You scared me little ones." She reached into her waist pocket, pulled out a few sweets, and placed them at the entrance. She whispered a few words to them, and they exited their home, retrieved the sweets, and went back in.

She turned to him and said, "I think this will be just fine. Make sure you put on the crest and the sword as well." She had chosen a darker red vestment than he had on, with minor gold frills. The pants were black, and the belt was black as well. It was fashionable without being arrogant.

"I will step out, but be quick. Pasha will be downstairs soon." Azarla scurried out to change as well. Olcay was quick to put on the clothes she laid out for him. The comfort of the cloth was immeasurable. Olcay knew spider thread clothing was a luxury, and it made him feel even more out of place.

He dawned on everything and looked at himself in the mirror. Not too long ago, he was wearing linen and leather and working in his father's shop. Looking at his face closely, he looked for any signs of facial hair.

"I already looked, nothing yet." Azarla snuck back in behind him without him noticing. He was startled.

"You're not going to get anything done if you keep doubting yourself, and I'm not going to let you. Keep being the man that stood up to the Heartless Council." Azarla aroused his heart and promptly took it away. "Pasha says you are making him late." As she adjusted his belt and sword scabbard.

On instinct, he quickly hugged her and ran down the stairs to see Pasha armored up and waiting. "It is best Olcay you don't make me wait like that," Pasha spoke from on top of his horse and was almost condescending.

"Yes, Sir Pasha, it won't happen again."

"Please keep distraction to your off time; we must go."

Fire mares were being held by stable hands at the front of the courtyard. He mounted one and joined Pasha at the front of the manor. They both disembarked from the manor and headed to the castle. The homes near Pasha's were lively with the families of the various staff. A small market was selling fresh bread, and some kids were out playing near some ladies who were dying cloth. Olcay trotted ahead to the baker. "Master Baker, do you have any sweet pastries?" Olcay had hoped to make it up to Pasha for making him late.

The baker looked over at Olcay and saw the crest. "Ahh, young Steward, I knew your parents, they would visit quite often; yes, I have a selection of pastries." He leaned over to see Pasha approaching and smiled. "Sir Pasha prefers these floral-scented cakes this time of year." The baker gave Olcay a wink. Olcay handed the baker the money and then quickly looked for a quick snack for himself as well. A minced meat-stuffed roll caught his eye. The baker wrapped them quickly and handed them to Olcay. "The cakes need to be wrapped to keep them moist for when he wants them." The baker suggested.

Olcay smiled and placed the wrapped baked goods into his satchel. "Please take this as well, young Steward." He handed him a small parcel of sweets. "Welcome to our community. Make sure you share it with someone." Olcay quickly nodded, thanked him again, and put the stuff into his side saddle before Pasha caught up.

As they got closer to the castle, he could see the morning guard waiting to join and accompany them as well. Olcay tried to keep calm as the crowds in the main city started to move through the markets. Olcay did not get a chance to explore during his last visit; he was not used to seeing this many people at once. Pasha diverted the group to a side entrance of the castle. As they went through the gate, Olcay saw an entire army of soldiers waiting for rank inspection. They all stopped near a platform in front of the group.

Pasha dismounted, and Olcay followed suit as they went in front of the crowd onto the platform. The group snapped to attention in unison as he touched the top step. The sound of metal clanging together was deafening.

"My fellow knights and soldiers, I have returned from my mission." The crowd resounded in adoration. He waited and then continued. "I see you all managed not to burn the city down while I was gone." I mild amount of laughter rose from the crowd. Pasha continued to talk about the news and his missions for the general orders for the coming day.

"I will meet with my officers to give them further instructions. Now for the most important part. Our King has given title to this young man as my steward, Olcay son of Demir." The crowd voices started to whisper, "He has already brought honor to my house and my crest by staring down the Heartless Queen herself." The crowd roared with excitement and approval.

"My steward will speak for me and represent me; so, his word is my law." Pasha's words caused Olcay to become flushed as he felt the feeling leave his face. Pasha continued, "You are all dismissed to your posts or in the care of your officers; my council meet me in the ready room." He then turned to Olcay and whispered, "Come with me and be prepared with your sword." Pasha whispered.

Olcay took the message to heart and had his hand resting at the ready on his hilt. They moved off from the viewing area to a side room before entering the castle. They walked down the halls past the armory and common areas. A couple of guards opened the door to the meeting room. There, several of the lead officers could be seen lined up in front of their chairs, each with an assistant squire next to them. As they came in, the group snapped to attention, placing their right fist over their hearts. Pasha found his seat and sat down. Olcay stood behind him. The back of Pasha's chair was tall and had several books, scrolls, quills, and a writing station. One curious item seemed out of place, and Olcay dismissed it... Olcay could only assume it was important after he saw a note 'be at the ready with this'. Olcay stood behind Pasha and prepared to take notes. Each of the assistants stood behind their officers and started to set up as well. He saw a few knights before around the castle the first day he visited, and some from the judgment. All were armored and ready; human, fae folk, the kingdom did not discriminate.

Pasha had the knights brief him on the incidents they handled while he was gone. Various brawls, arrests, and an infestation. They all had their attention on Pasha, but their eyes were drawn towards Olcay.

"Olcay, please brief them on the meeting you had with the Queen." Pasha requested.

"Do you wish to brag, young steward?" A voice sneered from the far corners of the table.

"As expected, Lady Jess, I am surprised you could hold out this long." Pasha chuckled back.

"Is it my steward's metal you wish to challenge? The kings? Or my own?" Pasha grieved.

She stood at the words. "I do not challenge you or the king, I just wish to know why this boy took the stewardship ahead of better candidates, and he is beardless no less." Her voice was harsh and dismissive. You could almost feel she was asking for the position herself. The room became uncomfortable as the others in the room either avoided eye contact or gave a glaring look.

Olcay stepped out from behind Pasha's chair with a wooden blade he found on one of the shelves that had the note attached and stood at the ready. Olcay felt Pasha placed it there for him, knowing this would happen.

"My steward seems to have taken your message to heart. At the same time, he thinks you are not worthy of his blade." Pasha's voice sneered.

Olcay felt a sense of horror as he thought the wooden blade was for him to challenge her as a bluff. He had thought this was part of Pasha's plan. Olcay did not know what to do but knew he could not show fear now and decided to stare her down.

The lady's assistant stepped from the side and bared his blade as well. Jess stood and took the sword from him. The bloodlust in her eyes was palpable. It did not look like Pasha was going to step in either. "It looks like we need a new steward after all." One of the officers commented.

She charged at him with her blade thrusting forward; he stepped to the side and swung at her chest, his wooden blade connected, and it knocked the wind out of her side. She fell, heaving from the lack of air. Pasha stood up with a laugh and said, "Jess, you can stand down." Pasha walked over. "I did not expect you to have it in you Olcay, and I also did not expect to have Lady Jess take it that far."

Jess stood up, caught her breath, and smacked Olcay in the back of the shoulder. "Ha, he is ballsy, as you have told us, Sir Pasha. He has a hit behind him; it must be from working in his father's shop." Jess commented.

"Well, I am sure Pasha has been working him hard at night, teaching him combat."
One of the other officers commented. Olcay had to take in the moment as the room
came into a frenzy of laughter. It was a prank on him, and he could only laugh along
with it.

"Olcay, the members of this room do not question your status as my steward; you
may confide in them as comrades and friends." Explained Pasha. "At the same time,
not everyone in the court may see you as we do; never be goaded into a fight you
cannot handle, but uphold the defense and honor of my house." Pasha's words were
very clear and concise.

The meeting continued, with Pasha receiving more briefings on events that
transpired while he was gone. After hours of lumbering briefs, an aid entered the
chamber to inform Pasha the King had summoned him to the throne room. After
dismissing the officers to their posts, Pasha led Olcay back into the castle itself
through the back entrances. To Olcay's surprise, he was in the main part of the castle,
offset from the rest; it was the private quarters of the king and royal family. The
rooms were well adorned and furnished but overall unused by the king himself. It was
now time for Olcay to get to work.

Olcay spent a portion of the day observing his peers and learning about life in the
castle. King Hakim himself was not of a noble upbringing and was, in part resented
by much of the nobility. When Ebedi fell, Hakim was already a prominent steward
himself. The Lord he served adopted him since he had no heirs. After the lord's death,
Hakim collected allies and eventually was named king by most of the broken states.

Hakim's kingdom was ruled by tolerance for the many races, and many found
refuge on his lands. Most would defect from other areas and even other continents;
the kingdom grew vast and powerful. Other lands also fell from lack of leadership or
were absorbed by the Heartless lands. To seek protection, many swore loyalty to King
Hakim.

Many were happy with the current state of the kingdom, and the few that were not
kept it to themselves. Hakim's judgment was always harsh, unforgiving, but always
fair and true. Olcay witnessed a criminal brought in for trial who desired a judgment
from the king. The strangest thing for Olcay was just observing it from the outside.
Nothing happens, or at least nothing can be seen. The king sits there holding his ax
and stares at the person. His eyes do go black, but he never stands or moves. The rest
of the room sits there and waits for it to be over so as not to draw his gaze. The man
fell to the floor in tears; his words were incoherent, and the guards dragged him away.

After the judgment, it was business as usual. The lords and guild masters filed into
their seating arrangements. Everything was done in the room publicly, as the King

never left his spot. Most fought about taxes or land incursions. In the coming weeks, as Pasha's steward, Olcay would learn how to represent Pasha within the hall. Pasha held several titles that gave him control of huge areas of land. Much of it contained fairy folk, gnomes, and other smaller races. It would explain why most of the staff at the manor are from smaller races. Olcay spent most nights learning the towns and their locations on the maps he had in his room. Some of the mystery villages he found were not far from his hometown as well.

The other lords never interacted with each other. The stewards were made to negotiate between the lands themselves. Olcay was glad he had Azarla there some days to help him keep it all straight. Pasha's focus was on maintaining the security of the kingdom, and his business affairs had started to pile up. It took eight days to get most of it sorted. For most of the reasonable requests, Olcay was able to take care of himself; for the more difficult ones, he was able to find time for Pasha to look them over. Working with customers his whole life, Olcay was able to make sense of most of it.

Every other day, he had training in the yard. As Pasha's steward, he was expected to maintain some skill in defending himself. He learned from the very best of Pasha's loyal guards, and it was hard on him to keep up such a schedule. A month had passed in the blink of an eye.

"I will need you to take a break Olcay, for a few days. The staff has voiced concern about your being up all night reading." Pasha scolded.

"I am just trying to get my head around it all," Olcay responded.

"It is too much, even for me, Olcay. After maintaining the people and their safety, the rest will sort itself out. Take Azarla and go through the markets; you have not learned anything about the city we are charged with." Pasha did not want to raise his voice, but he knew Olcay would understand. Pasha tossed a small purse to Olcay. "Your pay for the month. You made some excellent deals with the other Lords, so take these days off as a reward and not a punishment."

Olcay dismissed himself and felt some relief as he went up to tell Azarla. He found her in the study moving scrolls to shelves.

"Azarla, do you have a minute?" Olcay asked.

"Why? What happened? Look the scroll was on fire before I got there, and the water scrolls put it out so no issues." Azarla responded.

Olcay then understood what Pasha meant. Even Azarla was a bit overwhelmed and was starting to show.

"Azarla, we have been given the next few days off by Pasha," Olcay told her. "We are being rewarded, and we get a chance to learn more about the kingdom."

Azarla was relieved, but then despair set in. "I am not ready to go out like this! I have not bathed, nor have I done my hair. Can we meet in a few hours so I can at least get ready?" Azarla pleaded.

Olcay nodded as he knew he needed to get ready as well. He did not need to embarrass himself either. Word and gossip spread quickly in the kingdom, and he needed to make sure he looked his best. He went upstairs to get ready. He asked one of the staff, who was a water sprite, to help him fill his bath and a fire nymph to heat it for him. He felt mildly spoiled, but he felt it was the quickest way to get ready. It was the first time he has ever bathed fully submerged. He was used to rivers and lakes, but indoor plumbing was still not a thing in certain parts of the kingdom.

*knock *knock "Olcay... Olcay. Can I come in?" Azarla came in to Olcay's room.

Olcay was not prepared to be seen and grabbed a towel from the shelf next to him to cover himself.

"Sorry, I am seeing if the weaver spiders made my clothes for this outing." Azarla walked over to his closet. She was in her undergarments without a care in the world.

"Why are you using the weaver spiders in my room?" Olcay scolded. He tried to avert his eyes but could still see her out of the corner of his eye.

"You are the only one with them Olcay, and the cloth they make is fire resistant, which is useful for me."

"Why am I the only one?" Olcay's voice was concerned.

"Weaver spiders are not an abundant species and limit themselves by sets. A cluster of each color makes up a nest. They are of a hive mind, and all die if one dies. You were granted these and their fairy shepherd as a gift."

"That is terrible, I feel like I am some sort of slave owner." Olcay felt sad as he never knew of this.

"Olcay, this species cannot live in the wild as they are delicate and fragile. For generations, they lived in people's homes for protection. If one gets stepped on or eaten, it is over for the nest."

"Lin cannot be happy about this arrangement." Olcay argued.

"I am perfectly fine with the arrangement, Master Steward." Lin fluttered down from her door.

Olcay was taken back as he was still naked in a tub with two women in his room, and it was starting to feel a bit weird for him.

"I am sorry, Lin I did not know..." Olcay tried to speak, and Lin raised her hand for him to be quiet.

"I think you misunderstand Olcay. I don't choose where the spiders go, and they make their home where they are happiest. Your closet was that choice. Also, you did not try to brush them off when you first met. So that made you a worthy master to serve."

"Are you at least being compensated well?"

"Very well, clothing you, Pasha, and your mistress here has kept me well compensated, and the spiders are quite pleased with you as well."

"Oh, Azarla is not my mistress, she is my assistant."

"Mmm hmm. Right. Mistress, your dress has been prepared as you requested. I do ask that you stop feeding them sweets; it keeps them up all night." Lin scolded.

Azarla left with her dress, and Lin dismissed herself. Olcay knew he had to finish up cleaning quickly before he was interrupted again. He went to the closet and found the weaver spiders quite active with one of the articles of clothing. It looked like they were picking out his attire for the afternoon. The cloth was blue and black. It was something he would not normally wear, but he knew that the spiders may get upset if he did not put it on. As before, the fit was perfect, something he was not used to. Common clothing tended not to always fit right. A few of them jumped on and adjusted the buttons to line them up better on the spot.

"My sister has a friend just like you guys. Very helpful. Thank you." Olcay did not know if they understood. He was less bothered by them since he had gotten used to them. He would ask Lin later what he could get them. Olcay put on his sword from his family, and his wardrobe was complete. Just in time since Azarla was waiting at the door.

"That was fast," Olcay commented.

"Oh, I mean, I don't need to wait for my hair to dry; I just heat up and steam myself off. It also softens my skin." Azarla responded with excitement.

Azarla walked over to the closet to showcase the dress to the spiders. One motioned for Azarla to turn around; they noticed a hemline that needed adjusting and jumped on her to fix it. The tiny legs acted as needles to adjust the dress. Azarla smiled and said, "Thank you, little ones. Here." She unfolded a napkin with a piece of cake and placed it in the closet. The spiders pulled on a thread attached to the closet door and closed it.

Olcay and Azarla departed rather quickly to the main shopping district of the kingdom. The market was huge, with a wide variety of treats and items from around the world. It was a free trade market that allowed open tax-free trade on many goods. Money was made off the space and guild fees. Crime was very low in the city; with the guards and the king's judgment always looming, it kept most of the riffraff out of sight.

Olcay found the afternoon quite wholesome. He was able to restock on ink for his quill and get a few items for himself. Azarla eyed the smithing district, the heat and metal were all she had on her mind. "What is it about the forge that you like so much, Azarla?" Olcay asked.

"It was always the family business to work with smiths. I never knew my mother, but my father was always working in the shop. He would sometimes let me help heat the metal with him. We were close." She paused and closed her eyes, as if in prayer. Olcay felt he asked something a little too personal and felt bad about it. Azarla picked up on this and held his hand. "Olcay, it was a long time ago. He was a great father, and I miss him so, but I keep positive about his memory."

"What was his name?" Olcay asked.

"Sadly, he died without a contract and is an unknown. Even I cannot say it, for it will leave my lips before any noise is made. So, I say it in prayer to the forge. I hope to recraft his name again, so he can rest in peace." She held her hand to her heart again.

Olcay had to admit he did not know much about her culture other than their interaction with the smiths. He knew they lived in warmer areas and on volcanic lands, which would be unfriendly places for non-fire-based creatures to live. They were almost extinct when the old religions found them to be easy targets for casting blame. Some of this prejudice still exists. It was Ebedi of all people who stepped in and brought them back from extinction. His fascination was more personal and short-lived. Later, the guild would take up the cause to prevent them from becoming legends. Lost in thought, someone bumped into Olcay in the square.

"Watch where you are going, you whelp!" A drunken man, smelling of something rancid, sized up Olcay. His clothes suggested he was a noble or trader. Olcay gave a small bow and said, "I do apologize sir, I will be more careful." Olcay wished to avoid the issue entirely, as he did not want to give Pasha's house a bad name.

"No, you don't get out of it that easily. You give me your whore there, someone like you wouldn't know what to do with her." His voice was almost incoherent.

Azarla was not too happy with the comment and proceeded to light up her left hand to give the man the slap of a lifetime. Olcay grabbed her hand, and he received a little singe. "Olcay?!" she yelped.

"He is a drunkard and not worth your time. Besides, I think he would not survive your slap and I don't think you want to explain it to Pasha." Olcay warned her.

"You harlot, you were going to burn me, Sed! Pin! Take care of them." Two massive, brutish bodyguards came from his side. They had to be hybrids of orc or another giant race.

The scene started to draw a few stares as a few drunkards pushed for a fight and others went to grab the guards. Olcay put Azarla behind him. He did not have much of a plan other than to run if possible.

He turned to Azarla to tell her to run… "Lookout!" Azarla screamed, yet it was too late. The larger of the two had run up on Olcay and stabbed him in the chest. Olcay could not breathe as the wind was knocked out of him. Olcay hunched over the brute's arm. He heard Azarla scream as the other bodyguard went for her. She lit up both of her hands and started to fight the best she could. She heated up the area around her, and her aura caught the attacker's clothes ablaze. The assailant gave a snide smile; his skin was thick, and heat did not seem to affect him.

Olcay felt the point, but he could not feel the blade. He returned to his senses with the brute trying to get him off his arm. "Die already!" The points kept coming, but he only became winded and his ribs bruised. Olcay mustered up what he had and grabbed his short sword from his belt and swung up through the goon's elbow. The cold steel cauterized the wound solid and the arm fell to the ground. In a state of shock, Olcay looked to see that his chest had not been penetrated. Still feeling bruised, the pain returned. The hybrid-orc with his hand missing screamed in pain till he finally fell to the ground out of shock.

The guards had arrived to see the mess unfold. The bodyguard attacking Azarla retreated to his partner and went on the defensive.

The pompous drunk stood up and announced, "I am Milo! Grandson to the grand Vizard Vance and lord of the western lands, this thief tried to rob me along with his demon whore. They assaulted Pin, arrest them!"

The guards looked to Olcay, and without missing a beat, the captain asked. "Sir, are you alright?"

"Excuse me? Arrest him immediately, I order you!" Milo demanded.

Olcay returned his sword to his scabbard. "I am alright, Captain Jess. The drunken bastard decided he was going to run me through and harm Azarla; they even called her a whore."

"Why are you not arresting him?" Milo got up in Jess's face, and his spit was flying onto her helm.

Jess drew her blade quickly and busted Milo's nose with the pommel. He fell to the ground, shockingly confused and bleeding heavily from his nose.

"I am still wondering how I survived that?" Olcay winced in pain from the bruises and cracked ribs.

"It's your clothing, sir; I hear you inherited weaver spiders. Their threads are quite durable against blades." Jess commented. She then took out her blade fully, and the other guards followed suit.

"What should we do with them, sir?" The captain's eye pupils slitted like those of a dragon.

Olcay could see the tension in the air begin to rise. "I suppose arrest them for now and let it get sorted out later."

"You misunderstand, sir you were assaulted." She turned to Milo and placed the blade on his neck. "You have assaulted Olcay, son of Demir, steward of Pasha, and the one who has stared into judgment and pain, and you have assaulted Lady Azarla, his vice. Are you mad or insane?"

Milo and the bodyguard's blood left their faces. "He can't be, he is just a boy!"

"It would not matter if he were a common street beggar; you know the law, and then you tried to use your authority afterward... That is a death sentence. Olcay survived the king's judgment; could you do the same?" Her blade started to nick his skin, and blood started to trickle out.

"Captain Jess, Thank you. I would say that is enough." Olcay walked over to them and pulled Jess's blade from Milo's neck. He kneeled and looked into Milo's deadened eyes.

However, the kind gesture was short-lived. Milo, in drunken anger, went for Olcay's sword and pulled it out from the scabbard. Before Milo could react, the blade left his hand and buried itself in his chest. He fell to the ground again, not knowing what had happened. Pinned to the ground and gasping for breath. In between life and death, he was at a loss for what had just happened.

Olcay, in a bit of shock, knew that his sword would not harm him and reacted for his safety. His father's design idea for sure was a bit much, but it kept thieves away. He went back over for the second time.

"I don't need this on my mind today, apologize to my assistant Azarla, then to all of these nice people, and take your goons and enjoy sobering up for the night in a jail cell." Olcay was not about to have the death of a drunken idiot on his conscience. Neither did he wish to have someone look into the king's eyes for judgment; it was a little too much for one night.

Milo could only nod in understanding. Olcay took hold of the sword's pommel and twisted it, and it removed itself from Milo without a wound. The crowd that had gathered did not know what to think at this point, and even a few of the guards could only stare in awe. Milo was taken away to prison with his goons to sober up.

"You knew I was joking, right... about killing him?" Jess asked Olcay.

Olcay looked at her and could only stare. "No, I did not."

The captain let out a bit of a laugh, as he could only remain bewildered.

"So, who has to write this up in a report to Pasha?" Azarla asked.

"The steward has to handle this one and report to Pasha; a vizard is involved, and he will have to settle the matter." Jess said and then muttered, "It would have been less paperwork if they were dead." That part was only heard by the other guards, and they laughed at the notion.

Olcay was not looking forward to going home. However, he did not delay the matter and cut short his evening with Azarla. Pasha had been waiting at the steps to the manor when he returned. Olcay was prepared to be scolded.

"Are you both all right?" Pasha asked. "I was only told some of the details."

Olcay explained what happened and was commended for his action. "You were lucky this evening, we will need you to train harder, I will handle the Vizard issue myself," Pasha looked at Olcay's state. "Get yourself cleaned up and bandage those ribs till you see the healers."

Pasha then looked over to Azarla, who was in shock from the ordeal. "Azarla, get yourself looked at as well."

Azarla did not notice her dress was damaged from the fight. She started to cuss in various languages and was in tears. "I think she will be fine." Olcay remarked and laughed.

Chapter 16

Olcay was able to spend the next few days off with an escort in tow. Pasha did not need to lose his steward. When Olcay was done with his time off, there was no time for him to ease back in. They were both summoned back to the castle.

Pasha relieved the guards on duty and entered through the back door behind the throne. Olcay followed and was welcomed by an old site of the throne room; from this side, it looked mildly different. High upon the view of the room, he looked over to see the king sitting as large as ever. From the right side, up close, he gave off a stern vibe that sent a chill down his spine. As he looked around the grand hall, he could see no one has come in yet, and the other doors were sealed as during judgment. Olcay did not feel the same after it happened.

"It is about time Pasha you showed up. I have been sitting here for hours." King Hakim chuckled.

"Funny as always, my King. I hope you have been well. I see you change the room around again."

"I grew tired of the décor being here, so I changed it. It is one of my few forms of entertainment." The King muttered.

"Yes Sire, have you been briefed on the events that have transpired."

"Yes, my daughter and her new friend gave me most of it, and that talking mug filled in the rest on the other matters." The king lifted his brow and stared at Olcay, who was looking around the room. "I know it has been a few months, and I could not address it with you. I heard you decided to take on a queen this time, young steward." He leaned over and motioned for him to come closer. "Try slowing down on upsetting royalty, it may become bad for your health."

"Your Majesty, I understand." Olcay gave a bow, and the King motioned him back to Pasha.

"Can you open the room up for me, Sir Pasha?"

Pasha unsheathed his sword from the hilt and tapped a small stone between his feet. The doors of the room revealed themselves, and the nobles started to enter the room. A balcony appeared, and the princess walked out atop the crowd and sat on a small throne.

The various nobles and aristocrats lined up along the walls, some mingled in corners, others found chairs. A scribe came forth and read aloud the dockets for the day as one by one people came forth to bring items before the king. Olcay tried to take in what he could on his first day back, but ultimately succumbed to fatigue and yawned.

112

Pasha nudged Olcay and he went to refocus.

"Now, Olcay, I believe there is a matter of the young lord Milo." The king pounded his ax on the floor, and an echo silenced the room.

"Where is the house of Vance?!" The king announced.

"HOUSE OF VANCE MAKE YOURSELF KNOWN!" Pasha commanded.

Vance moved to the front of the king. He was an older man who had seen time catch up to him. His beard was white, and his hair was thin. His face was of anger and hate for the king but remained passive. Milo and his partners were dragged in shackles out in front of the assembly.

The orator stepped forward and spoke, "Your grandson attacked the steward of Pasha and then tried to use his authority to bring false charges against him. Even after the steward pardoned him, Milo attempted to murder him with his own sword. In addition, Milo tried to kidnap Olcay's female assistant to perform unbecoming acts on her purity. This has been corroborated by witnesses, a captain of the guard, and the silver oracle investigator." The orator stepped back to the side of the room.

"Is your house in order, Vance?" Hakim asked very calmly.

Vance looked at the floor and then looked to Milo. He struck Milo in the face with his cane, bashing in his cheek and knocking out one of his teeth.

"Your Majesty, my house is in order. I was unaware that it was this untidy. I have been away from the capital, watching over the land under my care. I came here under a different understanding of the circumstances." Vance gave a small bow.

"Steward Olcay, what say you on the matter?" The king addressed him directly and personally.

Olcay thought for a moment and decided he was not going to deal with being tricked into saying anything this time; he chose his words carefully. "Your majesty, I will have to yield to a wiser man on this matter as I am not ready for such a responsibility."

"Perfect." The king's aural presence emerged and warped the very walls of the room. "Olcay, you have yielded your will to pass judgment on the accused Milo and the house Vance, till a time you have found yourself to be wiser." The aura engulfed Milo, and he screamed in fear, but he was in no pain.

Olcay remembered how speaking brought him here in the first place, and now he regrets his words for the second time. He then remembered what Lady Tash said about how "speaking is equal to life and death." In front of the Hakim, things had become no different.

The passed-out Milo was dragged away by guards, his two goons were banished from the city, and Vance stood there and bowed out graciously. Olcay was feeling most uncomfortable. Pasha leaned in and whispered. "Do not worry; if you die before your judgment, they will meet an abrupt end."

"That is not the least bit encouraging. How do you keep up with these judgments?"

"Oh, I learned to shut up the first time around." Pasha's voice gave a little chuckle.

"Don't tire him, Pasha; he has much to learn still…" The king paused. The king's left arm moved to his ax and then resettled back to its usual placement.

Olcay took it as odd and almost chose to ignore it, but then he noticed that Pasha was gripping the hilt of his sword lower, as if he were preparing to lift it. Olcay then looked to the wall to the left of the king.

"The young Steward is gifted, almost no one in the room noticed you, come out and talk!" The king commanded.

The crowd was almost unfazed by a "skreel" from a shadow that bolted to the left side of the King. A cloaked figure masking as part of the wall was suddenly at the king's left side. The creature was dusted out of existence as it met the king's reach. "That was not very smart."

The king turned to Olcay and Pasha. "Can you dispatch the other one as well? I believe Sir Pasha has been training you lately. Let's see how you do."

"Draw your sword, Olcay!" Pasha commanded. Pasha lifted his sword, and the room closed. The guards in the room covered the nobles in the grand hall, and it all went silent. Olcay stood at the ready; his heart was racing, and he started to sweat. He felt something was off with the ground in front of the throne and jumped in front. The floor moved like ripples in a pond as if something was displacing the surface of the floor.

When it stopped, the floor returned to normal. It jumped up from Olcay's right, and a short blade could be seen. Olcay was ready and blocked the blade from his side. The covering over the being showed darkened yellow eyes. He felt a large hand on his shoulder. "Be at ease, Olcay." He turns around and sees the king standing behind him. "I realized this one may be out of your class at the moment. I will let you have the next one. Besides this one did not come for me, and I am quite vexed by this." The King struck the ground with the handle of his ax, and the area in front of Olcay appeared in the shape of a man-like creature and was dusted the same as the other.

Pasha placed his sword back on the stone, and the room reopened as it was. The king was back on the throne as if nothing had happened. "A whole week they were there waiting." The king scoffed, "The smell is the worst."

Olcay sheathed his sword. "Your Majesty, you knew they were here?"

"Assassins are a normal occurrence here; I am quite upset they were not here for me this time. So, we waited to see who they intended to attack. That is why we brought everyone in."

"To think you are starting your judgment debut here with an attempt on your life," the princess said from her balcony throne.

"Pasha, we will clear the room for today; please continue to investigate this." The king ordered. The nobles and vassals cleared the room. Many were relieved; others were annoyed. After everyone was cleared, Olcay returned to his post next to Pasha.

"Olcay, your story has just started, and someone wants to write you out. As you may have already surmised, I do not leave this room. As part of the agreement with the Heartless Council." The king's hand gripped nothing and something on the pillar where it sat. "We both need others to take care of business outside our rooms." The king motioned him over. "Please continue to serve as you have, train for what is to come, and solve this; not just for your own sake but for everyone. Become the wiser man who can make sound judgments. You will not have someone there to always give you the answer."

Olcay bowed to the king. "Yes, your majesty."

"Pasha, take him, work with your people, and the drunken mug. Work in my study if you must, so you will not be overheard." Hakim's voice was stern and serious at the moment. They both dismissed themselves and started for the exit.

Pasha turned to Olcay, "Olcay, you will be speaking with Vance in a few, please be careful on what you say this time." He walked ahead in the hall with the crowd of nobles as they closed out their business.

"Steward Olcay, a word." Vizard Vance had moved into Olcay's way and moved his arms, directing him to a small room to speak alone.

Olcay followed and shut the door behind him.

"I will get to the point Steward Olcay, what do you want? Name your price."

"I do not know what you are referring to, Vizard…"

"Please don't insult me and get to what you want for a fair judgment of my house."

"I would ask that you not take that tone with me."

"So, you want power, is it?"

"No!"

"What is it then?" The old man was flustered that he had to almost beg from someone he saw as beneath him.

"How about we start by leaving me alone. I don't care about you or your house. I was almost killed moments ago, and I do not need to mix words with you," Olcay was getting heated. "If your house was taught that not everyone has a price and maybe some manners, we would not be in this situation!" Olcay had a few things bottled up in him and did not want to deal with them anymore. "Your grandson tried to have me killed, then tried to kidnap my assistant, and then tried to have me thrown in jail. If I put a price on that, then that is what I am worth. Right now, I don't think I want to devalue myself."

"You will have to pass judgment someday, and I don't think I can wait around or trust a commoner like you to hold this power over my house for so long," Vance tried to bully the situation further. Olcay was upset, to say the least.

"Then you should have no house to worry about. No land to care for other than the fields you till yourself, the homes you build upon it, and the pastures on which you tend livestock. Live only off the land till such time as you understand the commoners that are within your care."

The room went cold, and they appeared before the king in the main throne room. "That took longer than I thought it would." Hakim smiled and lifted his ax from its placement.

"Vizard Vance, your lands are forfeit and your holdings seized till such time as your house has earned them back. I will place your family's estate, people, and land under Princess Lua's care till such time as Olcay feels to lift your sentence or later from your bloodline."

Vance looked down to find his belongings, clothes, and cane replaced with those of a common farmer. Olcay was mildly relieved that he did not say anything else in his rant, or this all could have been worse. Pasha was waiting for Olcay behind the king. Olcay was visibly upset that he was set up again. Vance was escorted to a cart waiting for him outside. It contained tools, farm equipment, food, seed, and some caged livestock. Milo was waiting there, mildly confused as to what had just happened to him.

Pasha looked to Olcay as he watched them leave the castle gates. "That was kind of you, Olcay; anyone else would have judged them harshly or looked for a favor." He smacked him in the head. "Next time, shut up."

Chapter 17

It had been almost a month since the incident in the throne room. Olcay started to get into a rhythm so he would not exhaust himself. Olcay was given the task of gathering everything up to this point on the attacks. It was a grueling ordeal as he did not know where to begin. The attack on his family was made to look like someone was trying to steal secrets. The attacker was a failed blacksmith who blamed his loss of business on Demir. It did not add up since he was from an entirely different region. The attackers on Yot were identified by the queen as hers, and she ordered the attack to prevent Ebedi's release. Azarla could not confirm if any of her projects could be used for such a task.

She claimed they worked on making farm equipment that could plow fields easier and kitchen items. Yot's death was extreme enough to make it look like an accident caused by his runes failing. Olcay knew after years of working in his father's shop that was not possible. The object on Yot's arm could not be identified. Olcay could only stare at the scrolls and books while combing the library. Barduk was with him and was starting to grow limbs from his cup shape. He looked like a treefolk or wood elemental of some kind.

"Barduk, is any of this making sense to you at all?" Olcay asked.

Barduk sat up from his chair, pulled a small flask from his side, and poured it into the reservoir on his head. "Olcay, I would be lying if any of this made any sense. The only thing that seems out of sorts is the apparatus that you found with Master Yot. I will need to ask the guild if they know anything," Barduk's bushy stems for an eyebrow furrowed in desperation. "The only people that can answer this are either dead or not available."

"Who is not available?" Olcay was confused by his choice of words.

"Embodiments of the crafts, vices, or passions might have answers, but they speak to no one," Barduk answered.

"Why is that?"

"They are neutral and serve their own self-interest."

"Who else?" Olcay wanted to get to the point, wondering why he could not get an easy answer.

"The young heartless that gave you the book might be of some help."

"What can you tell me about them? Maybe that might give us something."

"The only references to the Heartless are long destroyed, but I do have an account written on a scroll by a Lord that escaped them."

Barduk pulled from the shelf a tattered scroll with a broken seal and handed it over to Olcay. Olcay unraveled the fragile document, excited to see at least some progress. "This is the account of Lord Jertu of house Nefret." Barduk proclaimed.

I have been summoned home, Ebedi has been finally removed from power, and the council needs to move fast to take control of the situation. However, the drunkenness in the streets and the castle has become too much to bear.

Queen Yulia sits on her throne and yearns for her former husband, who was lost to her for all eternity as she also injected her sword to imprison him... I was walking one evening and glimpsed her frolicking and grinding Ebedi's statue prison. I tried to inform my brother, but he paid no heed to it.

———

It has been six months, and the council has become afflicted with a curse. We don't know where it came from, and it has started to worsen.

Lady Kirik was the first to lose her husband in a fire. She now sits in her chambers weeping; the wail fills the halls at night till morning for her one true love...

Lord Seket was the next, losing his children in an assassination attempt, he sits with his eyes glazed.

——

I have had no time to write lately, and I do not know why I must inform whoever is reading this. Lord Hakim came today seeking the return of his kidnapped wife. His brother, Lord Groun, turned him away, and a duel ensued. Both survived with the Hero Pasha taking up arms.

Lord Varish had become the next to lose his will and sat upon his chair, not caring.

I tried to get my brother to see what was going on, but he could only see that he wasted his life for some reason.

——

This is my final entry, as I must flee before this land takes me as well. Queen Yulia has convinced the council that they were cursed by Ebedi, and they must stand firm in his imprisonment. They needed to remove their own hearts to live longer to imprison Ebedi.

Lady Tash was the last to remove her heart. Losing her mother was just too much for her to take in these bitter days of despair...

Gradually, the people just started walking into the chambers and removing their hearts. The blood painted the floor. I fear I won't make it out as well.

Olcay could not read the rest, as it became too gruesome to take in. "Did he make it out?" Olcay asked

"Yes, he did, and now he is retired to a manor in the woods. I hear he has gone mad." Barduk poured another drink into his head and went back to reading a scroll.

"Why did they remove their hearts in the first place? Seems like something extreme to do." Olcay was digging for something.

"What reason would actually make sense? To stop their pain, to end their lives, anything you could think of would not make sense. What happened is they lived through it and took advantage of it." Barduk made his point clear.

Olcay picked up the book and thumbed the pages. "I wish we had more to go on; I remember it was Lady Tash that gave me the book."

"She was the youngest of them, losing her mother shortly after Ebedi was imprisoned." Barduk's voice was sad for a moment out of pity. "Her heart was dead with grief before she cut it away".

"Maybe she regrets her decision," Olcay mumbles to himself. He turns to Barduk to ask.

"What was the passage with King Hakim's wife then? I don't remember hearing about that story from the bards and poets."

"Ebedi wanted my mother to peer into his past to find out how this all happened to him and see if there was something he missed." A young female voice came from the doorway.

"Princess, I am sorry we did not see you there," Olcay replied.

"Not to worry, Olcay I know you are busy, so I brought you a snack to help you get through this." She had brought some items of fruit, slices of meat, and bread on a plate.

"You were asking about my mother?" Lua's voice was calm, as if she had rehearsed this conversation.

"Yes, we were looking at what happened when the council was created to see if we could find any references to the book."

"Would you like to see for yourself? It may make it easier." The princess's voice was muffled and restrained.

Olcay remembered when he first met Lua that she offered him the chance to see the past by touching Ebedi's statue. He only nodded his head. She took hold of the scroll in Olcay's hand; her eyes went black as he stared into the void, and he felt himself go. "Don't regret this." She cautioned.

His eyesight cleared, and he was standing in the great hall of the Heartless Council. The room was in better condition than when he was there last. He looks over to see the King in the middle of the room arguing with his brother, Lord Groun. The King was taller and more vivid in color than he had ever seen him. Both of his arms were the same size, and his ax had a shine. Lord Groun did not have much change from when Olcay first saw him.

"Ebedi is in prison; return my wife to me!" Hakim commanded.

"Know your place, brother; you know nothing of what we have gone through; your wife is the least of our worries," Groun replied.

For Olcay the entire experience appeared real but at the same time faded in and out. He had to focus hard for the image to be clear to see and hear.

"You best hold your tongue before I cleave it from your skull." Hakim threatened.

Olcay could barely make out a fight in the shadowy darkness. Hakim took up his weapon and leaped skyward. Groun took out his sword and took the blow from above. The sword cracked under the pressure. Hakim then pulled back from his blow, took the handle, and plowed it into Groun's chest. He fell to the ground and stared up at his brother. Hakim looked in shock as his blow went soft and sounded hollow in the plating.

"You bastard, what have you done? I only heard rumors, but you actually pulled out your own heart." Hakim took a step back. "What darkness are you in service of now?"

From the side, Pasha arrived. "Sire, we found her."

"Bring me to her!" Hakim's voice was in a panic.

The image moved forward in time to a dark room. Their eyes had to adjust, and Hakim saw his beloved. He fell to his knees in horror. "What has happened to her?"

From a corner of the room, Queen Yulia walked in.

"You! Heartless bitch, what have you done to her?!" Hakim's eyes darkened as if he were ready to pass judgment.

"Me? I did nothing; you have my husband to thank for this." Her voice was innocent and mocking him.

"What happened to her?" Hakim calmed himself but remained at the ready.

"After she tried to see his past, she went mad and fell into an Oracle paradox; her eyes never reopened." She stood beside Hakim and placed her unwanted hand on his shoulder. "Then he pulled Death from the aether to embody her." Yulia's voice began to whisper. "She did not take kindly to her imprisonment, but could do nothing to her enslaver." She could not bring death to him nor herself to be free." He became bored with her and placed her here.

She sat on a throne of black soot and bone. Her right hand was still flesh in color as the rest of her could only remain between being whole and not.

"What can be done for her then?" Hakim struck his ax to the ground to prevent him from kneeling. His heart ached as he looked upon his wife in terror.

"Ebedi is the only one that can do anything, but he can escape us at any time. We need to bind him to his prison to barter our lives and hers back. Will you join us? We need more power if we are to hold him." She held out her hand, but it was cold and lifeless.

"Bah, I won't become one of you, I have my daughter, and I won't let you do this to the people anymore."

"That is easy enough; we will hold ourselves here on our thrones, but you must do the same. We need power to hold the prison together. Our current efforts may not be enough."

Olcay's heart sank as he looked on as the world he knew started to reshape. Lua stood looking on, having watched this before.

"Why have you shown me this princess?" Olcay asked.

"In order for you to find answers, you need to start with the right information." She replied.

"Can you show me, Lady Tash?" Olcay asked. As Lua obliged his request, he looked back at Lua's mother on her throne, and she gave the slightest smile as the room moved forward again.

"Does it hurt little Lady Tash?" A sultry voice fawns over the great hall as a little girl weeps on the floor before the council. "We can make it stop hurting if you would give into us. Take your place so we can stop this curse from moving on to others."

Olcay looked on and noticed she was clutching something small in her hand. It was the book he had been researching this whole time. She clutched it as a mother would a child. "Can you stop it for a moment?" Olcay asked. The image stopped. "Did you see this before?" He asked

"Honestly no, I never get this far as I find this ritual distasteful," Lua answered.

"Lady Tash, had this book from the very beginning, was it from her mother or someone close to her?" Olcay murmured. "Can you pull us out then?"

Lua pulled back the veil, and Olcay found himself holding the scroll as before. He went over to the book and brought it over to Lua. "I don't know why we did not do this before. I could have you look at it."

"I never mentioned it to you before Olcay, but it could be dangerous for an oracle to be looking at something from Ebedi's reign. An unknown book and in an unknown language, that screams Ebedi; you saw how my mother ended up."

Olcay went cold, remembering Lua's mother's dark state. "I understand, but at least we are further than we started. Whatever happened to your mother?" Olcay regretted asking, but he wanted to know this time.

"She was pulled into another realm; we do not know where she is. The pillar her hand was holding onto that sits by his throne still holds her essence on our plane. The dead are drawn to her as a conduit to the afterlife. You have seen my father's arm?"

"I will have to assume the wasted arm in dark aura?" Olcay responded.

"He holds her to the mortal plane using the column his hand sits on. The power of death he draws from her he uses as part of his judgments, the same as the council draws on the curse for their rituals."

Olcay took down the notes in his book and looked them over. "I am sorry, I know none of this was easy. Thank you for showing me. At least we have a few answers."

"I fear I gave you more questions." Lua's voice fell silent, and she felt the need to cry.

Olcay realized he needed to take a moment as well to steady his composure. "Thank you again for sharing that with me."

"You would think it would be easier, each time I have remember I am only an observer." The princess was visibly upset.

Olcay grabbed the food Lua brought over to the table. Lua took the hint as Olcay tried to lighten the mood. Barduk found the bottle of mead for himself and began to pour.

To change the subject, Olcay asked, "Barduk? When is your condition going to clear up?"

"Who really knows? From the looks of things, I may just stay this way. I am not in any pain, and I am not getting a sermon from Grogg." Barduk continued to fiddle with the bottle until Lua handed him an opener.

"Did you find anything in the past that would be useful?" Barduk asked as he poured.

"Yes, the book predates the council, and Lua thinks it has something to do with Ebedi himself."

"So, nothing useful. I would say ask Ebedi, but he is imprisoned at the moment." Barduk mocked.

Lua was sapped of energy from the ordeal and grabbed a few sweets and started to eat. That afternoon, Olcay wrote up the incident as if he had found some old writing on the matter to report to Pasha. He was not going to get scolded for looking into the past with Lua without something to show for it.

122

Chapter 18

Fenya looked out the window of her home. Summer was here, the green around the mountain was very lush, and the tree line was thicker now. The sounds of the forest were muddled by the sounds coming from the forge. The constant banging of steel continued all daylight hours. Her once secluded home from the world now had guards posted outside additional barriers. They kept their distance to give the family as much privacy as they could. On occasion, an envoy would bring them information and letters. Ejder would sometimes play a prank on the guards and provide some entertainment. Last night she flew around the barrier and triggered it, causing the guards to run around all night. She left them a barrel of wine as a thank you in the end. Fenya missed her boys now that they were both out of the house. Oriel will be off soon for acceptance into the guild and still has not decided what she will do next. The discussions at night have been heated, to say the least. Oriel wants to move to learn more about other fire beasts and folk, eventually opening a shop in the capital. Demir doesn't want her leaving till the person behind the attack is found. In the end, the king and the guild will decide everything. Her fate is limited as the heir to Demir's bloodline and forge.

Fenya could only rub her temples and try to stay out of it all. She drank her tea with one of the female knights stationed outside her home. Alicsh was well built, with her long blond hair tied in a bun in the back, green eyes, and almost white skin; she probably has a fae family background.

"Do you have children, Lady Alicsh?"

"I have two girls and a son, Or'Fenya."

"What do they plan on doing for apprenticeships?"

"My son is to be knighted hopefully next season if he can keep his wits about his studies, and my girls dabble as artisans right now but are too young to know what they want."

They both paused as they could overhear an argument coming from outside, and the clanging of metal from the forge would interrupt them.

"I appreciate the company; however, my Oriel will be coming in a moment and will need some time with me." Oriel stood as if she was preparing the table and removed the items.

"Yes, Or'Fenya I will go check on the changing of the guards." Alicsh departed and opened the door to find Oriel running in at the same time. She kicked over the table in anger then went upstairs and Demir followed right behind her. He stopped at the base of the stairs and yelled to her, "We are not done discussing this!"

"Sweetie, why must you persist with this? You quenched her master seal; you need to let this go." Fenya's voice was imploring and assertive.

Demir turned to her, and his eyes warmed at the sight of her. He ruffled with his beard. "I am past that now; however, the guild wants her to get her papers before she can take on work anymore." He came over and sat next to her.

"We are on hold here, they won't come here, nor send her stuff till she meets the guild leadership. Also, she wants to go through the ceremony as well with everything going on." He could only feel her frustration.

"Well, I foresee us going on a trip then," Fenya said. He looked up to see the dark holes in her eyes.

"Fenya! What are you doing?" Demir was taken back, as he knew what was coming.

"A little trip will be fine. I could always look further, where you sleep downstairs instead." Fenya gave a sly smirk and rested her cheek on her hand.

"You mad woman." He chuckled. Fenya found herself in Demir's embrace.

"I will have Alicsh arrange transport for the six of us." Fenya ruffled through his beard and hair to adjust it.

"Six?" Demir was confused.

"Well, the three of us and three ancient, fiery family members. You think they would miss out on her ceremony as well?"

"I guess I will have Hix and Stix run things in town for now," Demir replied reluctantly.

"Olcay is back as well in the capitol and may have some questions."

Demir held her hand and her eyes went back to gold. Fenya felt lightheaded "I went further than I should have to make a point. Thankfully it all looks okay."

"Oriel, prepare your things! We have a trip." Fenya yelled to her upstairs in the loft.

"Already packed." She came downstairs, ready to go. Oriel's grin was ear to ear like a child that just got away with something.

"I swear you both have everything well-planned out." He reached over to open a bottle of mead. "I'll get the cart prepared; make sure you have a cushion for this trip," Demir muttered.

As he was leaving the house, he yelled back inside. "Make sure you have a container for Racheed; you don't need her catching the cart on fire."

It would be a long ride for them to the Kingdom.

Chapter 19

Olcay had spent the last few weeks after the incident introducing himself to the role he was given. The manor was easier to get around, the staff he learned all their names, and he had a knack for the job's day-to-day paperwork. He was introduced to a fae refugee town on the roof of the manor. The walls of the manor were also hollow, allowing for small roads throughout the house, which explained the noises he would hear some nights. In the castle, he would work with the other stewards and viziers on the administrative duties. Sir Pasha's accounts would disburse the funding for the military and security. Eventually, Olcay was given the chance to pay the troops as well. Olcay made notes of the people he was warned about; there have been no issues since Olcay learned to hold back for the time being. There were a few begrudged problems from when his parents were at the castle as well.

Barduk, mages, and scholars turned up nothing when it came to the book. The book was returned to Olcay, as they thought it would eventually reveal itself to him. They believed it was a message for him, which is why he was given it. At his desk, he looked at it and flipped through its rough pages. It was just a plain red book, nothing out of the ordinary or fantastical. As he looked, the room dimmed ever so slightly, and the torches took on a red hue. From his chair, someone reached behind and rubbed his chin with a thumb.

A sultry voice whispered, "Still no beard, I am disappointed." Olcay stood up startled and calmed when he turned to see the black sheen body of Ejder.

"Ejder! What brings you here!?" Olcay turned for a moment to allow her to realize she needed to form clothes. She smiled at his expense and gave him a moment to consolidate his thoughts as she formed a dress with her scales. Technically she was still naked, but only the illusion mattered to the young man still unfamiliar with the ways of a woman.

"No greetings? How rude! You are not going to get with anyone with an attitude like that." She looked to see his blushing face and realized she needed to give some more cover or he may faint. She continued, "I was sent ahead to secure accommodations; also, I could not deal sitting in a cart. Of course, my dear boy, your family will be arriving soon for your sister's entry into the guild."

Olcay turned around. "My family is coming here? Where are they staying?"

"I will take you afterward; they will be staying at a guest house down the road. Make sure you are there for dinner. They will be excited." Ejder remarked. Olcay was happy and mildly relieved. "I felt your sword strike through a half orc, then reversed through a human assassin, and finally unsheathed in defense against an angry shadow skreel." Ejder said, "What have you been getting involved with since leaving home? I heard a bard singing, you stared down the Heartless Queen herself as well."

Olcay felt like he was being scolded, and then she hugged him. She then looked him in the eyes. He could see them shifting from having dragon slits to looking almost human. She was tired from holding the form.

"We should get going, the metal behemoth gave you the day off." Ejder started to guide him to the door.

"How? I still have so much work to do." Olcay replied.

"I had a small chat about your trip with Pasha, and then he offered you time off to see your family." Her smile was a dead giveaway… she threatened him. Olcay knew he would be in trouble later. He thought to himself that maybe he should pick up a few sweets as an apology later.

A knock at the door and Azarla entered the room. "Olcay, I was just informed your family will be arriving in town for your sister's ceremony and you had the day off from Sir Pasha…" She stopped and saw Olcay embrace a well-endowed woman in a black scaled dress, her short hair gave off a sheen as if it were a crown. "I am sorry to disturb you, Steward; I had no idea you had called upon someone."

The room darkened completely, and a chill filled the once-sun-warmed room. Olcay, reading the situation, stepped in. "Azarla, please let me introduce Ejder; I believe we talked about her."

Azarla turned around, realizing her deathly error, and gave a small curtsy. "My humble apologies, Ejder…" She looked to find herself face to face with Ejder's eyes. Her scales flipped like a stone hitting a pond pattern that rippled down her body. It was as if her skin went through multiple changes at once. Her clothing disappeared momentarily and returned.

"Olcay, I think she is cute..." She ran her hand through Azarla's hair. "… and mildly familiar. Best you understand, young lass, I burned many for less, but Olcay took the time to save you, so I will hold off for now." Ejder brought the air in the room to a standstill to make her point. Ejder then kissed Azarla's cheek. Then the room went back to normal, and Azarla's breath returned to her.

"Olcay make sure you put on something nice for your mother. The carriage will be by soon to get you." Ejder evaporated out of the window and down to the street below. She turned, gave a small wave, and blew them a kiss.

Olcay turned to see Azarla in a bit of shock, and then she calmed herself. He gave a small chuckle. "Why would you think she was a prostitute?"

"I don't know, she was gorgeous, and I didn't know what to think, I mean she wasn't really wearing anything." She had her arms outstretched as she tried to explain nothing.

"What would have given you the idea I was needing the company of a lady of the evening?" Olcay turned his head and crossed his arms. They both gave each other a look and started to laugh.

"We'd best get you ready to see your family." Azarla's smile held back; she was still shaken. She only knew of dragons from the tales from her village and that they can be terrifying. She shuttered for a moment, then turned to Olcay.

Olcay just realized something. "I guess you have the chance to meet my father and sister for a forging job?"

Her eyes lit up and she remembered their contract. It was a star-struck moment for her then she recovered. "NO, I am not dressed or even clean for a job interview. Besides, you are seeing them for the first time in months." Azarla insisted even with Olcay's persistence. She planned to meet up with them tomorrow at the ceremony.

The carriage was waiting for him, and then they went to the accommodations where Olcay's family was. The king had several guest homes in the city itself for visiting dignitaries. The building was in the center of the main square, not far from the guild. The area had the best food and shops; it was a very generous location. Olcay could see in his field of view the faint blue aura of Fico in the distance. His family came into sight, and he was almost emotional. His mother was the first to embrace him after he jumped from the carriage.

Fenya gave him a quick look over. "You are looking thin, Olcay, are you eating well enough?"

"Hun, let the boy be; he is a big steward now taking care of the kingdom."

"He has a tenant now," Ejder interjected.

"We heard about the tenant. Is she cute? When will we meet her?" Oriel interrupted.

"Yes, she will be with us tomorrow." Olcay smiled and ushered them out of the road. Olcay took in the questions, and after the greetings, they went into the pub next door. It was a blacksmith guild pub, and it was fire-beast friendly. The walls of the pub had runes to prevent fires and the explosive damage that can happen. It was a rowdy place and had some charm to it. Even with all of the fire and heat in the room, it was cooled by inscriptions on the seats for guests to enjoy. "Master Demir! Or'Fenya!" A voice yelled out in the hall. "The pub went silent and then cheered in celebration! Demir looked to Fenya for approval, and she gave a smile and a nod. Demir was excited and announced in the great hall. "In honor of my daughter Oriel's

127

final trials and my son Olcay's stewardship, first round is on me!" Cheers rang out from the pub all over the square. The bartender and servers cleared a space for the group. Fico took a place in the rafters, where he found another Phoenix and other flying fire brethren. Ejder could be seen in the corner chatting with the beastman; if it weren't for her black scales, you would think she was blushing.

As the crowd settled down Olcay gave his family some details of what has happened to him but left out anything that will give them concern. The conversation changed as Ejder came back, then started to order food and drink to get everyone into a happier mode. There was a need for celebration with all they have been through.

The night started to get interesting when members of the guild started to challenge Demir and Oriel to cold metal bending to showcase their strength. Various-sized pieces of metal were piled in the corner. The bigger and thicker the metal they bent, the more the crowd would cheer. Oriel took on a few guildmates in arm wrestling, and the room started to heat up. Fenya even got in on the fun with some fortune-telling with cards. She never really peered into people's futures, but she darkened her eyes for effect.

Olcay managed to get away before the evening became too much. He had to stop a few guards from breaking up the party. It was the first time he ran interference using his position, but he knew that his family had reason to celebrate. A few more of Demir's old friends showed up, and it was going to be a long night. Olcay told the guards to let him know if it got out of hand.

Chapter 20

The artisans' guilds were a close-knit group across all regions of the continent. The Forge Guild was the most respected and oldest of the guilds. The halls were lined with metalwork, legendary weapons, and fabled tools. The emblem over the great hall was an ax, as it both symbolized a weapon and a tool. The inscription translated *'We discern the shape of metal but not how it shapes the world'*.

The family waited in the crowded great hall. They knew it would be a while. Demir was nursing a headache while he waited in the queue. Olcay and Oriel were taken in by the many wondrous items on the walls, there were also a few fiery beasts and folk among the crowd, which made for a fantastic sight. Many of them were there as registered companions or were seeking smiths to work with. Some tried to approach Demir but found Ejder in their way. Her aura seeped out and cleared a portion of the room. Only those who had contracts with high-level beasts themselves could tolerate the shock.

Olcay and Oriel went down a few halls to see the exhibits. Many of the items were encased in crystals to prevent theft. They even found a monument to their father on display. The previous helm of the great warrior Pasha from the last war was unscratched or marked, a testament to his skill. He took blows from monsters, fae, and magical swords… the helm remained mirror polished.

"I wonder what I could contribute here someday?" Oriel said.

"I am sure it will be magnificent," Olcay replied.

The receptionist came behind them. "Steward Olcay, Master Oriel I was sent to fetch you. You are at the front of the queue right now."

She walked them over to a side door, where the family was waiting. At the front was another master blacksmith of the guild, poised and ready for them. He was a short man, with both his beard and hair wild in the air. He dressed as a common smith, but his markings showed he was a previous Master of the Hammer. His voice was very articulate and dignified.

"Who comes before the guild?" The master spoke.

Oriel stepped forward. "I do, Oriel, daughter of Master Smith Demir and Or'Fenya." She gave a small bow, stood, and presented her arm, showcasing her markings.

"Who will witness your journey?"

"My brother, Steward Olcay." She announced it proudly. Olcay turned to her in shock. Oriel was ready with an answer, "As is tradition, one who is not gilded should be the one selected to witness and assist me. Plus, it would be boring if Dad was there. They will wait for us on the other side." She smiled and took him by the hand. Oriel signaled to the master that she was ready.

Olcay was humbled and stood next to her in front of the door. He felt awkward as he did not know what he should be doing nor how to prepare. The family said some quick goodbyes and departed through another door; the master smith looked at them both. "You may begin your sacred journey." He closed a curtain behind them to block prying eyes.

They walked through the first door and found themselves enclosed in a marble room, polished and as pristine white as the snow. In the back of the chamber, they saw a large metal door that was plain compared to the rest of the doors found in the great hall; ornamentation was no substitute for function. As she reached for the door, Oriel realized something was off and ignited the markings in her hand. There was a sizzle as the sweat evaporated from her hand; the door was white-hot; that lesson would have been painful.

Olcay did not know what he got himself into and remembered that a few of his scars came from playing in his father's forge. "This looks like fun," Olcay remarked.

Oriel pulled the door handle to find a humanized fire elemental heating the door with his hands. He disengaged heating the door seeing they had opened the door. His entire body was covered in a yellow flame. The shape of the flame was that of a slender male character. Olcay recalled that the color of the flame reflected the mood of the elemental beings, which can change over time. His eyes glowed blue and were very bright to look into. He was also wearing a leather garment, but it had to be something more durable to withstand his own heat.

"Brother and sister, I bid you welcome." He shook Oriel's hand and ever so slightly turned up the heat. At each level, another one of her symbols changed. He then changed his color to see the effects. He tested each rune and glyph, lighting them up one by one. He smiled in enjoyment of the experience. The elemental gave a nod of approval and stepped back to face Olcay.

"Brother, you are unbranded and unseared by the forge and the guild. You will bear witness to our sister's folding into our billet. This tradition goes back to our founding with the Un-bladed Brothers. You are tasked with keeping her grounded in life. In the end, a smith's purpose is to take care of their family, for without family our trade is meaningless. Keep yourselves united with the bonds you have forged together, and you may just make it through this."

Olcay could only nod in understanding. The only thing that played in his mind was saying the wrong things; therefore, he just made a mental note.

The elemental continued. "In exchange for your silence, you will be offered a brand that will be your acknowledgment of her pledge and any one question to be answered of your choosing."

He reached over to shake Olcay's hand. Olcay knew what was to happen next, but that did not make it any easier. They shook, and a brand of the ax seared into the web of his right hand. It was sharp but bearable. The elemental almost looked like he enjoyed it. Oriel was happy and hugged her brother.

"Please let us continue." He motioned them down the stone hallway and waved them goodbye. The walls were covered with broken weapons and armor. Failures littered the ground as they walked on. It was a sign that passing was not a guarantee.

A small chamber opened ahead of them with a stone gray room. Before them on a bench were placed a small kitchen knife, a broken spear for a guard, and a rusted plow. A dwarven smith stood before the items and inspected each one, then spoke, "What are these items to you, Oriel?"

Oriel picked up each item, inspected it, and placed it back. Afterwards, she stepped back and contemplated what she was going to say. "They are mine, Master Smith." Oriel stood as tall as she could.

"These are failures, your failures." He stared her down in a grim voice. "Why would we let failures into our guild?! We have no time to waste on a shadow of your father."

Olcay even felt that stinged a little too much and wanted to pelt the guy. Olcay tapped his sister on the shoulder to give encouragement. Oriel was grateful she had the moment to think.

"These are not failures!" Oriel argued.

"How can you say that? The spear broke when a guard tried to defend himself from a bandit. The plow failed the farmer and missed his planting, and the knife ended someone's life. You are responsible by the oath of your forge and contracts! We have no place for you here."

Olcay remembered the failures and they were hard on Oriel. She wept over them, and you could see the tears she was holding back now.

He motioned for her to leave and went to go towards the door. She reiterated, "These are not failures!"

"How so? What excuses do you have for me, your elder?" He said mocking her.

"I accepted the responsibility of what happened, so they were not failures. The knife cut as it was intended, the spear broke because he blocked a sword with the wooden shaft, and the plow was left out in the field to rot and was not cared for. If a smith calls these failures, then they should put up their hammers! Never call my craftsmanship a failure!"

The bearded dwarf gave a smirk and a little bit of a laugh. "You have the soul of the steel you forge. We are not gods, so nothing we make is perfect; we are not oracles, so we do not know what someone may do with our work. We are true to our work even when it fails. Please proceed, young smith." He guided them down the next corridor.

The next room was a fully operational forge. Around the room were the various other smiths from in and around the kingdom. There was a balcony where most of the leadership of the guild were. A large, framed man stood in the back and was recognizable as their father. At the front of the room, one of the guild heads stood. Olcay and Oriel stood in the middle of the well-lit, warm room. Olcay felt where he was branded was itching, and the sweat was not helping either. The ceremony looked as if it was going to start when one person in the crowd moved to the front. He was rougher than most of the others; he was unkempt, and his formal wear was faded and old.

"We came here to witness a forging; however, I feel forging something would be too easy a task for her."

"What are you saying, Grand Anvil Deniz? We have traditions!" A voice rang out from the stands.

"Traditions or not, this part is to be a challenge for the guild prospects."

"She has earned her markings like anyone else; let us proceed!" "I don't have all night for this; get on with it!" "She is too young to earn her membership."

The room itself became hostile as the arguments grew. Cloaks were coming off, and hammers were being held in hostility. The men, women, fae, and fire folk almost started to brawl. It had become chaotic. Oriel and Olcay were at a loss for what was happening. Oriel was so excited to be here, and now it was all falling apart. She could see her father tossing a few of the smaller smiths around the room. Oriel was needing to do something. She ignited everything she had then went over to the anvil in the middle of the room and pounded a hammer upon it with a loud

"CLANG" "CLANG"

Shouting at the top of her lungs "My mentors, elders, and masters; please don't argue over this. What challenge will satisfy you all?"

Silence befell the room as they stood in unison. *"You, young master smith, have rung your hammer upon the grandmaster's anvil. You will need to decide how to reforge our unity."*

Oriel looked to Olcay; he could only shrug at her in ignorance. She realized that the initiation had started but did not know what to say. Then it dawned on her what the elemental said at the door about the Un-bladed Brothers.

She recalled this tradition and the story of the guild's founding; it was hazy because she never paid much attention to it. A brother smith lived a normal life, providing for his family. He was commissioned to make a fancy blade by a local lord. The blade he made failed a lord in battle, and he died as a result. The brother was executed. His twin took it upon himself to refashion the blade with a Living Forge and present it to the lord's brother, both as repentance and humility for the action his brother's failed blade had taken. A simple story she'd long forgotten until now.

She turned to the on-looking crowd and spoke as if it were a play. "I seek the blade of my brother, who was slain for his failure, and I wish to reforge his honor at the Living Forge."

"What metal do you bring to reforge his blade? The forge has none to spare, and we are without any to give."

"I have metal to offer." Olcay presented the small quill Oriel made for him before he went on his journey.

"Olcay, thank you," Oriel whispered to him.

Grand Anvil Deniz spoke, "Then we ask that the guild's Living Forge come forth to appraise your offering."

The forge went cold as heat and light collected in the middle of the room from the walls and the floor; the forge itself took a female shape of skeletonized metal, and molten heat took form. The hand of the Embodiment of the Forge encouraged the offering to be placed on the anvil. Olcay complied and placed the quill there. He quickly returned to his place. It lifted the metal, inspected it, placed the metal within its shoulder, and began to glow. An ingot appeared in its hand after about a minute, and it placed it onto the anvil.

Oriel could see that she needed to forge this piece and started to work; she tied her hair up and put on an apron. "Olcay, I am going to need your help on this one." The masters stared on as they both began to work. Oriel started to give herself a quick morale speech and moved on to set up her station. Oriel looked around the room and saw that it was not set for holding in magic, and she will have to do this manually. "We have a second problem as well." Oriel said to Olcay.

Olcay understood, looking around the room, that the many safety measures he was familiar with were not present. The guild members were at a distance and did not need protection. If Oriel were to mess up, it could kill Olcay. Oriel was not planning on risking his safety for the ritual and was going to call it off. Olcay had other plans.

Olcay threw on all the leather garb and aprons he could find, and then for good measure, he dunked a barrel of water on himself. He held the metal with tongs and placed it on the anvil.

"I trust you can do this, so trust yourself." Olcay committed himself to the task at hand and was not going to allow his sister to faulter. Oriel nodded to him and started to cycle forging and hammering the metal. Oriel noticed that many of the usual runes or glyphs that provided assistance were not activating as well. It had been some time since Olcay had seen it, but the markings on her legs started to show as well. The room markings replace the need to use the ones on the legs. With having to move about the room, concentration was key, and you could not break it or lose control. Most blacksmiths did not need such precautions. However, the ambitious quill's metal layout made it difficult. To hold it together manually, a true test of skill was needed, which was no doubt planned from the beginning.

Olcay thought back to his younger days playing in the forge and working with Oriel. Reality returned as Oriel hummed bars from the Fairy Fire dance. The heat of the forge started to get to Olcay, and the sweat started to sizzle before it left his brow. Oriel knew Olcay would not give up on her, but it had to be extremely taxing. Oriel had no time and took the sharp metal they were working on and pricked her finger, and it began to bleed. She used her blood to draw the glyphs needed on Olcay's leather and forehead to cool him down. Olcay felt lighter. "Thanks, sis. Better hurry though this won't last long."

The blade in the end was plain, however refined, and was the most basic of forgings. After the final quench, she presented it on the anvil to the master's guild.

Master Deniz spoke, "A master must never forget that they were once an apprentice, and it is the most sacred position in our hallowed halls. Kneel before the living forge and take your final step into the guild."

She kneeled before the living forge and felt the cold of steel and the heat of fire upon her shoulders. The Living Forge turned to Olcay. "You have witnessed this blessing and the curse of which a smith must bear. As a gift, you will be honored with an answer to a question that is within my power to answer." Her voice was hollow as it came from within her chambers.

Olcay had everything he wanted to ask running through his mind. It was heart-wrenching as he knew that as much as he wanted to learn the secrets of the world. He kept the question in the here and now.

"I would humbly ask everything there is to know about this book." He pulls from his side pocket, the red book he received from his visit to the Heartless council.

The crowd and the forge looked upon Olcay in amazement and bewilderment. Olcay's eyes gave out a fierce determination. The forge turned to him and took the book from Olcay's outstretched hands. Her fiery hands cooled so as not to damage the book. She peered, closed her eyes, and handed it back to him. "Of all the questions of the infinite cosmos, you asked one I cannot answer." Olcay's disappointment was brief.

"Your question can still be answered by my kin. The Living Library can answer this question for you. However, her whereabouts are unknown to me as well. I feel that destiny and fate conspire this day." Her eyes became fired up as she struck the blade on the anvil. "Our time grows short, Olcay, as this ceremony still needs to be completed with a question from you."

Olcay looked around the room to see everything had stopped like before, and the air was thin and frightening. "Your question is private here, Olcay, so please ask me." Her eyes were soft to look at, and Olcay knew there was no ill intent in speaking this time. Olcay was happy that he was further along in knowing what he needed to know than before and could only be pleased. He took in a breath and asked…

The room had started again and was well lit. The cheering crowd of guild members roared through the great halls. Oriel was smiling in tears. She hugged Olcay and walked out the back door to the reception room, where the rest of the family was. The ceremony was over, and the protocol went out the door. They were carried back to the guild pub from the night before. The smiths and firefolk were all working on a second cask. Ejder had already finished the first and was arm-wrestling one of the masters for the next round.

Oriel stood up on one of the tables to give a toast. "Brethren, kin, and those who just snuck in! My brother Olcay never got a proper celebration for his promotion to steward, so here's to my brother." Everyone raised a tankard. "To Olcay! He stared down a king and a queen but still lacks the beard to get a stare from a woman." There was laughter and table slapping. You could see Olcay turning red. He gave her a brotherly tap on the shoulder out of spite.

"I wish Orion could have made it," Fenya said to Demir. She was missing her children around the house.

"We will have them all back during the end of the harvest. I also don't need to work as much with them gone; we can visit them." Demir replied.

"No, you can keep working I don't need you getting fat and lazy around the house." Her smile was in jest as she kissed him, and they took in food and wine. Around them, the drunken smiths started performing feats of skill and strength. A few in the corner were wrestling on top of a metal platform that was being heated from below. The idea was to concentrate on not burning and knocking the opponent out of the square. Some of the older smiths were arguing over whose blades were the strongest. Others were comparing scars and showing off the metal permanently imbedded in their skin. Oriel lifted the side of her shirt to show a massive scar from the incident with the cursed blade.

Olcay found himself taking a break and saw Fico and Ejder in the corner. "Olcay, how can we help you this evening?" Fico asked. Ejder and him looked to be having a warm chat, as two ancient beings would.

"What can you tell me about the Living Embodiment of the Library?" Olcay inquired. Fico and Ejder stared at each other in bewilderment.

"I myself have only met the Forge Embodiment here at the guild and have only heard of others, but many are older than the myth itself," Fico stated. "They tend to be neutral in all things and seldom interact with beasts, fae, or men."

"I never met her either, I only know she hordes a massive collection of books as old as time. I know the Immortal Ebedi wanted to find her during one of his conquests." Ejder answered.

"Thank you both; this is a lot more than when I started." Olcay looked as if he was going to depart as he was tired and was irritated at having no solid answers. Fico lifted his wing and stopped him.

"Why do you want to find her?" Fico asked.

"She is the only one that may know what this book is." Olcay pulls the little red book from his pocket. They both stare at it as he explains how he came into possession of it. They both listened intently with awe and concern.

"I would say you have had quite the adventure since leaving home; best not to inform your mother," Fico responded.

"I should roast Pasha in his suit for this. I told him to keep you out of harm." Ejder snarled, and her scales shifted again.

"I do not believe this was unavoidable. With the death of Yot, the attack at home, and here at the palace; I think we have bigger problems ahead." Olcay held her hand at the table. "Thank you for your concern. Just keep the family safe at home, and I will have Pasha here."

"What about Oriel? She wants to travel, build her skills, and reputation." Fico replied.

"What about Oriel?" A drunken Oriel plopped down at their table.

"Oriel, are you drunk?" Olcay asked.

"It's my folding into the guild and the start of my journey as a Master Smith. I need to celebrate. You guys here in the corner are bumming me out." One would think with her build, she would have had some tolerance.

"Sorry about that, I just wanted to ask Fico and Ejder about this book." Olcay lifted it and then tried to draw her focus.

"Books? Do you want to talk about books? Why don't you talk with Orion at the merchant's guild…Also, Olcay, your red maiden friend, just came and is looking for you." Oriel points over to the other side of the room. Olcay could not process the information at the same time and decided to forgo the first part till later and move on to the now.

"Azarla is here? That's right, I wanted to introduce you to her as part of the contract we have." He stood to look around the room.

"Contract? What are you doing with contracts at your age?" Fico asked.

"Well, he needed the experience sometime." Ejder smiled.

Olcay could be seen blushing in the low-lit room. "You two, oh never mind, it's complicated."

"My little brother is all grown up with a lady friend, and she is kind of cute. Mom doesn't want grandkids this early Olcay, best to hold off." Oriel laughed.

The conversation was halted as Azarla came to the table. "Steward, I came to check up on you."

Olcay could see she was waiting for when it would be socially acceptable to come over. She did not want to interfere before the ceremony and waited patiently till now. Olcay caught the hint and changed the subject. "Azarla, this is some of my family. You met Ejder and this Fico."

"A fond greeting to you, my young fiery lass." Fico gave a wholesome bow, and she returned one as well.

"I will have to say you are the first blue phoenix I have ever seen. My father worked with a violet one ages ago. Your plumage however is much more radiant."

"For a half-dragon and half-demon, you are quite fetching as well," Fico commented. The news shook the small table as they looked at Fico and then at her.

Azarla's skin almost turned purple in embarrassment. Phoenixes tend to have pure sight and cannot be fooled by most magic that masked appearances.

"My word, I did not notice before. That is why you were familiar to me, was it your mother or father? Birthed or hatched?" Ejder looked on more intrigued.

Azarla looked as if she was about to run out, and Ejder was going to continue the onslaught. Fico realized he had made a blunder and tried to change the subject. "Olcay, you had something to say?"

Olcay now had eyes on him, and he had so many questions to ask but did not want to press. "Azarla, this is my sister, the new guild Master Smith, Oriel. As promised, I would introduce you to her."

Azarla turned to Oriel in excitement and relief at the new subject. "I am looking to return to the forge and wish to offer my fiery skills to a master smith such as yourself. I only ask for standard guild wages; however, I would like to stay here in the capital to continue to serve Olcay as well. If this is not a good time for you, we can talk at a better time."

Oriel was very glazed from the elven fae ale and could only be described as well hammered.

"Okay, sounds good to me. How do we do this?" Oriel asked openly.

Ejder, taking advantage of the moment, leaned over and whispered in her ear.

Oriel laughed "Huh, well not my first time."

She stood up and ignited her arms, grabbed Azarla by the waist, and leaned in with an emblazed kiss. The contract appeared, was fashioned into light, and disappeared onto Azarla's skin. The moment passed as Oriel put her down. Ejder laughed as the rest of the table was bewildered. Olcay could only start to snicker, and Azarla felt a wealth of emotions at what happened. She took the closest ale and drank it down. Oriel then disappeared back into the crowd and danced the rest of the night away.

Chapter 21

The next morning, Olcay reported his news to Pasha about the Embodiment of the Library and asking his brother Orion for help. Pasha sat quietly at the table and looked through his folded hands. "Fascinating, at least we have a lead now. Report to Barduk and the King. I would say keep this confidential for the moment from anyone else. Anything else you want to report?"

Olcay left out the ceremony where he got the information and did not want to discuss the drunken smiths causing a ruckus afterward. Olcay smoothed it out… mostly. He will owe Captain Jess a favor later. Olcay looked back on the evening's highlights and remembered. "My sister may stay in the capital; I would request she has a pass to work and live in the inner walls near here for safety and our benefit."

"Benefit?"

"A master blacksmith of her level nearby may be of use; also, I know she wants to learn from a few of the local masters as well."

"Permission granted. Please invite your sister to stay here with us till she finds accommodations. After you finish with the workers' invoices, you can go tell your sister. Also, I have not seen Azarla since yesterday. Is she alright?"

"She needed a day for something. I will go check on her." Olcay held in a laugh as he remembered the outcome of the evening. Olcay dismissed himself and reported the book information to the King. He was preoccupied and was brief; he nodded in understanding from the report. "I trust you will fulfill your duties."

Olcay found Barduk in the library, moving around on his own. He was looking like a clothed older man. The clothes were made of bark and wood. His face also changed, showing a fuller beard of twigs. Barduk was more enthused by the news and wanted to come if the need arrived. "I cannot believe we are looking for the Embodiment of the Library."

"You told me it was a dead-end last time we spoke about it. Them being neutral and all." Olcay retorted.

"If that is all we have and you were told to seek her out, then that is what we will do. The embodiments are neutral and only seek that which they are a part of. They cannot be bribed or coerced into doing anything. Even if you found one, the likelihood they would even speak to you is almost nothing." He started to write notes on a scroll. "I saw her once years ago; I did not know she was it till after she was already gone."

"Where was she?" Olcay was mildly irritated that he had to backtrack on something he already dismissed.

"At an estate liquidation, I believe of an old baron, obviously claiming books."

"Well, for now, she is the only one with answers. I have a lead that may help us at least find her."

"Really?" Barduk was very surprised by this.

"I can't take credit for it, but my brother is a merchant for one of the book guilds and may be able to help. I sent a rider and hope to hear back in a few days."

"Then we will hope for good news," Barduk replied.

"I must excuse myself I have other matters for Pasha I need to attend to before I take care of family matters."

Olcay departed the wooden man atop his books and headed to the guild's private inn. It was the afternoon, and he could see that the party last night kept going till dawn. There was evidence of a few brawls, some drunken smiths still lounging, and nursing hangovers. Olcay saw his mother walking back from the bazaar to the inn and caught up to her.

"Mother, I see the celebration was long. I hope you slept well?" Olcay embraced her and kissed her cheeks.

"Well, I did not stay here last night; I would never get any sleep. I know your father needs to let loose and party with his guildmates. Having Oriel also there probably made it more entertaining." She rolled her eyes and motioned for Olcay to take the lead in the door.

"I know I could not stay long as well; I came to check up on everyone." Olcay realized why his mother let him walk ahead as a tankard flew by his head. She gave a little laugh, and he chuckled along, remembering she was a child at heart. "That would have hurt you know." Olcay laughed.

"I don't know what you are talking about. I just saw some riled-up smiths over the door window." She smiled and pushed him inside.

He took her by the arm to not be the only target and went inside the inn. The interior looked like the inside of a refuse bucket, and could see the inside was just as bad as the outside. The barmaids and innkeeper were poking people to wake them up so they could at least pick up. "Hey, hey, wake up. You still have your tab to pay!" The smith tossed his coin purse over and turned to sleep more. They looked up to the ceiling and found a few were sleeping in rafters and fixtures. Blacksmiths seem to party hard, and the state of the inside needed repair more than cleaning as they continued to look around.

Among the bodies, Demir was sitting having breakfast without a care in the world. He saw them approaching and kicked a few off the bench who had fallen asleep there.

Fenya wrapped her arms around her husband, and he stood to return it. "I hope you did not overindulge last night." She ran her finger through his beard to fix it up a bit. He looked at her like he had just seen the sunrise for the first time.

"The capitals' ale is weak compared to the dwarven ales we get back home; I was fine from the start." He ran his rough hand through her soft hair, a gentle moment.

Fenya noticed the room starting to stare at them and changed the tone. "Where is Oriel?" Fenya asked Demir.

"I think she was one of the few to make it back upstairs to her room before the brawling started." Demir motioned a few jabs, showcasing why the pile of bodies radiated from his seat.

"Best I fetch her so we can all talk." Fenya smiled and rolled her eyes. Fenya and Olcay went upstairs to Oriel's room, knocked, and entered. "I hope you are decent." She yelled out.

The smell of ale in the room was mild and stale; overall, the state of the room was normal compared to the rest of the inn. Two bodies are seen in the bed, one pale and tattooed, and the other red with her horns and wings torn from her dress. They were nestled together, one hugging the other. Racheed looked to have stayed as well and made a nest over the window above the bed.

"Azarla? Oriel?" Olcay and Fenya could only be in awe and laugh. The two ladies awoke with eyes glazed and hair matted. Their eyes met, the touching moment was short lived, and both could only feel embarrassment. They both turned their backs to each other and rushed to cover with the nearest bit of cloth. Racheed awoke as well and moved to the side of the bed to see what was going on.

Fenya needed to recover the situation. "Ladies, Father is downstairs. It would be best for introductions; please get dressed and we will be downstairs." Fenya scooted Olcay out the door as they both smiled.

Azarla jumped from the bed, "I am so sorry; I do not know what happened last night; I don't know how it happened." She placed one hand over her face while the other held a blanket to hide her body. She looked in the mirror and saw that her horns were extended and her wings exposed. Racheed took to the sight and started to dance. Her flames turned red, and the aura mimicked her horns and wings. Azarla retracted them to the disappointment of Racheed, who let out a small huff.

Azarla knelt down to where Racheed was. "I am sorry, little one. I was not ready to show that part of me to anyone yet." Racheed jumped away. Azarla did not want to have a bad first impression.

Oriel did not notice the exchange, and she was still playing back what happened that night, "I don't remember even coming up here last night, let alone knowing how I changed." Oriel let the bit of blanket she was holding fall as she forgot what state she was in. Azarla could see the entire outline of Oriel's markings. She turned so as not to stare further.

Azarla looked down at the state of her clothing and saw that her drake half had torn through her delicate clothing. "I have nothing to wear, and this barely covers anything." The rips in the sides showed the state of her scarred bosom and she gathered more cloth to cover it.

Azarla turned back to ask, "Do you remember last night at all, Master Oriel?"

Oriel still not aware of her nudity scratch the back of her head. "I am drawing a blank, I am soooo sorry. Don't tell me…what did I do to you?" Oriel covered her face not wanting to know what had happened.

"You made a contract with me," Azarla replied.

Oriel was relieved, but then was at a loss. "What kind of contract?"

"A blacksmith's contract." Azarla's body was turning redder than normal.

"Thank the forge! I thought we made a different kind of contract."

Azarla was mildly irritated by the usual notion but was happy that Oriel did not sound like she regretted it.

"Let's get downstairs before anyone thinks we are doing anything." Azarla tried to gather up anything else to cover her chest, as she was still not comfortable.

Oriel intercepted and stood before Azarla; her arms, legs, and breasts appeared firm and sculpted up close. It was as if her body had been forged by a grand master. Her skin was covered in tattoos and scars, which only increased its appeal. Whatever was covering her before is not there now. "If something happened, I don't regret it, and neither should you."

Oriel embraced Azarla, and their skin touched, and the warmth enveloped them both. Azarla gave off a bit of fire that Racheed reacted to in crimson red. Oriel's runes held off the flames. It was then that Oriel realized they had no clothing and went back to having modesty.

Oriel went over to her bag in the room. "I have an extra set of clothes that are fireproof for you, so you don't have to worry." She handed it to Azarla, and she went off to the next room to get changed.

After they both got dressed and started their way out of the door, they saw Ejder and Fico. Racheed was on Oriel's shoulder, showcasing her new crimson color.

"You ladies sleep well?" Ejder smiled and almost purred. They both rushed past her down the flight of stairs.

"You are so bad Ejder, putting them together in the room like that," said Fico.

"I do not know what you are implying, two young ladies were passed out drunk and needed to be helped to their room. What could have happened to them?"

Fico could only laugh.

Downstairs, the hall was cleared of the drunken patrons, and many started to sit at tables, scarfing down food. The ladies came down to find food waiting for them at the table. It was quite awkward for them as they came and sat down next to each other. Best to show a stronger front.

Demir's voice rumbled. "Guess we need to talk about your intentions with my daughter, demon drake." He stared down at the table, and there was silence in the hall.

Azarla could only feel uncomfortable. "And you, Oriel, what were you thinking?" Demir continued.

"I don't feel we did anything wrong, and it was a blur at best for us." Oriel's voice was cracking, and she did not know what to say.

He pounded his fist on the table, "I mean, you haven't been part of the guild one day, and you already forgot to register her before your contract."

The two were dumbfounded, as Fenya and Olcay could only laugh like two schoolchildren. "I am sorry Azarla, my daughter just got her license, and her registrations are usually done by me; did she at least do your contract with you right?"

Azarla nodded and smiled happily.

"Olcay already filled me in on the contract, so I guess now you are staying Oriel?" Demir muttered as he tried to consume some breakfast. "Do you have a place yet?"

"I talked with Sir Pasha, and he will bring her into the inner walls." Olcay replied.

"Guess we will head home and send your stuff." Demir's voice cracked as he knew what was coming.

"Mom, Dad." Oriel jumped over to where they were sitting.

He hugged his daughter, "At least come and visit once in a while."

He turned to Azarla. "Young lady, if you get bored and want to sling steel, come down and visit me as well."

The moment was fleeting as a messenger came to Demir; he had one stop at the guild before he went home. Fenya went out to grab a few things from the market for the trip home and to visit the Oracle Temple. The others stayed and talked about Oriel moving to the capital.

Chapter 22

Demir was still aching from the night before. He had pushed himself a little too much considering it had been some time since he was out with his guildmates. His head was pounding from playing some drinking games, and he was feeling disoriented. Demir knew it would be ages before he would be back in the capital. A summons from the guild is not necessary considering his status, so it had to be serious. He intended to stop by the guild to say goodbye to a few friends before heading home, so it worked out.

As he stepped through the door, he felt the nostalgia of his former stomping grounds. He caressed the massive steel door he had made during his apprenticeship. At the time, it was a massive undertaking involving several artesian guilds and smiths. The smell of heavy soot and sweat filled his lungs and fired up his enthusiasm. How he missed the larger forges of the guild. He always loved making giant armor and armaments. Even at this early hour, he could see the apprentices scrambling to set up their areas. The heat of the building started to evaporate the morning dew from the outside walls and grass.

The fire partners were also working hard, taking in food and energy before they could start heating the forges. Demir noticed a few faeries, some beast folk, a dragon newt, and some ember slugs. Even though he wanted to remain in the background, a few of the apprentices and partners noticed him. Some were in awe; others frantically panicked. Demir decided to approach one that was trying to look busy pounding a cold piece of steel. He smiled and decided to have a little bit of fun with the young man.

Demir cast a wide shadow on the young man before him. He almost collapsed from Demir's presence. "By what are you called an apprentice?" Demir's voice bellowed through the great hall and all but silenced the room.

The young man found it hard to even look up, as if staring directly into the sun itself. "I am Madox, a Journeyed Smith from the North."

"What are you working on there?" Demir asked with a gruff voice.

The young man all but swallowed his tongue and was able to squeak out an answer. "Preparing blank steel for the alchemist and magic guilds Master Demir."

Demir picked up a blank and inspected it. "Yes, I recognize your work. I receive a shipment each season." He placed it back down and started to pick up each piece. Demir looked over to see the young man's arms. "What are the purposes of your runes and glyphs?"

Madox stood up, almost at attention, and regurgitated the words from his classes. "Our runes depict our mastery level in our craft, and our glyphs protect us from what we work on according to our rune level."

Demir walked over to a post near the young man covered in writing. "Then why have our forges lined with runes and glyphs if we have them already on us?"

"They protect those who may walk in our presence so they may not be harmed, as not everyone may carry the weight we are burdened with."

"Why tattoos then? Why not just use writing or waving magic words around like magicians use?" Demir picked up a long piece of metal and imitated a wizard casting a spell.

"Our power is found in our worded flesh; the surface is etched with the bonds we make with our brethren, our fire keepers, and our guild."

"Why can't someone just copy our runes, and glyphs and then run the magic that way? Should be just as simple." Demir placed the metal he was holding back on the table.

"You have to have the capacity to hold the magical weight on one's body, the fortitude to see it through, and the wisdom to make the choices on where to set it right."

"If we have all these things in place, why do we pray?"

"We pray to settle ourselves and feel the harmonics of what we prepared." Madox felt an accomplishment in being able to answer the questions so far.

"Why do you choose to remain here?" Demir's tone had changed.

"I do not understand." Madox was put off by the question, and his demeanor calmed.

"Your steel has made it to me for several seasons now; it does please me to work with well-prepared materials; you should have moved on by now. I read your arms and can see you are ready to be folded into the billet of a master craftsman."

Madox looked to his feet and then to the sky for a way to avoid answering. "I have not found a bondable fire partner as I am limited." He admitted.

"How are you limited in our home sanctuary? Surely someone here can fit your needs." Demir's arms were stretched out, pointing across the great halls.

"My compatible partners are limited to the beast kin… specifically female beast kin." He tried to whisper, but it could only carry through the quiet hall.

"Ahh, you fear the commitment of the mating bond required?"

"No … No… Yes." Young Madox almost blushed in shame and put his head down.

145

Demir rested his hand on Madox's shoulder. "There is no shame in this. I have seen worse capability issues." Demir pulled him in close and whispered in Madox's ear. "Which one is she?" He held the biggest grin of his life as he drew out the embarrassment even further.

Madox could see he was not going to get out of this without an answer. "She works at the reception of the great hall." He answered.

"Then it would be best if you said something soon." Demir smiled as he pointed out the gathered crowd that came in closer to listen to the conversation. "Disperse, you gossip vultures, and back to work!" As they all left. Demir looked to Madox, who was still trying to process everything that was happening. "Madox, I expect you to move up or out. Don't disappoint me." Madox gave him a nod as Demir noticed part of a new crowd gathering behind him.

Demir ushered Madox off as he began to turn to meet his new observers. "Grand Masters of the Forge, Hammer, and Anvil; how may I help you this morning?" He gave a small head bow as well as sparked a small release of his runes. There was a small surge of heat in his presence. The Grand Masters did the same. The weight of the room shifted and almost pulled several to the floor.

The masters had equal say over the guild's hierarchy and business. Each is given the title based on merit, vote, or skill. The Master of the Forge, Crost was shorter than the rest. His beard rested down to his belt line. A scar over his right eye. Master of the Hammer, a beastman Gyrax; tall and slender, his runes and glyphs blended in nicely with his fur coat. Lastly, Grand Anvil Deniz.

Gyrax addressed Demir. "Master Demir, thank you for answering our summons. We need to discuss a request from the king in regard to the death of Master Yot." Demir's face soured. "We will need to talk in private about this."

They walked over to a side wall next to reception. Demir glanced over to see Madox talking with a young lady at the desk. Her hand covered her mouth in shock. He could see her tail wagging in excitement as he entered a door that appeared from the wall.

Down a hallway, they entered a windowless brick room. The light in the middle of the room was over a body draped in cloth. On a table next to the body, he saw the remains of the apparatus that was found with him.

"Can you help identify what this is?" Gyrax asked as he pointed at the item.

Demir picked up the item with little hesitation. His runes and glyphs reacted and subsided. Demir responded. "It looks like he was trying to work outside his means. These are the markings I carry."

A voice from the side of the room asked, "Why would he want to be using your markings?"

Demir looked at the other masters, and they gave him the nod to answer the question.

"My markings are unique as I can bond with any fire partner and have stable results." Demir seemed mildly irritated by the questioning, as few have not heard of him. This person also seemed not to be part of the guild.

"Who else has your markings?"

"Only my daughter and I have these markings." Demir continued to examine the item.

"Who found this?"

"Your son found this when he was investigating with General Pasha."

"General Pasha? Few would refer to him as a general in this age. I am not in the habit of talking to shadows on walls, at least not without a few drinks in me first." Demir folded his arms in defiance.

A cloaked figure moved from the corner of a shelf. The small stature was displaced by the aura that emanated from the figure. Demir's eyes grew, and he uncrossed his arms. "Why are you here…" Demir's voice was stifled by an oath he once made never to speak their name. "You could have just come to me and asked in person; we didn't need to drag the guild into this, or you could have just asked last time you saw me."

"We have a massive problem, Master Demir, that affects us all. There is a traitor somewhere in the guild or the capital." The figure's voice was stern and upset. "I need you to confirm everything for my investigation; your guild has too many secrets that may bring the downfall of the kingdom."

Demir calmed his mannerism and asked, "What do you need to know?"

"The Heartless Council members are in a state of paranoia and are attacking smiths and others they find to be a threat to the encasement of Ebedi. Additionally, the attack on your family by Holens seems to be orchestrated by someone, and the convenient death of Master Yot wraps up the investigation." The small figure paused and continued, "Is the Heartless Council's paranoia warranted? Can the Immortal Ebedi be freed?"

Demir said without hesitation, "No, even with every master smith here working with my markings, that maniac could never be freed by our will alone." Demir continued, "He is immortal, and his prison will degrade with time, but it will never happen within our generation or the next few on top of that."

The Master Crost interjected, "If you add in the binding imprisonment placed by the council and the king, the monstrosity placed over Ebedi's enclosure, and your warden, whom you place in charge, the entire thing seems ridiculous."

"If there is someone out there that believes they can free him, then that is enough to convince the council that it is possible. It was a ridiculous idea, drawn up by men like you, that you could imprison Ebedi in the first place. Yet it happened." The figure's voice was firm and logical. The room of masters shuddered at the thought of the immortal's return.

"What about the traitor you mentioned? Do you have an idea of who it is?"

"The investigation from General Pasha is ongoing, but we are working through the suspects. Holens and Yot had no prior connection beyond this interaction. Your work location had no effect on their income. It was orchestrated by someone that can cover their tracks."

"Are my children safe?" Demir's voice was filled with concern.

"Your son is under the stewardship of Pasha and after recent events, he has shown he can handle himself quite well. Your daughter, I am told, will stay here under their care."

"Orion?"

"I do not believe he is a target; we are taking precautions. We have dispatched a few trusted members of our legion to watch over him."

Demir knew there was not much that could be done. He would need to wait for now. He looked over toward the corner at the figure on the shelf. "Have you been well?"

"Yes."

Chapter 23

The once-grand empire's capital city of Fenrom. Its size and might were around for centuries. All the greatest discoveries and innovations came from Fenrom. The primary source of it all was the Immortal King Ebedi. Those times were also not safe, as with every new advancement, war and death came to other lands. The price became too high for some. Much of it was lost after the great wars. Mechanical marvels, high metal towers, and magical innovations. Those who knew passed on or became one of the heartless; their secrets were gone. Fenrom was still rich in resources, and all roads and trade routes passed through there. If you wanted to be a prosperous merchant, you had to make it in the guild at Fenrom.

Orion took to choosing his field of apprenticeship at a young age when he found a talent for bartering and selling at his father's shop. Traveling tradesmen took to Orion and offered him work around the time he would apprentice. His family's prestige gave him a boost and made his chances of entering a guild easier. It was his eyes that gave him that bit of push that brought him to Fenrom. The golden rings in his eyes did not give him oracle sight, as many would think, but they did give him luck. Children of oracles have a chance to receive the gift or not; but in rare cases, they have rings around their irises. No power or magic came from them, just superstition and customs.

Orion was still working his way up the ranks and taking on traveling work so he could visit home, but he never settled down in the big city. His apartment was close to his place of work, near the book district. Each apprentice had to work through each district for a probationary period of time before they could settle on a place to work. He already did well in metals and farming sales and was now working on books and paper goods.

Orion received correspondence from his mother from time to time, keeping him up to date on news. Some of it he thought to be pure fantasy, like the incident with the Heartless Queen. However, the bards in the tavern sang of it enough that he knew his little brother was moving up. His thoughts were holding him while staking crates, and Orion did not see his supervisor approach him.

"Orion, you have a messenger here waiting for you in the lobby." Orion looked puzzled, as he had never received private massages before, and went down to the lobby to find him. The messenger was covered in a heavy cloak; he had been riding for days through mud, and tears showed he rode unhindered. Orion noticed his clasp bared the emblem of the king.

"Are you Orion, the brother of Steward Olcay?" The rider asked.

"Yes, what is this about?" Orion asked with caution, not knowing what to expect.

"I have a message from the Steward Olcay for you." He pulled the scroll from its leather case; the red seal was unbroken. "I will be at the Orc'n Cavern Inn for three days waiting for a response to deliver back to the steward." He departed quickly and left Orion in the lobby.

Orion took the message to a side room to read it privately.

My Brother Orion

I hope this message finds you well. If you have not heard, Oriel has received her entry into the guild and will take up a store in the kingdom. Mother and Father have returned home and are as well as they can be. Unfortunately, this message was sent in haste for your assistance. The rider should have told you he would wait for three days for an answer from you.

I have been tasked with finding out who ordered the attack on our family. As of now, we have only one lead. A small red book that no one can read or use divination to answer.

We were told we could find answers from the Embodiment of the Library. An ancient being that may be able to help us. As luck smiles on you, you are working on your book trade. We have reason to believe someone in that area would know where or how to find her.

For your safety, tell no one why you need the information. I hope you can find her.

Love your brother Olcay

"My little brother. Looks like responsibility has found you." Orion gave a smile and then proceeded back to his station. Orion knew nothing and did not know how he could help, as he was still working on his own status. The book district was vast as printing started to take off and became its own district. He was never allowed in the main halls where the customers came, so he knew nothing of the inner workings.

"Orion, what is it the rider wanted?" His supervisor asked. Orion rolled up the letter and closed the ribbon.

"My brother, as you know, is a steward of the great hero Pasha now; he sent me inside information from the palace."

"Interesting, care to share?"

"No way! It's my ticket to moving up in this place. I am going to make a huge sale." Orion gave a sly smile.

"You know I have to approve all of your sales and commissions, Orion; you are not getting around me on this one." His supervisor grinned and stroked his long black beard. Orion played the part and frowned at these words.

"Fine, you roped me in on this, but you owe me big." He put his arm around his supervisor to whisper. "My brother is coming up to locate some books for the royal library's collection. He wanted me to locate them before his trip up here."

"That may be a problem; we have a high-profile guest here right now, and they get priority on all books when they are here."

"Higher than the Kingdom, sir?"

"Yes! The kingdom gets a discount, so they are not a priority. Our esteemed guest always has priority access."

"Just let me look around and not bother them."

"No way, Orion you are overstepping your bounds."

"I would hate for Pasha's steward to come all the way here for nothing and have you explain it to him. You have heard the bards? My brother has stared down the Queen of the Heartless; he won't take any excuses either." The golden rings of Orion's eyes gave a little flash.

The supervisor was not going to deal with it. "Look, I better get twenty percent on this one, and I will give you the papers to enter the storeroom."

"Ten, or I'll forget your name on the letter I have to send back to him." They shook hands on it. Orion went home with his papers to change, as he did not want to look like a worker when he went. The book district's patrons were nobles, magic users, writers, and collectors. If he needed to find his answer, it would be there. He thought to himself that Olcay would owe him for this. He will need to pay off the percentage to his supervisor. It was early afternoon, and the second rush after lunchtime had started. He rounded the corner and found the queue empty and a guard standing watch.

"Is the storehouse open?" Orion inquired.

"Yes and no. There is a political guest inside, and they paid for privacy." The guard answered. Orion's plan was falling apart. He had to think on his feet.

"No worries then, I am here for inventory and should not be a bother." Orion showed his entry for the storehouse.

"Ahh, you are a worker; why are you dressed like that?" The guard asked.

"You know how it is they don't want us looking shabby in front of the customers. It's the look of a good merchant." Orion replied. The guard unlocked the door and let him in. Orion could only think of how easy it was.

The guard was suspicious but decided to let him pass. He leaned toward Orion's ear. "Look, I hope you know what you are doing. She is very... weird when it comes to interruptions."

Orion acknowledged the warning with a nod and slipped a small coin pouch to the guard. As he went in, he found several of the head merchants piled around what he could see as a customer. Orion knew they would be distracted and went to the sales logs to see if he could find anything.

"What do you mean the series is incomplete?!" A female voice shrieked in anger. "What is the point of reading it if a volume is missing?!"

"My lady, we have sent someone to bring us a copy from our warehouse in the next town." The merchant was beyond frightened. As he continued to try and appease the customer.

Orion could barely hear what was going on but was happy for the distraction. He would be fined if he were found here and be bumped down in his apprenticeship. The sales logs did not give much information other than a normal number of sales. The sound outside was getting hostile as the customer's voice became louder. Orion could only think she must be a spoiled noble's kid. After a bit of time, the storeroom was quiet, and Orion could finally focus on what he was doing.

A body flew through the wooden paneling of the wall next to him. He saw that it was one of the guild leaders. He was bleeding and unconscious. Orion could see he was still breathing. He moved to look through the hole in the wall. He could make out a stack of books in the middle of the room, piled high, with a thin figure standing on it. Orion did not want to be there anymore. Out of nowhere, he found a pair of hands grabbing his collar. The guild leader was alive, "What are you doing in here?! This is no place for you right now!"

"Sir, what is going on?" Orion was panicking as more people were sent flying from the room.

"The Embodiment of the Library came for her delivery, and it was missing a book. Now she is shutting us down till we get her book."

"All of this over a book?" Orion was starting to regret coming.

"We put up with it because she pays us well. This was the first time in ages we missed a delivery."

"I can see why the standards are so high now for this part of the guild," Orion commented.

"Don't do anything foolish; she is calm right now and will be fine... maybe."

"Calm? Maybe?" Orion's voice was high pitch in displeasure. He could only think, 'Olcay what did you get yourself involved in?' Orion thought to himself that he had to get out, and the closest door was through the main storeroom, or he could be thrown through the wall itself. He made his way out of the room and moved across the wall towards the door.

She noticed him; the entire room erupted in pages and books; they formed a paper body around her like that of a giant spider and rushed to intercept him. Orion tried to run and found himself pinned to the wall. In the faint light, he could see it was only paper rolled up into a spear shape that had him against the wall. He could barely see amidst the flurry.

"Who might you be?" A soft voice crept up on him and descended from the ceiling. Orion could only make out the shape of a female riding a massive spider. However, it seemed to be made of the books from the storeroom. Orion went to speak but was interrupted. "Please don't lie to me... I will know." She shrilled.

Orion took the threat to his life in all seriousness, she would know he was lying. "I am Orion malady."

She interrupted, "No titles... but how would you know how to address me... continue."

Orion was utterly confused at this point, "I am just an apprentice of the guild."

Paper wrapped around his neck and started to strangle him, and he could not breathe.

"Liar! Apprentices are not allowed in here! No, he speaks the truth. Let him talk." The grip around his neck loosened.

Orion was going to need to change it up quickly. "I was sent a message to locate you."

"Me? This is unexpected, what for?"

"I do not know, my brother Olcay is a steward and had asked if I could find you; that is all I know," Orion answered.

"Intriguing; I will wait here. I do not get many gentleman callers." She answered.

The massive paper spider and other malicious forms folded back into the books, and they re- stacked themselves where they were. The disheveled room was destroyed as the light from the windows and lanterns returned. She then walked over to the stack of books in the middle. She pulled a book from a crate and started reading.

She motioned to him. "Go, also have someone clean up in here, thank you."

Orion calmly walked to the door and left. He found the other guild leaders outside with guards, wondering what was going on. They saw him leaving and stopped him.

Orion spoke first, "She was very upset, I managed to talk her down, and she wants the place cleaned up." The leaders were pleased with the news, and Orion managed to slip away to find the courier to give him the message.

153

Chapter 24

It had been a few days since Olcay sent the rider to Orion, and he was anxiously waiting for an answer to return.

Brother Olcay,

I would have to say the bards and scribes here have started telling tales of you all the way to the Northern Sea. I am glad to hear that you are doing well. To answer your question, yes, I found the books you wanted to order. They will be waiting for you here.

Hug Oriel and congratulate her for me. I hope to hear from you soon.

Orion

"What do you think, Pasha? Barduk?" Olcay asked.

"The northern sea is quite a trip for a hunch, Olcay; you may have secured her whereabouts but not an audience with her," Pasha replied.

"I know, but we have exhausted the capital's resources, and there may be answers there." "The northern sea city of Fenrom has many resources not found in the capital, and the merchant's guild may have answers," Barduk replied.

"Then prepare yourself; in three days, we will journey to Fenrom. Send a rider ahead to tell your brother to prepare for our arrival."

"You are coming as well?" Olcay asked. He was hoping to be on a solo mission this time.

"Yes, there is not much for me here in ways to protect the King. Also, we need to get this mystery solved before anything else happens. I will trust you to plan our route; you will need to go there covertly so as not to arouse suspicion, and get it back to me tomorrow."

Pasha had started giving Olcay more responsibilities befitting his station as a steward. He was getting the knack of doing the paperwork and the payments. Olcay dismissed himself and went to tell Azarla and Oriel.

It did not take long for Oriel to get set up with her shop. Pasha was able to arrange some space at the forge for her within the manor's grounds. There would have been an issue with having two smiths, so the manor's master smith was promoted to grand armorer for the castle guard as a reward for his years of service. He humbly accepted the promotion. Oriel's father had sent her tools and extra steel to get started. At night she stayed in a guest room at Pasha's manor, but she was looking to renovate the areas next to the shop for a home of her own.

Oriel's new forge was in a great spot close to the inner market, just down from the manor. The newest smith was becoming a celebrity and had started drawing a crowd of inner-city residents like back home. A loud bang of metal could be heard blocks away. Olcay muscled his way to the front of the store and could see a few palace guards holding the entryway. At first, they stopped him from entering, but when they saw Pasha's crest on his lapel, they let him through.

"Oriel!" "Oriel!" "ORIEL!" The constant banging drowned out his calls to his sister.

He moved to the front to see if she would at least notice him.

As she turned to place the steel back in the fire, she screamed. "Olcay! Don't sneak up on me like that. I could have hit you."

"Olcay's here?" a muffled voice yelled from the forge.

"Azarla? Are you in there?" Olcay investigated the warm forge, trying to see where her voice was coming from.

"Yes, I am coming out; turn around. Oriel, can you grab me a leather cloak?"

"Olcay, can you draw the shutters quickly?" Oriel pointed to the windows.

Olcay went over and shut them down. The crowd's disappointment could be heard. A small metal door opened from the side, and a very naked Azarla popped out and was immediately covered by Oriel.

"What brings you here, Olcay," Oriel asked.

Olcay was flushed from both the heat of the room and the barely covered Azarla. "Ah yes, I have a mission and could be gone a few months, and I wanted to let you know."

Azarla's eyes began to tear up, and she started to almost cry; she was now torn between the two contracts and was hesitant to speak. Olcay understood the matter. "Azarla, no worries; you can take care of stuff here for me and work with Oriel. I know you have been waiting to get back to the forge for a while now, and our contract can end if that would make it easier for you."

"Olcay." Azarla's eyes began to fill with tears that became steam immediately. "You are so sweet, but my bond with you is strong, you have saved my life a few times already, and I cannot abandon our contract."

"How about we go with you, Olcay?" Oriel suggested.

"What? No! You just opened a shop here."

"Well, I wanted to travel anyways before I fully opened and settled in the city. I can bring my basic tools and earn my keep along the way. Azarla and Racheed provide enough fire; besides, I need to have the place renovated so Azarla can change in peace without being embarrassed." Oriel had this all planned out and was looking forward to getting out.

"Clothing will still be an issue on the road; even the leather won't hold up after too long, and Azarla cannot be naked out in the open," Olcay interjected.

"That is why you can use this." Oriel opened a small metal box that was housing Racheed. The box contained a massive cocoon of webbing." Oriel seemed pleased with herself.

"How am I going to use this?"

"Azarla told me you have weaver spiders; you can ask them."

Olcay realized he was cornered and decided he would go along with it for now. Olcay knew he would need to talk with Pasha about this and find an excuse to bring them along. Pasha would want to travel quick and light.

"I will talk with Pasha about it, just be ready in two days."

"What about Racheed's thread?"

"Deliver it to the manor; I will try and talk to Rin, but I do not know if it will work."

Olcay felt conflicted about it all; he was not going on vacation, did not want to drag his sister into this, and did not want another incident with Azarla, who has been through enough already. In the end, while walking back to see Pasha, he came up with the idea of having them under the guise of escorts. The incidents involving the throne assassins and the attack on the Drunken Head were going through his mind. At least it gave him the cover story he needed while they traveled. Olcay gave his explanation to Pasha, and he agreed with the plan; he added that having a smith with them could help answer questions that he couldn't. Since the attack on Olcay's home, seven smiths had been attacked and five others were killed. Having Pasha near his sister was also a bonus for her safety.

Olcay prepped a covered wagon for the journey with three fire mares for the long trip. It would let them travel as commoners and allow the mission more secrecy. Bringing Oriel to work along the way as a traveling smith helped with the ruse as well. The cover wagon also hid Pasha; he could sit in the back if needed to travel comfortably and not draw attention.

Even with all the prep work and secrecy, Lua was there to see them all off outside the manor.

"Princess? I guess you heard we are leaving for the North." Olcay asked.

"Come on Olcay! I am an Oracle; that was easy to find out, but my father told me to come here with a present." She smiled.

"A present?" Olcay was confused.

"Not for you. For your sister." Lua turned to Oriel and opened a parchment.

"Me?" Oriel replied. Not knowing what to do she gave a knee before the princess.

"The King extends a royal invitation upon your return to take your father's former station as Master Smith to the King."

"Your Highness, I am honored, but I am too young for the title."

Lua looked around and saw no one was looking and lifted Oriel off the ground, saying, "Nonsense, you are forging with Racheed and Azarla now. When you return, he believes you will even be better. Olcay can you please teach your sister about my ways?"

Pasha approached from the manor in a cloak covering his massive frame and interrupted. "Olcay will not be doing anything of the sort; you have meetings, Princess, and we have to go."

Lua handed Oriel the king's seal with a hammer and anvil. Pleasantries concluded and the princess departed.

"Olcay is everything prepared?" Pasha asked.

"Yes Sir, everything is as I detailed to you yesterday."

"Then we depart before the market square becomes too crowded. I will sit in the back until we leave the city." Pasha maneuvered himself to the back, and Olcay blocked him in with a few crates.

Olcay led the crew in the covered wagon out of the capital towards the northern toll roads with no issue. When they got past the first checkpoint, Azarla moved to the front and sat next to Olcay.

"So, what do you think are the chances of finding what you're looking for?"

"I hope we find more answers there and can at least put this ghost chase behind us."

"How are things in the shop going?"

"I guess I never could get used to working without clothes. They tend not to handle the smoke and soot. I enjoy the work, but it interferes with some modesty."

Olcay gave a mild chuckle as to avoid thinking the obvious. "So, what color do you get when you work with Racheed?"

"It took a few days; spiders are not my thing, and Racheed is larger than average as far as spiders go. In the end, she glows a bright pink and red. Quite fixating."

"Oh, I almost forgot, I got something for you for the trip." Olcay takes a package from behind his seat.

"Really? What is it?" Azarla was excited with the gift.

"I was able to convince Rin to make the cloak for you, the weaver spiders worked hard to get it done. Just make sure you bring them something sweet when we get back."

"Thank you, Olcay! Now I don't have to worry about my clothing burning up or getting damaged." Azarla's excitement would have to wait, as she was not going to change in a moving cart. Olcay looked to the back.

"How are the two doing in the back?" He asked.

"Oriel is adoring Pasha's armor and equipment. I guess your father's earlier works." Azarla remarked.

"Yes, I don't know much about it since its record was kept at the palace after my parents left the capital. I know it has gnomes or another fae handy work as well." Olcay commented.

"Well, hopefully, he does not need to use any of it on this trip out." Azarla placed her hand on her chest as if in prayer.

They passed out of the main land of the capital and made it to the well-traveled highways. Massive roads spread across the world to move the old armies of the immortal king. Mostly for show, as he never needed an army to back him. The advantage now is that cities loyal to King Hakim were connected by these same great roads and infrastructure, allowing for great wealth for the kingdom. Each city's governor held nobility ranks of Duke and were all bonded to the King in battle as he had no other living family beyond the princess. The Heartless territory did have the same roads, but they have been reclaimed by forests and land.

After the day's travel, they made it to a small village that benefited from the road. "Oriel, you're up, and remember the plan." Oriel moved to the front, switching places with Azarla. "The village had one guard at a fenceless shack. "Travelers, what brings you here?"

"I am Oriel daughter of Demir traveling north on business and would like to enter for trade, accommodations, and smithing work for the local farmers."

She handed over her guild seal and travel permit to the guardsman.

"Master Smith, I bid you welcome. A smith of your rank may be more than some of these farmers can afford."

"My father had a saying. 'A farmer's metal needs are more important than an army's, as an army cannot eat their armor'. I will not overcharge them." She gave a cute, charismatic smile.

The guardsman returned her paperwork and motioned them into the village square. The plan so far has been to keep the mission a secret under the guise of a traveling blacksmith going to collect materials in the north. Olcay was to play her assistant.

158

Pasha was to remain motionless if seen. Oriel was to explain she was delivering the armor to a nobleman if someone were to see him by accident. He would only move at night or when they stopped in a thicket if he needed to get out.

Oriel quickly set up a small stand in the village circle. Olcay and Azarla set up a small table with farming tools and other kitchen stuff for sale. One by one, the villagers approached as this well-built young lady in leather garb started pounding molten steel. Oriel set up a small, enchanted stove for Racheed to sit in to heat the metal, and on the ground, she laid out a makeshift blacksmith circle. Not that she needed it for farming tools. In all, she repaired quite a few tools, sold some kitchen wares, and made some metal puzzles for some kids. Azarla was able to try on her new fireproof cloak; it was black and gray. The pattern was matte, as the usual silk look would attract unwanted attention. It was still stylish, and Azarla could only hug Olcay in thanks. The first stop on the journey was quiet and peaceful.

The small group continued to stop at many towns along the way, keeping up the ruse. A few guardsmen or village chiefs in some villages wanted to be bribed, given taxes, or given protection money. To prevent issues, Pasha simply instructed that they pay, and he would send a messenger back to the capital to handle the issue later, after they left. He instructed Captain Jess to follow three days behind them because he knew she would love to arrest or dispose of any corrupt locals.

Currently, there is no need to jeopardize the mission over minor issues. Oriel knew she was going to get the money back and did not complain. She knew what was coming for those corrupt individuals later: judgment. It was only around halfway through the journey that they ran into their first real issue.

"Pasha, we have a tree in the middle of the road," Olcay whispered to the back of the cart.

"Ladies, come inside with me, Olcay, if they want money, just hand it over to them. If they want more, grab my blade under your cushion." Pasha instructed.

As they rode closer, sure enough, about a dozen bandits came from the thicket. The leader came from behind the tree. "That will be far enough, young man. Hand over your valuables and we may not torch you and your cart." The man was a scraggly mixed race of dark fae and beastman, with hair from head to toe that was matted and dirty. He had noticeable scars; telltale signs he is a fighter.

"Well, we would not want that." Olcay took off his purse and tossed it to the leader.

"Chyne, that was a little too easy. What is in the cart?" a second man said from the road.

"I have guild wares that are locked in curse boxes for travel; I would hate to have my stuff stolen." Olcay said with a smile.

Curse boxes are used for major deliveries; they are very expensive and quite volatile. It is one way to keep stuff from being stolen by bandits. If anything, that should have been the end of the conversation.

"I smell others in the cart; they smell pretty." Another beastman bandit said from the side of the cart.

"I think my men would like to meet the pretty ladies you have in the cart." He bared his teeth and gave an unsightly grin.

Olcay, knowing that this was about to get out of hand, grabbed the handle of the blade under his cushion and vanished before their eyes. Olcay moved from the front of the cart to inside the cart, next to everyone.

"How many did you count?" Pasha asked.

"I counted twelve."

"Good, watch the ladies and do not step outside," Pasha commanded.

Olcay pulled his own blade and took up a defensive posture near Azarla, with Oriel holding him close. "Do you think we will get out of this?" Azarla asked.

"Pasha was paying them a kindness by giving them a chance to leave; I am more concerned now with cleaning blood off the cart," said Olcay.

Pasha jumped from the back of the cart and was immediately surrounded. He disposed of his linen cloak and tossed it to the side.

"Look, Chyne, we have ourselves a fancy one here. Shiny too, not a scratch on him."

"Not much for brains knight. Must be a noble's kid playing dress-up, no combat skills probably." The bandits all started to laugh. The bandits continued to mock him and started to draw blades, bows, and clubs.

Pasha laughed at their words and let it bellow out to the point of rumbling the forest around them. "My goodness, it has been such a long time since anyone did not know who I was by looking at me. I have no battle marks because I have never been hit by a worthy blow." His voice went dark, and a few stepped back. Pasha pulled his sword and placed the tip upon the ground upright, and it began to hold stationary as he backed off.

"I would usually just smack you around and leave you for a wondering patrol; unfortunately, you threatened my companions, and my oath to Fairies Guardians would not allow you to leave here alive."

"What bullshit is this? We have you surrounded, you noble brat!"

One of the older guys stepped back and dropped his weapon. "You idiots, that's Pasha, the Shining Reaper of the Forest. We are all dead!" He started to bolt towards the thicket.

"I see someone remembers me." Pasha cackled with laughter.

Two of the others looked like they were in old uniforms, probably deserters; they dropped their weapons as well and ran down the road. Not to be swayed by this, the leader yelled for everyone to attack at once. At that moment, Pasha's sword glowed red and accelerated in all directions; it then returned with a hum and stopped back where it started. The blade was clean and untainted by blood. It was over, as eleven of the men around the wagon were cut down and four fell from the trees. The sprays of blood covered the area in a red hue. Only one bandit stood left holding his sword unscathed. Blood seeped into the ground, and flowers started to grow in and around the bodies.

Pasha turned to see the young man's hands shaking and his legs barely supporting him. Pasha grabbed the hilt of his blade and approached him. As he walked, vines began to sprout beneath his heels, and plants spread out.

"Well, this is a first for me. Usually, my blade never spares anyone." Pasha tips his blade up and knocks the sword out of the young bandit's hand. "You have never scarred, maimed, or killed anyone in your life?"

Tears flowed down his face as he felt death's gasp, and he shook his head in acknowledgment.

"Go back to your mother, boy, till your fields, and die old," Pasha said as he put his blade away. Blood lust subsided as the young man fell to his knees on the ground from the shock.

"I have no one, Sir Pasha, and no fields to till." He cried and bowed down.

"If you feel you have no hope, I can reconsider cutting you down as well," Pasha responded.

The fear returned to his eyes. Pasha returned to the cart and pulled out a scroll and wrote something down, he then went over to the money pouch held in the dead leader's hand and rustled a few coins from it.

"Go to the next town and give the scroll to the guardsman at the town, stay in the inn with the coin and wait for someone to retrieve you there from the capital." Pasha hands them to the would-be bandit. "We were never here, if you speak of this, my sword will find you and cut you down before you can finish my name. Now Go!" Pasha commanded

He departed down the road as fast as he could into the distance. Pasha returned to the cart. "You can come out now Olcay; we need to move this log and continue."

The log rolled away easily to the side of the road, and they resumed their course. The ground around them had become a field of flowers, and none of the bodies could be seen. The only evidence of the massacre was a blood streak across the wagon wheel.

Olcay resumed sitting upfront, and Azarla re-joined him. Oriel sitting in the back across from Pasha.

"I only read about Fairies Guardian in a ledger once, but it did not have anything else about it," said Oriel.

"As it shouldn't, Master Smith." Said Pasha. The scornful tone subsided quickly. "Sorry, that was rude of me. You are the daughter of the master that created it and one of the few that can even repair it if the need ever arises."

"No worries, I know some owe their lives to the secrets kept in the steel, and as a master smith we protect ourselves as well with those same secrets," Oriel responded.

Pasha felt he was being too harsh on her and decided to give her a chance to inspect the blade. Pasha pulled the blade out awkwardly in the small space of the wagon and handed it to her. Oriel was excited but tried to hold restraint as she could see Pasha was in a moment of vulnerability unfamiliar to him. Oriel held the steel in her hands; her runes discharged, preventing the various activations of the blade. It took to her as she was kin and calmed itself in her hands. The lines of the blade, the pattern, and the steel told her the story; it was both beautiful and horrifying.

"I cannot believe my father would make such a thing. How many died?" Oriel shed a tear, and her voice cracked as she could see all that happened with the blade. The patterns in the blade suggested that Demir himself wept while making it.

"Enough, and that is all that matters." Pasha took hold of the blade and returned it to its sheath.

"I am sorry for your loss." Oriel went over and hugged Pasha, and he could only return the embrace. "How did he get the materials?"

"No worries, young master; they were given willingly, and your father freely made the blade." Pasha's voice was very moved and relieved to share the knowledge with someone new.

Oriel sighed in relief as she placed her hand on the hilt and gave a small prayer. "I hope I can craft such a piece just as wonderful and precious."

"I hope you never have to master smith," Pasha replied.

Chapter 25

It always felt cool in the summers in the northern regions. Farming was sparse, and many made their income with trade or crafting. The Northern Sea city of Fenrom was the center of the merchant's guild. It was part of the great expanse of the Immortal King during his reign and subsequently was never changed. The ruling noble was a Duke Deice, who kept the peace. He was also the guardian and warden of the Immortal King's prison, held under the palace. It is said to be the most cursed location on the continent. Many still braved living and working there since the merchant guild would not depart.

From outside the walls, you could see they expanded towards the sea on both sides. The massive towers, remnants of the glory days of the city, were falling apart. The duke and guilds bickered over who needed to pay for the state of the city.

Olcay approached the great gates to the city and was held up by a never-ending line of carts to enter.

"What should we do, Pasha? This could keep us here past nightfall, and we will be left outside till morning." Olcay yelled back to him.

"How far is the next crossroad?" Pasha asked

"It is just up ahead."

"Take us to the western gate. We will make our way easier through there."

Pasha took to writing something on parchment paper, placed his seal on it and handed it to Olcay at the front of the cart. "Hand this to the guard that stops us."

After a minute of driving, a patrol halted the cart for inspection. The captain was handed the scroll that Pasha had written. The captain saw the seal and returned it to Olcay and motioned him to pass. "Show that to the guardsmen at the front of the line. Don't stop till you get there."

They were stopped only three times heading to the gate and each looked at the scroll and left them alone. "Pasha what did you hand me? No one is opening to read it?"

"It's an executioner warrant," Pasha responded.

"A WHAT?" the other three exclaimed.

"It was the quickest way through; a king's seal would draw attention, I cannot push you to the front to blow our cover, and pushing to the front without the merchant's guild's approval would also cause problems. Our mission is still a secret."

"Still, this feels weird." Olcay retorted

"Someone delivering an execution warrant cannot be halted and gives us more than one cover for the time being. At least till we see the duke." Pasha's words were still not comforting.

Just as Pasha said, they made it through the gate without any issues. The suns were setting, and they found an inn for the night to set up for the rest of their plans. Pasha was able to sneak in the back unnoticed and was able to have a bed for the first time in a while.

In the morning, a messenger came to Olcay's room with an invitation to the palace for all of them, including Pasha. Olcay delivered the note to Pasha in the barn where the wagon was being stored.

"Not much would get past him about us entering the city. There's no point in making him wait; breakfast will be ready when we get there." Pasha replied.

The inner palace itself was a spectacle to behold, with high, rising towers with no reasoning just jutting upwards. The remnants of the Immortal King's mighty city, as impressive as they were, now just a shadow of themselves. Olcay remembered the drawings of the old city he found in the palace library. The wealth of the city was removed, and the King and Queen went to their thrones to both hold the peace and keep the main resident imprisoned.

Riding into the main courtyard, the gate was closed behind the covered wagon. Only a few guards and a large, husky, bearded man stood atop the stairs near the entryway. His hair was unkempt for someone of nobility and looked to be needing sleep, as well as his eyes seemed puffy and glazed. His face was scarred from battles and time.

"What brings you here, Sir Pasha?! With an execution order, no less." The duke's voice was stern and commanding.

"Maybe a pompous old farmer needs to return to his fields and die in his freshly tilled ground." Pasha's voice grumbled in defiance.

The three did not know what was going on as Pasha leaped out of the back of the wagon and rushed, blade drawn, up the stairs towards the duke with unholy rage. The blade ignited the air around it, and the point came within striking distance. The duke parried the blow with a short sword pulled from his side and struck downward with another massive blade in his left hand. Pasha recovered his blade and blocked the blow, and it shook the ground; the stone slab cracked the ground under the pressure.

"You usually would have gotten closer than that."

"You usually would have knocked me down."

"I guess we are not the men we were before."

"I will have to agree there."

The duke reached down and helped lift Pasha from the ground as they both looked at each other and felt deep nostalgia. The two embraced and laughed as two warriors would.

"You would usually let me know you were coming. What is going on, my friend?" said Duke Deice.

"It's best we eat breakfast and discuss this somewhere more secure," replied Pasha.

The three realized it was just two war buddies that were just reminiscing and exited the cart. They went to give a bow but were abruptly stopped. "None of that here; I cannot deal with it today. The companions of Pasha's are of mine as well."

The palace's inner walls were massive and well decorated compared to the King's palace in the capital. Massive tapestries and paintings to the point of being gaudy. Deice noticed how Olcay, Oriel, and Azarla were staring at the amount of it all.

"Not my taste in decorations, just leftovers from the previous owner. Just never got around to doing anything with it all." His voice echoed throughout the great halls. "Even my wife had to leave this place and go back to our homeland to keep her sanity." He laughed, saying, "One time she burned down an entire section of the castle and it repaired itself, furnishings and all."

The dining hall was just as ornate as the rest of the palace, and the abundance was starting to become nauseating. Each utensil was beyond description and purpose.

"A little much isn't it?"

"I tell you; we keep finding more and more of this stuff, and even if we dump it, it just keeps coming back as if it returned itself. After a while, you just forget it's all here," said Deice.

"Why is there so much?" asked Olcay.

"The Immortal King Ebedi is an enigma. Any attempt to find out is futile. I recall two oracles, one from the past and one from the future, attempting to read him once. Eyes switched colors, and they went mad seeing the opposite timelines of each other." Deice chuckled at the thought, but he was trying to hide how he was disturbed by it.

"What happened to him after the fall of the council?" Olcay asked.

Deice stood up and took a long piece of bread and held it like a sword, as if he were fighting an army around him. His voice went low as he started to spin his tale. "The great war was just starting, as the council grew mad with one tragedy after another. People began ripping out their own hearts, consumed by the insane aura they exuded. The nobles themselves were worthless and fell as well. Lord Hakim was one of the few who stood their ground as the world started to fall. Working with the smiths, he created the Final Judgment ax he holds today." Deice paused for a drink and continued. "Alongside the king, myself, Pasha, and others fought to free the

165

council of their madness. In the end, we were only able to halt the bloodshed. An agreement was made that a seal needed to be maintained to hold Ebedi and contain the cursed tragedy that was befalling everyone. Unfortunately, the great seal needs to be constantly held. You saw them both… quite tragic."

"Sir, that did not answer his question. So, what happened to Ebedi?" Azarla asked.

"Let an old man have his fun with storytelling. It is a very boring answer… he is down the hall and down a flight of stairs, where he has always been." Deice pointed with the piece of bread down the hall.

"What? Like, is he dead? Or in a prison?" Oriel asked.

"Why would he be dead? The bastard's immortal. You get the concept, right?" Deice scoffed.

"I understand the immortal part. But how many legends have an immortal, an undead monster, or an ever-living demigod, and they are taken down by a hero or a spell?" Oriel responded

"True, the "immortal" bit gets tossed around easily; however, Ebedi is the real thing. He will outlast us, his prison, and the test of time." He sat back down and started to rip apart the medium-cooked ribs.

"Can we see him then?" Azarla excitedly asked.

Deice's mouth was full, and he took a drink. "I can take you, no problem."

He stood up, took a roasted leg of a massive beast, and started towards the door; three of them got up to follow, and Pasha remained sitting. They waited for him a moment, but he motioned to go on ahead. "I have seen him already; it's not much of a show."

Deice motioned them on straight through the hall and down a flight of stairs, then they went to a courtyard with a massive door. The gate was covered in padlocks of all types and colors. "What is with all the locks?" asked Olcay. "The locals place them there for luck. In hopes, they will help keep Ebedi sealed." Said Deice.

Oriel looked over to look for the master's mark and found the building was constructed by several guilds and high-level smiths. She noticed her father's mark as well. It was encouraging to see it this far from home. Deice took out one of his blades and pushed it into the actual gate lock, and it opened. The massive doors' locking mechanism roared as the foundation itself moved. Inside the wall retracted several gates. The group waited until Deice started walking in first. Down a few flights of stairs, the four continued. They saw a few guards holding chains on the walls.

"Each one is attached to a mechanism to collapse the chamber. If they fall or get pulled from their spot, then the trap will spring."

"Seems like a lot," Azarla commented

"I wish we had more to hold him." said Deice.

The hallway went up over a curved floor, and they began to climb the outside of a dome. At an opening, they found themselves high atop a massive chamber where the path opened to a balcony. In the middle of the expanse was a single metal statue that looked like ceremonial armor that had sword hilts embedded in each segment. Olcay recognized it as the same one at the palace. Sitting across from him was a single man sitting in a plain chair and staring at the statue.

"There he is, The Immortal King Ebedi."

"The man in the chair?" Olcay asked.

"No child, Ebedi, is bound in the statue; the man is an observer of the Heartless Council, charged with watching him and setting off the chamber's collapse if the statue budges."

"You just said he is a heartless?" Azarla asked while clutching her chest.

She looked on as the man was hunched over on the chair; his eyes were empty, and his skin was almost gray. He stared at the statue motionless and without distraction.

"Yes, poor bastard, he has been here as the Queen's eyes since the beginning. No point in talking with him, pale eyes, and all, so we gave him a chair at least. Never moves as well, kind of weird. We just leave him be. So, tours over, let's head back." Deice motioned them back down the stairs.

"How did you end up as the caretaker of this land and warden to Ebedi?" Olcay asked out of curiosity.

Deice smiled and said, "I was the most trustworthy, I suppose. Pasha commented before, I was a farmer... I still am. I plow the fields outside the palace and sell my goods at the market. I had the least desire to hoard the wealth of the former palace. It would have thrown everything into chaos with a war over the wealth. Most of the information and technology are too dangerous to be held by anyone. I was seen as the least likely to use it. The guilds here needed to be held accountable to the common man as well, so King Hakim judged me to rule here."

He continued to walk them back out of the building, all while telling them bardic tales of his adventures and prowess. The three smiled and gave their thanks for the tour. As they departed and returned to the surface, they could only start to feel a mild pressure being lifted that they had not noticed before.

Pasha was waiting on the surface, sitting on a stone block. Deice locked up the prison doors, and they all went over to where he was.

"Well, I know you all did not come all the way here to have me show you around this awful place. So, what brings you all out here so far north?" asked Deice.

"We came to find the Embodiment of the Library to help shed some light on a mystery," Pasha responded.

"She does not like guests; you should have been told that, and she rarely will speak with anyone even if you find her. You may have traveled here for nothing, my friends. On top of that, she tore apart a building last week over a missing book. You should leave her be." Deice's eyes were wide and disturbed.

"I was owed a question from the Embodiment of the Forge that she could not answer," Olcay responded.

"I would say that might get you an audience with her, but there are no guarantees," Deice responded and continued to walk back to the castle walls.

"We will find out tomorrow; for now, I secured our accommodations at the inn. We will be on our way." Pasha said.

"You never had a stomach for this place, did you, Pasha?" Deice chuckled.

The group left the duke at the footsteps of the palace and moved out the gate in their cart. Orion was there the next morning at the city center waiting for them. He was dressed nicely in a well-made black long coat. His guild crest was marked as a metal shield on his left shoulder. He was fidgety, waiting there early so as not to miss them, and he was afraid the guild leaders would give him trouble if he was late.

"Orion! There you are, brother." Olcay yelled across the courtyard.

"About time you showed up, what have you gotten me into?" Orion responded.

"Your supervisors will forgive you for escorting us today."

"Us?" Orion had not noticed that a party was with Olcay, and they came into view through his tunnel vision.

"I will introduce Sir Pasha, Commander of the King's Army, Azarla, my assistant, and you know your sister." Each was guised in a linen cloak over their frames.

"Oriel? Azarla? Sir Pasha! I am so sorry. Olcay, why did you not tell me they were coming with you? You do know there is some protocol at the guild with royal visitors?"

"Our mission is a secret for now, and we need to keep it that way," Pasha replied. Orion nodded his head and understood. He quickly embraced his sister.

"Congratulations! I am sorry I could not make it to the ceremony." There were quick smiles all around with the family reunited.

"No worries," Oriel responded.

"Best we get a move on before we draw attention," Azarla whispered.

"Yes, yes. I will take you down to the paper district. She will be there waiting for you." Orion explained

They followed Orion down several streets in the city. Each area was very efficiently laid out next to one another. From raw materials to finished products, they were separated as if cataloged. You could almost buy anything here. The two biggest locations in the city were the banking market and the commerce market. The area they needed was not very far and was easy to find. History says ages ago the Immortal King created ways to print books faster and cheaper, allowing for the world to share knowledge, an age of enlightenment in a dark time. The Embodiment of the Library at the time was a smaller being with no distinction among her kin. After the number of books increased, she grew past almost all but death. When the Immortal King was imprisoned, she secluded herself in this city to keep close to the main influx of books.

Next to them, they could hear and see the mechanical district. The area contained technology the guild has been trying to recreate since the age of Ebedi. Gears, steam, and some failed flying contraptions littered the area. The air hissed loudly and clanged repetitively. The guild leaders were trying to reverse-engineer most of it. The area's former occupants made up most of the victims during a heartless raid, and much of it lay in shambles. The hope was to bring life back to the former capital of the world.

The culinary markets were not far, and the group could smell spices, sweets, and meats. It was a definite must-visit for them if everything went well. Olcay had to think that Orion was training in all these areas to get his merchant license. He had to learn all the areas and how they interacted with each other. Overall, it was to give the merchants a worldly view.

At the end of the district was a massive building of wood and stone. Outside was a small table with a bookkeeper accounting for shipments. He was older, frail, and had an attitude that came from the stress of the position. The party approached and stood at the small table.

"How may I help you today?" he remarked.

"Guild business; I am escorting some guests to see the book warehouse," Orion replied.

"Do you have papers?" He squinted at them and looked them over and smacked his tongue on his teeth as if he was not impressed.

Pasha, not wanting to waste time, placed a gold-sealed scroll of the king in front of him. The foreman dared not open it and just pushed it back into Pasha's hands, saying, "Orion, please take good care of our guests."

It all seemed too easy to them, but the way the journey has been, they were going to take what they could get. The air was musky in the warehouse, as it was not like a library where everything was neatly organized on shelves. Books were packed in boxes and on tables. Workers were binding and printing and paying no attention to them.

Spotting their target was easy enough. She was sitting there on a stack of books amid the warehouse. The workers and the customers paid her no heed as they went about their day. As they approached, she came into better view. Her hair, skin, and clothes were those of curled pages of scrolls and books; bindings made up most of the color her pages lacked. The height of the books she was sitting on was higher than Pasha.

She resembled a younger woman with very distinct features. As she shifted, the pages of her body moved to give an almost mechanical movement as she turned the pages in the book she was reading.

Orion pulled Olcay off to the side to have a quick talk. "There she is. Just don't upset her." Orion said.

"Upset her? We were told she may not even speak with us." Olcay replied. "Look, I am just letting you know. I was here when she let loose a horrific wave of creatures and magic when a book was missing in a series she was reading. I was part of a cleanup crew; it took us a week to get back in here." Orion said in frustration.

"What did she do?"

"The contents of her library began to leak out and started attacking us in the warehouse looking for the book."

"How is that possible?"

"What I found out from the guild is that she is the culmination of all written knowledge, known and unknown; she is not swayed or deterred. As an embodiment, she has anything and everything within her. Look, Olcay, she almost ate me alive with a giant spider, but I convinced her otherwise. She is aware you were coming here, and that is the only reason I am alive right now."

"Why did you not mention that before?!" Olcay replied with discomfort.

"You made this out to be urgent and needed to be a secret. I was hoping to have more time to talk to you before we got here. Olcay, all I can say is that lying to her has consequences. Just be careful."

Olcay reported the intel back to Pasha, who was trying to figure out a solution. "Well, she is expecting you, so it would be the best start." Pasha went over his plan of action. He had the ladies stand near the door in case they all had to flee. Hopefully, with Azarla and Racheed, they could burn the books to make their escape. Orion was going to clear everyone out of the warehouse. Olcay was given Pasha's sword just in case he needed to pull back. After the last worker left the warehouse, they started;

Pasha placed the Fairy Guardian next to Olcay with the point down. It began to float just like before. As Olcay walked, it stayed behind him a few steps within range.

The Embodiment of the Library sat upon her books, still unfazed by all the activities happening around her. Olcay slowed his pace as he could see the books beneath her start to fidget like frightened animals, and they began to hiss.

She placed her finger to her lips to hush them. "Why do you approach me, Olcay, son of Demir?" She spoke.

Olcay was taken back by that question, but remembered his brother already said she was expecting him. "I am here to learn an answer to a question." He responded.

"What makes you think I will answer?" Her head did not move; a second set of eyes formed from her forehead. Those eyes panned upward and showed a murderous intent.

"Your kin the Forge sent me here for an answer to a question she could not answer."

"Forge? Why would you ask her? The hot head knows nothing." She became irritated, and her pages began to unfurl.

Olcay had to think. "The ritual my sister was going through required me to ask a question as part of it."

Her eyes began to flip like pages in a book. "Ahh yes, then you were not insulting me; continue." The pages began to return to their places, and her face settled together.

"No, I would never do such a thing." Olcay felt some relief.

"What is this answer you seek?" Mildly curious, she placed her book down and placed her elbows on her knees and her hands under her chin.

Olcay reached back to the satchel he was carrying and pulled out the little red book he was in possession of. She looked down, jumped from her tower of books, and stood in front of Olcay.

Olcay handed her the book, and she began to move through the pages. "How is the Heartless Council doing these days?" she asked.

"They seem to be doing well; I have nothing to compare them with." He replied.

She started to pace back and forth with the book between him and the stack of books she was sitting on. Her eyes began to flip like pages again, and the writing on her skin started to change and become organized.

"I am in a dilemma, Olcay. You said you had a question and handed me this book; what is it you wish to know?" The paper-crafted figure moved around, adjusting her shape.

"It was placed in my pocket for unknown reasons, and many have died recently. I thought by knowing something about this book I would have answers."

"I can only imagine the story you are making that led you here. Promise me your story when it ends, and I will answer you." Her eyes adjusted and furled.

Olcay was cautious, he felt something was missing from this that she was not saying. "What would that involve?"

"You have the makings of a great story of drama, tragedy, and adventure. Most books these days are filled with numbers and ledgers. I need something better. You only need to write your journey, and I will feel it as it happens. Give me that, and I will have you an answer."

"I see no harm in that. You have yourself a deal."

"Good, you can call over your friends. I will not interfere in a story I wish to read as it unfolds." Her paper face folded into a massive smile.

Olcay walked back to the party and informed them that she would answer the question. They gathered near her cautiously but relieved.

"Olcay, I would have to say I do not have your answer here." The Library answered. A look of disgust came over their faces. "Why are you upset? I don't have it here with me, but you can pick it up…"

"Why can you not just give it to us?" Olcay asked.

"The author of the book never wrote down the translation of the book, hence why I do not have an answer for you."

"Where is the author?" Pasha asked.

"…in me." She whispered.

"In you?!" They all exclaimed.

"He is one of a selected, enlightened few allowed in my hallowed halls. Return the book to him, and you will have your answers." Her patterned clothing unraveled, and the pages of her chest started to split down the middle. "I find it unfair that he refuses to share his knowledge with me. Maybe you can do me a favor and convince him."

The group began to think it over, as it was something they were not expecting to do. In the end, they needed to push forward. Olcay and Pasha stepped forward. "No, no, I will need them to join you as well." The Library's outstretched hand pointed to Azarla and Oriel.

"I cannot allow that!" Pasha voiced and took a defensive stance near them.

"Why not?" The books around the room started to slither like snakes, wrapping around her legs to form a serpent-like body.

Pasha realized his error and stood down from his defensive posture. "I do apologize; may I ask why you want them to join us?"

The Library calmed herself for a moment, "I found them fascinating, and the aura they give off tells me they have great stories to tell as well."

172

Pasha turned to the young ladies to see what they had to say on the matter; he was not wanting to press further against the Library, but he was not going to put them in harm's way. Oriel looked at the now slithering paper monster. "Will we be safe? Can you promise us we will be returned unharmed?"

"Of course, it would be rather rude to harm my guests while they are visiting my inner self." The Library unraveled to her original form as the books left her; they reformed back into piles. "I will warn you that I am vast, and you can get lost easily. If you need anything, look to the books for help, and you should be fine. Also, no magical items are allowed; I don't need to have you discharge in me and burn me up." The thought of the journey started to get less appealing.

"The author you are looking for can be found in comedy; just ask for assistance."

The whole thing seemed very rushed as she ushered them over to the stack of books she had been sitting on, which now began to move like riled worms. The pages and binders started to move around them, and they merged with the pages and then dissipated.

Pasha was prone on the ground, lifeless. Olcay went over to shake him up, but there was no response. Azarla and Oriel, both still groggy from the transfer, came over to assist. "Is he dead?"

"I don't know; his armor is always on him, but I am getting no response. Can we turn him over?" Pasha was surprisingly light for a man in full plated armor. Both Oriel and Olcay remember moving large metal pieces around the shop, and this was almost too easy.

"We should get the helmet off," Oriel suggested.

Olcay was hesitant. He has still never fully seen Pasha's real face. It was always covered by the helmet or mask. Was he hiding a scar, a flaw, or a disfigurement? Would he be upset if he awoke to see them without his coverings?

It was an emergency and could not be helped. Oriel propped up the back of Pasha's head as Olcay began to release the catch holding his helmet on. The scruffy beard underneath made it difficult to maneuver it off his chin as well. When he got it released, he lifted it off Pasha's head.

The smoothness of Pasha's face was that of finely crafted marble, each hair perfectly aligned with the next. The group did not know what they were looking at. Only when they were close to the face could they see that it was a mechanical face and neck.

A small knock came from the side of the chest as a small hatch opened and a tiny figure came out. She stood no more than two hands high. She was a fairy folk, pale from lack of sun, with reddish hair, and with no wings. Dressed in a leather garb with various metal links. She was just as out of it as the rest of them.

She turned and looked upward towards them. "I did not expect for us to meet like this."

Back at the book warehouse, Orion was still standing in front of the Embodiment of the Library. He just witnessed his brother, sister, and the others fold like paper into her pages. She then picked up a book in front of him and went back to her perch. Orion kept his tongue, remembering what happened last time and wanting to avoid confrontation.

"No questions? Outburst? Cries for help? Very disappointing." She moved her book to the side. "Why not you? I find you amusing and will need to be entertained while we wait for them to get back."

Orion needed time to process it all but needed to answer her. "I overheard that the embodiments are not very talkative, yet I have had the privilege twice to speak with you."

Her body started to ripple again with her pages unfurling and then hold its shape. "Your brother and sister have interesting stories to tell, and I am curious if I can get a third." She chuckled as she started to stack a few books. "The other three, I think, will have a few chapters themselves to contribute to their stories."

She hopped down from her perch and got uncomfortably close to Orion. Her eyes were a folded mess of letters that were in constant flux with her mood. "You are a luck oracle, are you not?"

"Luck Oracle? You mean the rings around my eyes? Children of oracles have a small chance of getting them. No real power, I am told." Orion chuckled.

"Yes, that is what you have been told. Guess that bit of history is no longer written anywhere." Her lips smiled and darkened. She then lifts the book she was reading to cover her face.

Orion, at this point, could not resist and asked. "What is a luck oracle?"

"Now we have a reaction." A smile folded from her lips. The lighting in the room changed. Her voices were taunting, "Where do we begin?"

Hello Pasha

The fey town was nestled in the farthest corner of the forest. The overgrowth provided significant camouflage that hid the village for generations. Even the war with the Immortal King did not rustle the finest blade of grass, and it went widely unnoticed. Elif, the youngest of her siblings, had taken flight for the first time from her hollowed-out ash home. The fey had a gorgeous slim figure and long amber hair that needed to be tied up to keep it out of her gold-colored wings.

She was sent to market in the large oak tree at the end of the glade. How such a simple errand could turn from a moment of joy to unfathomable horror.

As Elif woke from her shock, a severe pain emanated from her back. She tried to flutter up and fell immediately straight down. Her wings were torn to shreds. The shock started to subside as she remembered a raid was happening. "Kobolds!" Elif remembered them from stories. She remembered being knocked from behind as she passed the tree and falling to the ground into the bushes as she lost consciousness.

Gray and red-skinned creatures half the size of humans, wearing tattered garments and pieced-together armor. The nasty creatures pushed suddenly into the glade, snatching fey from the ground and air. The terror of the kobolds rang out as they made short work of the defenseless town. They used rusted tools to hack into trees and logs and short knives to cut off their victims' wings, as they would get stuck in their gaping, pointed teeth. The horror inscribed itself on her soul as she saw her own fate being written.

She looked around as her fog lifted; she was snatched out of the air and was staring down the gullet of a salivating monster when a blade struck through its skull like a stone into a pond. The kobold's blood burst through the air, and she fainted. Elif's eyes began to focus again as she saw a massively plated knight wielding an immense sword making short work of the remaining invaders. Covered in blood that glistened off his already mirrored helmet, he turned to her and knelt down. "Are you alright, little one?" A spear penetrated his side as the last kobold cackled its death cry and was dispatched with the stranger's gauntlet. Elif fainted once more.

Elif's eyes open to an unfamiliar metal ceiling. Her shock was still holding, as she did not know what to feel. A yellow crystal on the ceiling illuminated her surroundings. She was in a soft bed covered with a blanket. She sat up and found herself stripped of her clothing and covered in bandages. She felt the bandage on her head, where she was now missing part of her hair, ripped from her skull. Her wings ravaged from her body as she remembered the cackle of the Kobolds as they played with their victims before consuming them. She grabbed at her mangled, bandaged head and began to sob.

"How is my guest holding up?" a small voice said from the corner. Elif yelped and covered herself with her blanket.

"No worries, little one. You are safe here. No harm will come to you, I swear."

Elif pulled down the blanket to see a small gnome standing at the door. His clothes were those of a working gnome. He had metal bracers on all his joints that were encrusted with stones. He had a massive dark mustache that stretched across his face and no beard on his chin.

"I guess introductions are in order, I am Pasha. Head of his majesty's royal guard and general to his armies."

Elif chuckled mildly, for if she burst out laughing it would have aggravated her wounds.

"The great Pasha of legend? Sorry I cannot stand Sir Knight." Elif let out a giggle again. "As funny as this all is, thank you for bandaging me up." She let out a small cry. "Did anyone else survive?" Her questions were tripping over each other, one after another.

"I know a few were able to fly away in time, and others burrowed in deep enough to escape. I cannot hold the nasty creatures alone and will need to get back to camp for reinforcements to exterminate the last of the infestation."

"You are amusing, Sir Pasha; what can a gnome do against those nasty creatures?"

Pasha was amused and gave a grin. "Best you get rest. We have a long road ahead, and we are on foot till I get back to my horse. We should move you to the main room before we leave, where there will be fewer vibrations."

The gnome held out his hand to the young fey and helped her to stand. The pain was less, but it still ached. The door opened into a massive hollow metal shell with four other doors across and up above them. Stairs brought them up to a platform in the middle of the room. "Where are we?"

"Inside my armor." Pasha scoffed. "We do need to get moving before any more of the kobolds show up."

He stood in the middle of the room and attached chains to his bracers. Elif could see that the chains locked onto gears throughout the walls of the armor's interior. A set of stones illuminated a phantom image of her forest home in front of him. "Please have a seat and hold on." Elif found a chair bolted to the floor of the platform. She used a small leather belt around the chair to hold herself in.

"We'd best be off." Pasha stood in the middle of a set of gears and began to walk in place as they turned. The room was a technical marvel of gears and magic. His first step she felt from her seat as the room shifted, then the armor began to stand and walk. "Watch from the seeing stone in your chair behind us. I don't need to be surprised again." He pointed at a small hole in the armor covered by a cloak from the outside. Elif remembered the spear that impaled the armor. It was then that she realized this little gnome, no bigger than herself, was really the famous hero of legend, Pasha. Elif's shock, which had been ever-lingering, subsided as she fell asleep again in her chair.

"Wake up! I swear you are the sleepiest fairy I have ever met." Pasha rustled the fairy in her chair.

"Where are we now?" Elif was still dazed and confused.

"We are at the encampment; I have sent my people into the forest to clear out the infestation and find any survivors."

Elif began to cry again, "I am so sorry; I did not believe you. The stories never mentioned you were a gnome."

"And they never will. You are one of only three people that know I am a gnome."

"But how did this all happen? The clockwork suit, the armor..." She had questions.

"That will be for another time. For now, you will stay here with me till you are better and you find your kin." Pasha's voice offered her comfort as he rested his hand on her shoulder.

The night passed with blood-curdling wails from the dying kobold screeches. Hours passed, and the fighting started to subside. A few of the tenant guards approached.

"Sir Pasha, we have collected what you asked from the town; also, the remnants of the kobold plague have been exterminated." The young captain presented Pasha with a red felt bag. Pasha took it from him. "You are dismissed." The captain left Pasha's field tent after giving a salute. Pasha pulled the sack close to his side, and he opened a panel in his armor to retrieve it.

"Elif. Can you come here, please?"

"I will be out in a minute. I need to get dressed." Elif still had difficulty getting clothing on or over her shoulders. Her scars were still swollen and sensitive from the attack. The pain reminded her that she was alive, and she found comfort in that. She emerged from her room in the right thigh and saw Pasha next to a sack about his height.

"My soldiers collected all they could find... are you ready for this?"

"It would happen eventually." Elif's tears started to fall before she could get any closer.

Elif climbed to the top of the sack and pulled it down to release its contents. The wings of her fallen fairy kin and friends spilled out onto the platform. Like shattered stained glass, they reflected the light from the room and gave off an eerie feeling. Elif held in her emotion the best she could, yet tears flowed even more as she went through them. She spouted off their names; Pasha then wrote them down and placed them upright in a box like books on a shelf. Among the wings, she found her mother, uncle, cousin, and friends. In her tears, she composed herself and looked at all of them, filed neatly like specimens in a collection.

"My brothers are not here…" a mild sigh of relief mixed in with anger. "They probably went off drinking again in a nearby town."

"The last of the kobolds that attacked your village have also been killed. As of right now, we are looking into what caused them to be this far from their homeland and how they got by our checkpoints."

In the midst of it all, she found her wings, and she relived the ordeal in her mind— the pain, the shock—it was too real again for her. She rubbed her shoulders and felt the tenderness of her scars. The reality finally came over her as she began to bawl when the pain and anguish overcame her. She went over to hold her mother's wings. Pasha placed his hand on her upper arm, avoiding her wounds, to console her. She turned to hug him. Taken back, he returned the hug until she stopped. Her cries echoed throughout the armor. They could never be reattached, and she would be flightless for the rest of her days.

Time passed; she dried her tears and then looked up through his massive mustache.

He looked down and asked, "What do you want to do with them all? I am not familiar with your culture, and fairy wings are not something we can just leave lying in a field."

She placed her hand on one of the metal beams holding the body together. It was rough and started to show signs of wear.

"Can you use them here?"

"That is most generous of you…" The barbaric practice of using fey parts to augment armor and weapons ended centuries ago. It was one of the few things agreed upon in a great war so long ago. Fire creatures refuse to work with it as part of the ancient pact, and only the most skilled could even attempt such a crazy process.

"Please bring honor to their deaths; allow them to become part of this creation to help prevent the next tragedy."

Not to deny her request or lose this advantage, "I have a blacksmith friend of mine that is crazy enough to perform the task. I will get with him when we return to the kingdom."

"As long as you swear you will always protect the innocent and use them for good, they are yours." Elif was in a mortified and grieving state.

Pasha hoped she would return to her senses after some time. He could see in her eyes a resolve that needed to be acknowledged. Pasha kneeled to her level, produced a small penknife, and cut a few strands of his mustache and placed them in his hand. He pricked his finger, then hers. The blood dribbled out, and he grasped her hand. "Bound by this blood oath before you, I swear it."

She never expected such an oath, but it reassured her of her decision.

It was a few months before Pasha found his way to the kingdom. Elif stood by in amazement; Pasha's movement within his contraption was second nature to him. He interacted with people and performed his duties with great skill. In battle, the suit reacted effortlessly with his motions.

Elif was healing well with Pasha's nursing. The flesh where her wings were started to scar over, and the muscles she used for flight began to stop seizing.

At night, with the armor laying down, she could walk the length of it and see it all. One of the areas was a small kitchen, library, spare rooms, and a tinker's forge. Most of the other areas were never used since they were used for storage or the mechanics of the armor. Over time, Elif started to help with the regular maintenance of her new home. It was backbreaking, but it kept her mind busy.

"Elif, we will be in front of the king tomorrow and the other members of the nobility. Try to keep it down while we are in chambers."

"I understand Pasha."

Pasha was on hiatus after the last kobold clean-up. The damage needed to be repaired before he could return to his regular duties. Elif's offer was still playing in the back of his mind as well. He would need the king's approval and the guild's to use the wings for his equipment.

Even then there was only one person capable of doing the feat. Elif was aware of the requirements and knew that it was a huge risk even asking such a taboo thing. It was a restless night for them both.

The King's main hall was crowded for festivities and well decorated, more than usual. It was the princess's birthday, and many had come to bring her gifts and receive an audience with the king. Pasha was not scheduled to have an appearance, but he would not miss this opportunity. Behind the main throne were the king's unused chambers, and the young princess Lua was waiting.

"Pasha, you came! I was worried you would miss out on the food." Lua screamed excitedly. Pasha noticed the attendants for Lua were at their wit's end with the young princess, and he dismissed them.

"Did you bring me back anything?" She asked.

Pasha reached into a small satchel and pulled out a book wrapped in ribbon. She grabbed it and hugged him. "I guess we need introductions," Lua said.

Pasha noticed that for a moment Lua's eyes changed when she was clairvoyant. "You know you should not be looking into the past until you have had training," Pasha replied. Pasha pulled a lever in front of him to open the chest plate to reveal the open cavity. Elif was taken back by this, but she trusted Pasha and followed his lead.

Pasha gave a slight bow from his perch. "Princess, may I introduce Elif of the fey," Pasha commented.

"Elif of the fey, Pasha's armor has shown me you are without a home and in need of a purpose. You are also entrusted with his secret." Lua stood tall for a seven-year-old as she made such a serious face. "For your continued silence, I shall offer you… fairy cakes as compensation," Lua said.

Pasha snickered as Elif could only take in what the little girl was saying. "As for your request with the taboo wings, I shall aid you. But we must be very best of friends."

Elif smiled and nodded in acceptance of her offer. Lua went back to the party and played out the evening.

"She is very mature for her age," Elif commented.

"When she lost her mother, her eyes came into their own, and she had to grow up from there," Pasha said.

"I only heard of the oracles of gold and silver light. I have never seen it up close. "She carries more than she lets on."

"That is why we have our station, for her protection."

"What of the king?"

"He is another matter; just watch what you say."

The evening settled, and the guests left to continue the celebrations in the street. All that remained was the King upon his uneven throne. Princess Lua was playing with a small puzzle she received as a gift. Pasha entered and bowed before him.

Pacha, please seal the room. We need our privacy."

Pasha placed his sword within the stone next to his station. The room walls became flush, and the doors and windows became whole and smooth.

"Remember what we talked about, Elif." She nodded in understanding.

"Pasha, please don't keep me waiting and introduce our guest." The king commanded.

Pasha pulled the chest plate lever and opened his armor. He was inside, kneeling along with Elif.

"My King, I present Elif of the Fey, a survivor of the town attacked by kobolds not too long ago. I have been her caretaker while she heals."

"Kobolds, nasty vermin. Their methods are grotesque and vile. My daughter has already told me much about you, young Elif, and she has taken a liking to you." He tilted his head slightly to get a better look at her wings. "I see their methods as always violent."

Elif had a flash of her trauma and then let it go and maintained her composure.

The King's hand removed itself from his ax, and he gestured to Pasha. "You may speak to the King," Pasha said to Elif.

"The princess is most kind and very sweet, your majesty." Elif raised her head slightly to get a full view of the king. The field of view changed as she saw the vastness of the room shrink next to him. "Has the princess conveyed my request?"

"Yes! Lua has. I do have a bit of concern with the request you ask of me, Elif of the Fey." The king's hand returned to his ax and gripped its hilt. The room went cold, and Pasha went gray.

"The ancient law forbids the usage of fey materials in experiments and weapons. This was made to protect your people; why would you bring this curse upon the kingdom and the princess?!" King Hakim rose from his throne, removed his withered hand from its column, and gripped his ax.

"I cannot allow this to go unjudged." The king's voice rumbled in the empty hall.

Elif did not know what to do. Everything was wrong—the air, the light—it was overwhelmingly out of place. She could not speak and could not get a reaction from Pasha. Elif fluttered her limbless wing stubs to get away. She felt she had failed her lost family and friends.

The king brought up his ax to bring down a heavy blow. His size and aura were immense, and she was crushing under the air as she was trying to breathe. Gray darkness engulfed the room, coming from his eyes and rage.

Elif collapsed and could barely catch a breath. Out of the corner of her eye, she could see Lua playing with her puzzle box, and as she solved it, black smoke came forth, producing a kobold next to the young princess. Lua fell to the ground, scared, and braced for the assault. The nasty creature went unnoticed by the king, and Elif could only hold her breath and pull the lever of the chest plate closed. Pasha was now beside her... lifeless. The armor held as the axe blow rang throughout the armor. Elif could only move enough to grab Pasha's arm and get the sword arm to throw the sword in the armor's hand toward the occupied kobold. The pressure lifted, and Elif found herself kneeling before the King as before, with Lua playing in the background. A dream? An Illusion? It was discomforting and definitely violating.

"Pasha see that she is properly housed, fed, clothed, and trained. Talk with Demir about your request with my blessing."

"Thank you, your majesty," Pasha replied.

Lua walked over with a small package wrapped in cloth. "As promised... fairy cakes as compensation." Lua giggled as she placed them at Elif's feet. "They help with the headache afterward." Lua then turned around and puffed up her face at her father. "Really? That was a little much, you know. That kobold even scared me."

"It's best we leave and get to rest," Pasha said. Elif could only nod in understanding as she tried to wrap her head around what had just happened to her. The tiny princess could be heard scolding the giant king in the background.

Our journey continues.

www.ingramcontent.com/pod-product-compliance
Lightning Source LLC
Chambersburg PA
CBHW060645260626
47161CB00008B/3010